Shadows Revealed

Rohan Monteiro always knew he was not meant for a nine-to-nine job in an office. He wanted to be Flash Gordon, Batman and Bon Jovi at different points in his life, but since none of those were considered viable career options, he decided to be a writer instead. This gives him very little fame and very little money but it allows him to spend most of his time avoiding people, which is heaven for an introvert. It also allows him to read a lot of books as 'research' and make up stories. *Shadows Revealed* is the second in an urban fantasy series set in modern-day Mumbai.

CELESTIAL CHRONICLES
BOOK 2

Shadows Revealed

ROHAN MONTEIRO

Published by Westland Books, a division of Nasadiya Technologies Private Limited, in 2025

No. 269/2B, First Floor, 'Irai Arul', Vimalraj Street, Nethaji Nagar, Alapakkam Main Road, Maduravoyal, Chennai 600095

Westland and the Westland logo are the trademarks of Nasadiya Technologies Private Limited, or its affiliates.

ISBN: 9789371978101

10 9 8 7 6 5 4 3 2 1

Typeset by Jojy Philip, New Delhi
Printed at Thomson Press (India) Ltd

Praise for *Shadows Rising*

'The only thing thicker than Mumbai's traffic is the plot and action in Rohan's jhakkas debut novel about a semi-immortal chap who gets sucked into a kidnapping scheme. Big, boiste rous and absolutely bonkers. Just like the city of Mumbai.'

Sidin Vadukut, author of The Dork Trilogy

'Humour, irreverence and action. This book does everything you don't expect.'

Anand Neelakantan, author of The Bahubali Trilogy

'Myth, magic, mysteries and more than a little hard-boiled noir. It's a potent and exhilarating mix.'

Mike Carey, author of *Lucifer*

'A breath of fresh air in the crowded, elbow-jostling landscape of Indian mytho-fiction. His wry, self-deprecating, ironic style breathes wit, humour and freshness into a classic tale of paranormal investigation.'

Ashok Banker, author of *The Forest of Stories*

'Noir and ancient myth rubbing elbows and told with a reverent purpose—Monteiro has made something special with Curse of the Yaksha.'

Sam Sykes, author of *Seven Blades in Black*

'The crazy, immersive, fantastical debut of the year.'

Kevin Missal, author of The Kalki Series

'An amazing adaptation.'

Koral Dasgupta, author of The Sati Series

'Not all heroes wear capes. Some swear like sailors and kick ass while doing so.'

Saksham Garg, author of *Samsara*

'An innovative, witty, page-turner of a spin on Indian mythology. A must read for mythology fans!'

Trisha Das, author of *Never Meant to Stay*

Dedicated to my mom,
who after reading Book One told me:

'Please stick to non-fiction.
I don't find these kinds of books interesting.'

Yaksha: Male nature spirits, seen throughout Indian art across religions.

AUTHOR NOTE

Welcome to Book 2 of the *Celestial Chronicles*.

So, look, sequels suck. I get it, really. With the possible exception of *Terminator 2*, every movie I've ever seen was always better than its sequel.

If you've not read Book 1, you might be wondering, why am I picking up this book at all? Is it simply because of the gorgeous cover? Or am I just a masochist who enjoys starting a series in the middle and trying to piece together what happened at the start?

The answer is: no, you aren't. Or maybe you are, but it has nothing to do with your choice of books. This book in particular.

I guess the best way to think of this is like watching a James Bond movie. They always open up with him wrapping up a mission in the first ten minutes before the story really begins. And these ten minutes are enough to tell you all about him, and set the tone for the rest of the movie.

The same trick works here. Think of chapter one as the bit you need to read to understand the book, plot, characters and everything that happened before.

An epic tale awaits, but for now, the stage is still being set. In the spaces between words, in the silence after footsteps, in the pause before the strike—that's where the real story lives. The shadows don't just hide; they whisper secrets, conceal motives, and shelter truths too dangerous for daylight.

Settle in. Watch the corners where light fails to reach. Listen for the rustle of movement in the dark.

You are about to discover what the shadows reveal.

PROLOGUE

Delhi

The bar was crowded. Obscenely so, with hundreds of people in their teens and early twenties swaying to the music and fiddling with their phones.

It was clear that the bearded man standing in the doorway, frowning at his surroundings, did not belong there. It was also clear that telling him so would have been a mistake. His face was a black thunderous cloud as he stared at the people gyrating around him.

This was what passed for entertainment among mortals? Minimal clothing and swaying to loud incomprehensible screeching? The bar had hit a new low.

There! He spotted his dining companion for the evening—a large-boned woman sitting at the back. He had half expected her to turn up dressed in deerskins and bark.

Thankfully, she had chosen to dress according to the times, the way middle-aged women of this generation typically dressed. The garish make-up she was wearing indicated that she was either a tremendous optimist or had severely impaired vision.

She glanced up at him and waved. For a brief second, he was tempted to spin on his heel and walk out of there. Cavorting with someone like her would be an affront to everything he stood for.

But no. He had come too far. He would suffer her presence a little longer. Steeling himself, he stepped forward.

Before him, the crowd parted. Not so much Moses parting the Red Sea as a knife through particularly anxious butter. There was something about him that made the happy youngsters want to give him a wide berth. A couple of them looked ready to take offence as he strode past them but their anger wilted as they saw his face. He looked harsh and unforgiving, unsmiling and eager for blood. It was the face of a man accustomed to power; of being obeyed. And if the young in the most populous capital city in the world had learnt something, it was this—recognising those with true power.

Her table was already laden with food. The woman had been gorging herself for a while now, judging by the mounting pile of bones she had tossed into a plate. He could see the juices running down her face and onto her neck as she ate. She wiped her hand on her dress, not seeming to care about the stains it left on the thin fabric.

'Have you had dinner yet?' she asked, speaking with her mouth full and extending her arm at him. It was a gesture he found offensive. Did she really imagine that he would shake her hand? Demean himself any further than he was doing at this moment by even talking to her?

Her fingernails were long and yellow. A faint glamour made it look like she actually had petite human arms, but he could see right through pathetic magic tricks like that.

A smirk played on the woman's face as she watched him. Slowly, she dropped her hand and grabbed a massive lamb shank. If she had taken offence, it didn't show. She merely let out a loud belch and continued to slobber over her meal.

He felt a tiny prickle of disgust as he watched her smacking her lips, eating with her mouth open. In that moment, he couldn't imagine a more abhorrent creature than her.

'Do you really have to eat like that?' he hissed as he sat down. It had been a long time since he had eaten meat or even imbibed alcohol, and the smell of both was repugnant to him.

Far from being embarrassed, the woman appeared delighted by his discomfort. She flashed him a brief smile, her teeth gleaming viciously in the dimly lit room. They looked like they had been filleted away to points—every one of them.

'You have better things to worry about than my eating habits, don't you?'

Could she have found out somehow?

'I don't know what you mean,' he said stiffly.

She snorted. 'Are you really going to sit there and pretend you don't know what everyone in Heaven and the underworld is talking about right now?'

He sat silently, refusing to answer.

'Fine, I'll spell it out for you. Ashwatthama lies defeated and in chains at the bottom of the ocean. By that damned Yaksha no less!'

So she had heard!

He swallowed bile as he looked at her more closely. To think that he was forced to deal with a Rakshasa of all people.

But, despite her lineage, she had her uses.

'The Yaksha is insignificant!' he said dismissively. 'Don't worry about him.'

'Don't worry about him,' she mocked. 'If only it were that easy! I thought that Yaksha had been stripped of his powers and was suffering a fate worse than death, consigned to that hellhole of a city! And now? Not only has he been pulling the wool over every one of your eyes, he also took out Ashwa-fucking-thama! Wasn't he your golden boy? Your great Chiranjivi? How the fuck do you explain that little upstart ruining all of our plans?'

'I'll thank you to not swear in my presence,' he said, affronted.

'And I'll thank you to get your fucking affairs in order.' She leaned forward, and the fetid stench of her breath nearly made him gag. 'You told me this was under control! This whole debacle has drawn undue attention to me and my kind!'

'There is no way any of this can be traced back to you. Or to me. My allies in the Celestial court ...'

She gave him a pitying look. 'Do you even have any allies anymore? From what I heard, the Axe has been getting his hands bloody. How much longer do I have before he starts killing my kind on principle?'

The Axe. Like anyone with a lick of common sense, the demoness feared Parashuram, the enforcer of the Gods. Capricious and short-tempered, the sage was deemed insane by a number of his peers. He was a walking extinction event in a loincloth. When you methodically wiped out twenty-one generations of warriors just because your dad was killed by one of them … It was hard to put a label on what he was. Calling him a serial killer would be like calling a cyclone a bit of wind.

Parashuram was a dangerous being to cross. If he even suspected the two of them, it was as good as being dead already.

So why didn't he feel fear? Did it mean he was insane?

That wasn't possible. His was the path of righteousness. He would not give in to his fear and stray from his dharma.

She was right. His plans had been effectively thwarted. The Yaksha was a black swan. He would not underestimate him again.

'The plan remains unchanged,' he said, his voice hardening. 'Stick to your side of the bargain.'

'I will keep my word,' she responded. 'But I need assurance that you will take care of him. Do you even have a plan?'

The bearded man sneered. 'The Yaksha has made too many enemies in his wretched existence. I've already found someone willing to deal with him.'

'If he defeated Ashwatthama, he won't be easy,' she warned.

'Neither is who I have in mind.' He smiled for the first time since entering the bar. It was so out of character that the woman blanched.

'They hate him even more than you do.'

CHAPTER ONE

Keeping a diary is a very human trait. To reduce anxieties, set goals and use as an outlet for their emotions—all the frail and supposedly wonderful things that make humans appealing. Or so I've been told.

This isn't one of those. I am Akran, the first of the Yakshas. I'm not going to feign modesty because it's expected of me. Everything I'm writing is good advice you shouldn't ignore.

If you are reading this, I'm probably already dead. Pay attention, for you will likely be next.

—The Private Journals of Akran

'K, duck!'

My hastily yelled warning fell on deaf ears as K took the fireball straight to the chest. The blast sent him flying into a stack of crates balanced precariously at the pier's edge.

We were standing at the docks in Mumbai, near the Western harbour. It was almost twilight, the ideal time for a fight like this to take place. Poor visibility and the urge to go home after a hard day's work would keep most people away from the ruckus, minimising civilian casualties and saving me the headache of explaining the dead bodies.

The demon turned around at the sound of my voice and raised his hand, snarling as black flames enveloped his fist.

'Whoa, big guy, calm down. I'm not looking to fight.' I was, of course, lying, but when you are wholly outmatched and going head-to-head with a demon, a few white lies don't count for much in the cosmic sense.

I don't think he cared either. The fireball struck and disintegrated the little illusion I had put up of me flapping my arms, trying to reason with him. The real me was beside him, trying to shove a fully charged magic card below his feet.

Yeah, I'm going to have to explain myself better.

The quick and dirty summary? I'm a Yaksha, a magical Celestial being that has been living on Earth for a while, give or take a couple of thousand years. It wasn't by choice— there was a crime (I was innocent), a sham of a trial (think Chicago Seven facing judges from Allahabad) and a valiant and spirited defence by yours truly, but eventually, I was stripped of my powers and exiled to earth.

That was a long time ago. I made the best of a bad situation, learnt a few fancy card tricks (the exploding kind), made a few friends and most importantly, survived.

Then, a short while ago, I regained my powers. They pulled me out of a tight spot at the time, and I got cocky. I also began to believe the 'great power, great responsibility' shtick and declared myself the guardian of my little corner of the globe, Mumbai, and vowed to protect it against anyone who sought to do it harm.

In hindsight, that might have been a mistake.

In the six months since I made that declaration, there had been a massive upswing in the number of supernatural incidents. Most of those were minor—the occasional demon slipping through for a quick snack, a couple of Celestial voyeurs fascinated by humans interlocking their bodies like lego pieces, etc.

But occasionally, a big fish made his way in—like this guy here.

On the face of it, he wasn't too much to look at. Just a regular run-of-the-mill construction worker who seemed more gorilla than man. He had a brutish look and a bent iron crowbar around his neck, courtesy of K, who had naively assumed that bonking a demon from behind would solve our problems. All it did was piss him off.

By way of a quick introduction, K is Kama, the God of Love, a title that suggests far more dignity than he's ever possessed. Besides invisibility and making people fall in love, annoying people is his superpower. That last one he has reserved just for me, for some reason.

He is also vain, exceedingly proud of his appearance and would hump anything that moves. Possibly even things that don't. Oh, and he is my best friend. I can always rely on him being somewhere nearby during a fight. Not because he is brave. Gods, no! More like, you know, how fish in an aquarium press their face to the glass for some weird-ass reason? Well, that mindlessness is K in a nutshell, and the whole world is his fishbowl.

Given a choice, I would rather that he was useful instead of just nearby, but we work with what we have.

Right now, he was picking himself up from amid the crates he had landed on and fastidiously checking if his clothing had suffered damage.

If the bent-but-not-broken bar wasn't a good enough clue that this was no ordinary human being we were dealing with, there were a few other hints: flaming footprints, for one; the distinct sulphur-and-brimstone smell that he emanated; and, of course, the complete lack of concealment on the astral plane.

More exposition needed?

Sigh.

Okay, here we go!

We don't all operate on a single plane of existence. Humans, being among the lowest forms of life there are, tend to only see what's in front of them and exist entirely on this plane. Beings who dabble in magic, or 'sensitives', often have dual sight—an ability to see this plane and possibly one or more others, which often vary. Cats can see three planes of existence, which could explain why they appear so insufferably smug most of the time.

Being a Yaksha, I can see nearly seven planes of existence. Maybe there are more—they don't matter anyway. All it means is that people with 'true sight', or 'the third eye', are better able to pierce the veil of illusion when you encounter one.

Thanks to an incident from a really long time ago, K was possibly the only person I knew who could cloak himself entirely across all seven planes. Even a top-tier demon, or God, can't spot him if he chooses to hide. It makes him incredibly useful when he doesn't do stupid shit like attack demons head-on with a stick.

This chap was a demon. On the higher planes, he looked significantly taller, with bloodshot eyes and a copper tinge on his body. His teeth protruded from his upper jaw, stretching beyond his chin, while his lower body resembled a giant serpent. He looked like he was out of sync with what the modern, fashionable demon was meant to be wearing.

The dispelling of my illusion had left him confused and angry. He let out a low growl that sounded partly like frustration and partly like hunger. I sympathised—kinda. A while ago, I was forced to swim a considerable distance to an oil tanker and realised how badly out of shape I was. I may be a semi-immortal being, but natural laws still apply. You eat too many doughnuts, you start looking and feeling like one.

I had thus begun intermittent fasting and the results, while positive, did tend to make me cranky. Crankier than usual anyway.

The cards I had shoved under his feet exploded, making him trip and fall. That was my signature move—blowing tiny, brightly coloured pieces of paper up. Sometime in the last two hundred years, I realised that playing cards were particularly well suited (no pun intended) to my abilities. All Celestials have a mana well—a pool of energy we could access. With a little bit of effort, this mana can be stored in various objects. The larger an object, the more the energy would dissipate; too small, and it would crumble under the weight of the power it was infused with. Playing cards are the ideal balance of utility and storage. They are just the right shape, come in standard sizes, are easy to carry and can be easily replaced at any convenience store.

Because of a long and unfortunate series of events, my mana pool has been shackled. What I can access is essentially the drippings of a leaky tap—a tiny dribble barely enough for any major spells, but if I could accumulate and store mana every day, it would allow me to perform higher-order spells.

Over the past few centuries, I had powered up several decks with all sorts of minor spells. In the weeks before this fight, I had also used up most of them. It was insane how fast I burned through them, fighting off enemies.

The demon was now back on his feet. I hadn't really believed I could take him down with my crummy little deck. This was just me stalling while I tried to figure out the next steps.

I had spent weeks practising how to throw cards perfectly. To make them slice the air as I flung them. To master every game of chance, every underhanded shuffle, every little practised motion that would make them a set of deadly weapons in my hands. I had learnt from the best card sharks and street magicians how to palm a deck, so it looked smooth and impressive. It was not about wowing an audience. Well, maybe it was, but the stakes were higher in my case. I had enemies in high places—ruthless, implacable foes who hated my guts and would never quit. Because of them, I had learnt to posture like I always had something more up my sleeve. One final card trick. One fatal weapon in reserve that I would not hesitate to use if push came to shove.

But all of this meant diddly-squat when fighting a demon.

Most demons are interested in causing mayhem. Several of them, particularly the larger ones with animalistic tendencies, lack a sense of self-preservation. They are used to being the top dog and settle challenges the old way—ritualistic combat, possibly even eating the heart of their vanquished foe. Looking at him, I had no doubt that he was one of those demons.

I can hide myself from humans without breaking a sweat, but demons are another matter entirely. The only reason he hadn't spotted me yet was that he was still using his five basic senses to try and find me. Coming to our dimension tends to be a disorienting experience. It was an advantage we needed to press quickly.

K had finished examining himself and finally deigned to look at me. His clothes and hair were singed, but otherwise, he looked none the worse for wear. Celestials are notoriously hard to kill. He jogged in my direction, extending his veil of invisibility to include me.

'Any ideas?'

I shook my head. 'It might help to know what we are dealing with. Did you pick up anything?'

One of K's secondary abilities was a form of low-level telepathy, a perk of being a fertility God—he used it to charm, seduce and sway any number of men or women into his bed when the occasion demanded it. This was our first attempt to use it as a means of intelligence.

K's brow furrowed in thought. 'I'm getting something. Wait. Hang on!' He stretched the moment out before making a dramatic pronouncement.

'He's furious at someone.'

I glared at him. 'No shit, Sherlock.'

'I mean, really mad.' He shot me a look. 'I think he dislikes Indra.'

Huh! Maybe this demon wasn't so bad after all.

'Indra' was the title for the leader of the Devas, the minor Celestial deities responsible for things like wind, water, fire, etc. The chap who held the title of Indra was usually the one in charge of rain and everything that came with it—lightning, thunder, etc. As a de facto leader, Indra was also responsible for rallying the troops into battles with demons, aka Asuras, every few years or so.

Unfortunately, most Indras were dicks. The bar to become one wasn't very high, and most abused their power to chase women or use humans as playthings. More often than not, it was also why the Devas were always losing every battle they got into and running to the big guys (aka the Trinity) for help.

I disliked most of the Indras I had met. Knowing this chap also felt a certain degree of animosity towards them made me feel an immediate rush of brotherly affection for him.

'Maybe we have been approaching this all wrong. Here's a chap who just got to our realm, and we have been attacking him. Let's try and start a dialogue about what he really wants.'

I had barely completed my sentence when one of the demon's fireballs exploded five feet away from me.

Unable to see us, he had begun throwing fireballs randomly. Small fires had already started to spread in various parts of the docks.

The warm brotherly love dissipated quickly.

'This could be a problem,' K murmured. 'We are violating the First Law by even being here.'

I nodded. The law of concealment, also known as the First Law, was a decree laid down by the Celestial Council at the start of the Kali Yuga. Celestials living on the mortal plane need to comport themselves in a low-key manner. Fighting a fire-throwing demon at a public dock may not have been quite what they had in mind.

The First Law existed to prevent humans from discovering supernatural beings. Which was deliciously ironic, considering humans would willingly hand over their privacy, location data and deepest secrets to faceless corporations just to play Candy Crush.

Throwing fireballs in the middle of a shipyard kinda defeated the purpose of the First Law. If the existence of the Gods was revealed to humans, there would be blood on the streets. The human race was simply incapable of dealing with it at this point of time.

By and large, demons had the good sense to stay away from the mortal realm. Seriously, when you tend to be a plus size through no fault of your own, do you really want to be body shamed by skinny Gen Zs mocking you on TikTok? More often than not, they would just dismiss them as some crank in a Halloween costume. This generation did not share the same fear of demons that humans once held.

Which isn't to say demons weren't dangerous. They were. Insanely so, in fact. The problem was that by the time humans figured that out, a few thousand people would already be dead. And governments tend to take notice when stuff like that happens. This was Mumbai after all, not Manipur.

'I'm going to call Sars,' I muttered, extracting my phone and thumbing the dial. It picked up on the first ring.

'You've reached Sars.'

'Sars, it's me. Found the disturbance. It's a slightly bigger problem than we first thought.'

'Gimme the deets.'

Sars was the third member of our little group. She was a Celestial and an Aspect of Saraswati, the Goddess of Knowledge. While the original Goddess tended to be stately and held herself with great poise, Sars was the opposite. She was quite literally a cooler, Gen Z version of the Goddess. Sars symbolised hidden knowledge—she made an appearance in the late '90s when the internet was just beginning to bloom across India. Her lifeblood was the trade of information and secrets, and she was really good at her job.

'Angry demon, reddish tinge, seems to have a mad-on for Indra, big teeth.' I could hear her keyboard clacking as she added all the data parameters and started her search. 'He's wearing a leopard skin around his waist and nether regions.'

'Tell her the leopard skin isn't doing a great job,' piped in K helpfully. 'He's flashing the whole dockyard.'

I sighed. 'Sars, K wants you to know …

'I heard',' she interrupted. 'Anything else?'

'K tried hitting him on the head with an iron crowbar, and it didn't work.'

The clacking paused. 'You sure it was iron?'

A reasonable question. Iron and silver were both harmful for most Celestials. Iron wounds healed slowly and agonisingly; and holding anything silver for too long would give us a red, itchy rash and a bad case of silver poisoning.

'Very sure. It made no difference whatsoever.'

'Got it. Where exactly are y'all right now?'

'Close to the docks.'

'So, it's safe to assume there's water nearby?'

'Umm, yes. Why?'

'Hmm.' I could imagine her as she spoke, dressed head to toe in black, talking into one of those shiny new-fangled wireless headsets, legs crossed in her classic lotus position, blowing bubble gum as she stared at her screen. 'It's most likely to be Vritra.'

'It's Vritra,' I mouthed to K.

'I don't know a Vritra,' K whispered back. He stared at the demon thoughtfully. 'He looks like a Bob. I'm going to call him Bob.'

I sighed. 'We don't know who that is, Sars.'

'Ancient drought demon, builder of dams that blocked rivers. Described as a Vedic serpent or dragon.' She gave a low whistle. 'He isn't supposed to be here.'

'Well … yeah, I could have told you that, given that he is a demon.'

'Woo-hoo! Here, Bob!' K was running around, making this sound with his lips that you typically make when you are trying to get stray dogs to flock to you. 'Who's a good boy? You are! Yes, you are!'

Vritra did not look like a 'good boy' from any angle at that moment. Eyes red, he snarled and tried to catch Kama again, who ducked behind a different set of crates.

'I meant that he isn't supposed to be alive. He was killed by Indra a long time ago.'

'Is that even possible?'

'Not from that side. Someone here is holding the door open.' I could feel the frown in her voice. 'Akran, this is …'

'I know, I know,' I growled. The dead are supposed to stay dead, be they zombies, Jesus or anything in between.

A resurrected demon meant there was someone out there actively bringing them back to life—a troubling prospect.

'Sars, do you know any way to stop him?'

'He received a boon. He can't be harmed by metal, wood or stone, nor anything dry or wet, nor during the day or night.'

The day and night clause was a popular one among demons. Fortunately, there were still a few minutes before twilight turned to night.

K had made his way back to me.

'How did they kill him the last time?'

'A sage named Dadhichi donated his bones.'

The demon had wandered away, no doubt still looking for us.

K leaned forward. 'Just so I'm clear, is she asking us to …?'

'No! Sars, there are no sages nearby, and even if there were, I doubt they would be willing to donate their bones.'

K poked me in the ribs, an act that is incredibly annoying at the best of times. 'I don't think whoever he is needs to "donate" the bones.'

'You are suggesting we—what? Extract them forcibly?'

K gave me a sulky look. 'The first rule of brainstorming is that we shouldn't shoot down anyone's ideas, no matter how outlandish they are.'

'I don't think that would have worked anyway,' Sars interrupted. 'Dadhichi's bones were supposedly as hard as diamonds and imbued with mystical powers.'

K nudged me again. 'Why don't you blast him with that ball lightning thing you've used in the past? That should work.'

That was a good suggestion. Why didn't I do that?

A while ago, a particularly nasty bad guy named Ashwatthama attempted a yagna, trying to resurrect a demon. My friends and I interrupted the grisly sacrifice he was attempting to perform, managed to rescue the victims and won the day. It had felt like a victory at the time.

Unfortunately, the half-completed yagna had broken something fundamental in the forces of the universe. The metaphysical fabric that separated our dimension from the demon realm had weakened, resulting in this influx of demons popping out of the woodwork. And my powers were on the fritz. They worked on occasion but not in a consistent fashion.

Suffice it to say, this was not one of those occasions.

I took a deep breath as I turned to face K. 'I don't think I can do that anymore.'

To his credit, he didn't react badly. K was one of those people who, if you told him the world was ending the next day, would shrug and immediately go back to eating a sandwich or whatever else he was engaged with at that moment. When you are deliriously in love, you tend not to worry about most things. When you are a God of Love… you are often just delirious.

'Guys,' Sars called out. 'If you do have a plan, I suggest you do it now. The window of twilight is closing fast.'

K's suggestion had given me an idea though.

'K, distract him. Get him to one of those electric poles.'

K's face brightened. 'I can tell him some jokes?'

'Yes, whatever.' I was already running as I spoke.

K's jokes were usually as funny as Ebola. If they were anything like the ones he normally cracked, the demon would probably welcome a quick death. 'Sars?'

'Standard containment protocols. I know. I'm already on it.'

Good. I wasn't quite sure how she would do it but Sars would find a way to keep this off the evening news. Which left me free to focus on my solution.

Maybe I couldn't throw lightning around. But we had a few conveniences in this era they didn't have in the good old days. Such as electricity.

In other words, a loophole in the metal, stone and wood weaponry boon protecting him from harm.

Celestials and electricity didn't mix well. I avoided most forms of technology since I was always worried I would short them out. I also had a pair of nitrile gloves stowed in my pockets.

'Hey Bumblebee,' K called out, and I supressed a groan. I hated that hanging out with K meant I actually understood he was pointing to the guy's yellow loincloth. I was perfectly happy not getting all his references.

Maybe there were 'jokes' involved, in the loosest sense of the word, but I doubted it. K's unique brand of humour is often only fun for himself. Besides, I'd heard most of his wisecracks over the past few hundred years and he was running out of new material.

Vritra however was new to this. Like a caveman being exposed to incessant honking in Bangalore, the whole experience of listening to K's taunts was a massive attack on the senses. Red faced and furious, he charged at K, who was now making a beeline towards me.

I reached into my pockets and pulled out my last two cards. They contained a simple spell—edges as sharp as shuriken—but that was about it, no fancy sparks or anything. These were for blade work, nothing else. I was really scraping the bottom of the barrel here.

I flung the cards upwards. They gleamed as they spun through the air and sliced the wires, like tiny razors bringing them down, crackling and spitting several thousand volts of raw electricity. Vritra stood there with a puzzled frown on his face.

His meaty palm reached out to grab the frayed cable right where the green and red bits stuck out. We watched him as his expression shifted from puzzlement to anger and then pain. For a split second, it looked like his anger would let him ride through the effect of fifty thousand volts coursing through him, then his eyes rolled back into his head as he toppled over and spasmed like a jellyfish.

'Did it work?' K asked as he peered over my shoulder at the prostrate demon.

I knelt by his side and placed two fingers on his neck. There was still a pulse.

I had hoped the current was enough to kill him but all it did was knock him unconscious.

Sars was still yelling through the phone. Apparently, we had only five minutes of twilight left.

I turned to K. 'I'm out of ideas—unless you happen to have a fancy diamond knife or something?'

'Would a ballpoint pen work?'

'We can try, I guess.' I patted myself down in the hope of finding anything else I could use.

K was staring out at the docks with a funny look on his face.

'I might have another idea,' he said.

'What is it?'

'Remember the first rule of brainstorming?'

'K, I'm not going to shoot down your idea unless it's an incredibly stupid one.' Which it most probably would be, I added silently. 'But right now we don't have enough time, so stop dithering and just tell me already.'

K gave a deep, melodramatic sigh. 'Very well then. But you aren't going to like it.'

CHAPTER TWO

The Buddhist text Tittha Sutta (written in 500 BCE, during the Buddha's lifetime) tells the parable of the three blind men who visited India and touched an elephant for the first time. Each one guessed what the elephant looked like based on his limited experience. One imagined it as similar to a snake based on the trunk. The second touched its leg and declared it was an animal shaped like a tree. The third touched its tail and described the elephant as a rope-like creature.

~~The story is meant to show how humans tend to believe and insist that something is absolutely true based on their limited experience, while ignoring other people's experiences that may be equally valid.~~

Let me try this again.

Buddha was too polite to just say that people are idiots. I'm not Buddha.

The story is meant to show how incredibly stupid people are when they draw half-baked conclusions.

And that's exactly what happened when we fought that demon Vritra.

See, the Tittha Sutta isn't just about elephants, it's about how we shape the world through perception. The universe, at its core, is a vast web of energy fields, chaotic and unseen. Across history, humans have sensed these forces and given them form through myth, ritual and Gods. The powers we worship, the demons we summon, even the quantum mechanics we now study—they're all our clumsy attempts to grasp the same cosmic energy. Like those blind men, we see only pieces and call them truth.

Take Vritra, for instance. He walked, talked and dressed like a typical Indian demon. Badly. His facial features today resembled how we would describe monsters in the ancient Vedic texts—long canines jutting beyond the bottom lip, horns, red eyes, the works.

But a demon raised in a summoning circle in London looks completely different. They might wear a tux and carefully sip Earl Grey while speaking in a delightful, cultured manner. They would have manicured hands, tiny little elegant horns, an occasional goatee and may sometimes sprout a forked tail.

So, what's different? Are there two very separate realms of Hell, and we got the ones with no dental hygiene while they got the cultured ones? Or is it that demons, like everything else, are shaped by how we perceive the chaotic energy we call Hell? Our expectations, our myths, our fears—they mould the unseen into forms we can understand.

These may sound like mere trifles to worry about, but there's a point to this rant. Perceptions matter. Immensely. Part of the reason the Gods of the subcontinent have survived while dozens of others have bitten the dust is because of our perceived strength. Our unity against all external enemies.

Ashwatthama's yagna broke something fundamental in our access to the energy of the cosmos. Not for those in other realms. Not for those who are outside of the mythos we are a part of.

Which means for the first time, we are the only pantheon in the universe that is vulnerable. There is a big gaping hole in our defences. An empty vacuum instead of a vibrant collection of godly powers.

And nature abhors a vacuum.

—The Private Journals of Akran

It was close to 9 p.m. by the time Sars joined us. She had picked up one of my spare card decks and brought it over, which I was grateful for because I felt naked without them. We were at Papa Panchos, a tiny café in Bandra which had the best lassi and keema parathas. Fighting a demon had given us a healthy appetite.

'So, what did you finally do?' Sars enquired as she grabbed a couple of menus. There were close to ten helpings of apricot custard on the table, and K was working his way through them all by himself.

'I had a bunch of rather creative ideas,' K began with the enthusiasm of an old person wanting to share their vacation slideshow.

'Which included somehow extracting one of Vritra's bones and fashioning it into a blade, puncturing his lung and letting him drown in his own blood …'

Sars froze in the middle of grabbing one of the dishes from the table.

'Feeding him to a bunch of pigs, kidnapping some pigs while we were at it, tying up the farmer who lent us his pigs, going out on a date with the farmer's wife while he was tied up …'

K looked up with a wounded expression on his face. 'I got a bit distracted,' he mumbled.

'Eventually, Akran came up with a simpler plan. Air. He needed air to breathe. So, we used a plastic bag to … well, I'll spare you the details.'

Sars gave K a horrified look. 'You choked him to death?'

'No, no, Akran choked him. I just helped.'

Sars looked a little green at the thought. I couldn't exactly blame her. Choking someone was not something we had done before or wished to gain more experience with. You might be forgiven for thinking divine beings like ourselves are a little more blasé about spending the lives of others, particularly demons, but that's not true. Having lived as an exile among humans for so long has made me soft. I'm not willing to automatically assume demons are bad and relish killing them.

Her face softened. 'You didn't really have a choice with this one, Akran. He was a drought demon. He would've drained the water from the air, drunk it from the rivers and hoarded it for himself. As long as he was around, crops would've withered and died, and droves of people would've perished from thirst. Vritra was powerful enough that the Devas needed help stopping him. You made the right call here.'

I said nothing. Sars was right but I couldn't help feeling like I had handled the whole thing badly. We didn't know how he had gotten there. An interrogation might have provided a scrap of information, some tiny clue as to who was behind this. We had just killed our best lead.

'Speaking of how we saved the world, again,' K continued, 'now might be an excellent time to decide if this is a line of work we intend to continue pursuing …' He shot me a quick glance. 'Given that you have no reliable powers at the moment.'

I considered this as I chewed my last morsel of food. We were not operating from a position of strength anymore. No significant powers meant I was better off doing what I had been doing for the past few thousand years and just staying hidden. Too much attention on me was never a pleasant experience, especially when a few members of the Celestial court were still looking to make a name for themselves by permanently erasing me.

'Of course,' continued K, 'if we did have a friendly ally or two, things would have been different.'

The other two members of our collective were on a break. Shukra had been through a kidnapping and some serious torture by the big evil monster of our last great adventure—he was due for some R&R.

Deanna, my Valkyrie girlfriend, who was technically the most competent warrior among us, was also away for a while. She had hinted that she needed to spend some time back in her Scandinavian homeland to deal with a jealous ex who also happened to be a thunder God. We had parted amicably, but I had the distinct feeling I was not going to see her again. She had seemed distracted and snappy when we had last spoken, and I was happy to give her space to work through whatever issues she was dealing with.

Which left the three of us. Left to himself, K was usually ready to bolt and let the world take care of itself. Only in our company did he feel bold enough to engage in murderous mayhem.

Sars was happy to trot along if the occasion demanded, but her real skill was providing intelligence. She was our oracle, we needed her safe and sound. And while she was the Aspect of a Goddess of wisdom, compared to her, K and I were old men. When you've lived a few millennia, 'back in my day' technically also covered the stone age.

And then, there was me. First among the Yakshas, slayer of Shambha-la, keeper of the Celestial weapons, and feeling pretty darn useless. I knew that the powers of all Celestials were on the fritz since the yagna, but given my proximity to Ashwatthama, mine had essentially shut down. I didn't quite know how to turn it back on.

'We leave Deanna and Shukra alone for now,' I said aloud. 'Let them come back when they are ready. For now, we will take things as they come.' I turned to Sars. 'We have a bigger problem here that we need your help with.'

She nodded. 'Someone's resurrecting demons!'

'How is that even possible?' asked K, his mouth still half-full. 'Don't they go back into the void or whatever once they are dead?'

'We don't know what happens once a demon is killed,' Sars began. 'We've theorised that their essence gets discombobulated, but ...'

'Be that as it may,' I interrupted, 'this isn't supposed to be possible. Shukra told us last time that doing something like this requires the Sanjivani mantra, and he is pretty much the only person who knows it.' But then, a thought struck me, and I looked at them in alarm. 'Is Shukra safe? When did we last hear from him?'

'I called him just an hour ago, right before I headed here,' Sars said. 'He hasn't been kidnapped, coerced or tortured.'

Okay, that was a relief. I felt responsible for Shukra's last kidnapping.

She hesitated for a moment. 'There's something else I need to tell you about. I've been monitoring a couple of servers on the dark web. Chatrooms, forums and bulletin boards that mention paranormal activity. It ranges from crackpot theories about lizard people to a few more plausible ones involving Celestial sightings, etc.'

'Lizard people are real by the way', K said. 'They can't move their mouths in the same way as humans so there's a catch phrase that you make them say to test if they are humans—Ka nama ka laajerama.'

Sars ignored him. We had hit upon a sure-fire method to know when to ignore him. Usually, it was when his lips moved.

'Three nights ago, at 11 p.m., a message was put up on a hub used by an assassin guild in South Asia. A landlord's pet labrador had turned rabid and needed to be put down. A vet responded at 3 a.m. the next morning, confirming he and his colleague would handle the problem. The payment was fixed at eleven million in reds.'

'The whole assassin business seems a bit slow if they are putting hits out on dogs', K remarked.

When I was in the company of people like Sars, I knew I wasn't the smartest person in the room. I was too old school to understand a lot of newfangled tech references, and comparisons to a blunt instrument wouldn't bother me at all.

Sar was still looking at me expectantly, so I felt obliged to respond, 'Sars, this sounds like some teenagers dicking around. It's not relevant …'

'Rabid means an urgent mission. A vet is a contract killer. You have two assassins either working independently or together in the city'.

I frowned. 'So? There are probably eighty or more murders committed daily. Why is this something we should get involved in?'

She pushed a white manila envelope towards me. 'An encrypted attachment was transferred between both parties. I was able to snag and make a copy. Unfortunately, the file was also deleted from the hub immediately after, and all references to the message itself were scrubbed.'

I took a look inside the envelope. There were four grainy photos, all black and white, all shot from a distance with a telephoto lens. They were all pictures of me.

Okay, now I got why it mattered.

'There's a contract out on me?'

'A rather large one as it happens.'

'Eleven million reds?'

'Eleven million dollars' worth in uncut stones—rubies, emeralds, diamonds and sapphires.'

'Are you serious? That's an obscene amount of money!'

'The going rate for most elite targets.'

I leaned back and thought about this for a bit. Most Celestials weren't comfortable with paper money; they still preferred tangible currencies from ancient times. The payment indicated that one or both parties involved were Celestials. Very wealthy Celestials.

'Any other details?'

'I could only extract the photos. I cross-referenced the aliases used by the people accepting the contract. They have a series of high-profile kills attributed to them. Some other words in that message may or may not be clues. "Landlord" is typically code for the Gods because Earth belongs to them, as far as they are concerned. A labrador is …'

'A Yaksha, since we were their attack dogs,' I finished her sentence. I was surprisingly intuitive once I knew the context.

'You might want to get out of town,' Sars said.

I stared at her. Running from professional killers with unlimited resources and an eleven-million-dollar motivation to end me seemed like such an overreaction.

'Sars, you have got to be kidding. I'm not going to run from some two-bit …'

'It's not a two-bit assassin, Akran. Whoever these people are, they are very expensive contract killers. Which means they are professionals. You've been under surveillance by someone who knows you are a Celestial and has the means to finance a very lucrative hit on you.'

'That kind of budget would likely mean a paper trail,' I said as I gave her a meaningful glance.

She gave me a helpless shrug. 'I don't know how to start looking. They could have safe houses and private transport, nothing that would show up on the usual databases. This level of funding provides them with unlimited opportunities.'

K raised a hand. 'Are you sure you don't want to rethink the whole let us hide till it all blows over strategy?'

'I'd rather get in front of what's happening. Running from these guys rarely works.'

K gave me what he believes is his 'serious look'. 'It's just that these fellows seem more competent and tech-savvy, while you are more of a viking as far as technology is concerned.'

He had a point. I have witnessed the rise and fall of entire civilisations but nothing has made me feel as obsolete as watching teenagers use TikTok.

'The incident with the demon and this thing may be connected. Maybe the person resurrecting demons is the one who wants you dead. You did stop the last yagna that happened,' Sars said.

'They don't seem related. Granted that the timing is suspicious but it's quite a leap to assume that the person hiring contract killers is also the person raising demons.'

'Maybe it was a distraction,' K interjected.

I frowned. 'A distraction?'

'You know, get you chasing your tail, or in this case, a demon, in point A while they commit dastardly deeds in point B. They know you are a glutton for punishment where paranormal activities are concerned. In fact,' he became more animated as he warmed to his theme, 'there may be a whole orgy of activities taking place right under our … noses, that we know nothing about because, you know …' He made a vague pointing motion, 'Gallant knight, horse, windmills etc.'

'Or,' Sars interrupted, 'it was a precursor. They are toying with you. You know how a lot of them like playing games.'

I did. Centuries of idleness has made a lot of Celestials petty. An elaborate game where I'm running from one perceived threat to another before they deliver the final coup de grâce sounded like something they would enjoy. If I wasn't the nice, kind-hearted chap I was, I might have enjoyed persecuting an enemy or two in the same fashion. It was a deliciously divine form of torture to inflict on someone.

'Coming back to what you said about resurrecting demons, it's not true that the Sanjivani mantra is the only way,' Sars began. 'I did find one more mention of something that might be used to bring the dead back to life.'

Her phone buzzed before she could finish. Her expression turned grave.

'Seems like K was right!'

K immediately looked interested. 'About the horse?'

'About it being a distraction,' she rose from her seat. 'Someone was murdered at the other end of town; about the same time you were dealing with Vritra.' She gave me a sombre look. 'It's one of ours.'

CHAPTER THREE

*T*hree primary races populate our realm: humans, demons and celestials. It's like a cosmic sitcom that nobody asked for but everyone's stuck watching.

Humans are the participation trophy of creation. Back in the good old days, their ancestors could squeeze out a decent century and a half. These days? Most humans tap out before they hit triple digits, which is honestly merciful considering what they've done to the planet. Their one evolutionary advantage? They breed like rabbits They're basically the universe's way of saying, 'If at first you don't succeed, try, try again ... several billion times.'

Celestials are 'immortal' the way a Nokia 3310 is 'indestructible'—technically true until someone really commits to breaking it. Their main role by and large is to float around dispensing wisdom nobody asked for while avoiding actual responsibility. Their population remains charmingly small, mainly because Celestial–human *relationships produce exactly what you'd expect: awkward family dinners and only rarely a few offspring.*

Demons round out this ménage à trois. They've made a career out of showing up uninvited to both Earth and Heaven, like that drunk uncle who crashes every wedding and somehow always ends up starting a fight at the reception. Their periodic invasion hobby has earned them a permanent spot in mythology—not because anyone wanted them there, but because they're impossible to ignore. They're essentially the universe's way of reminding everyone that things could always be worse.

The ironic bit? We're all stuck in this cosmic arrangement, but we avoid each other like inmates in a men's prison shower—everyone sees the soap on the floor, but nobody's stupid enough to bend over and pick it up.

It's not exactly The Good Place *but sometimes it feels like it.*

—The Private Journals of Akran

The house was a private bungalow facing Juhu beach. You would not stumble upon it by accident, because it stood off the main road and had virtually no traffic in its vicinity. The beach itself was quite secluded. The ten feet high walls surrounding the house ended in glass shards. There was only one way in—through the iron reinforced gates in the front. Motion-activated security cameras recorded our entrance.

'This chap took his privacy seriously,' K whispered.

The premises had four large Dobermans, all of whom had been drugged. The lawn had several iron objects strewn about. This was standard practice among Celestials. For reasons not entirely clear to us, iron tended to block/inhibit our powers. A few pieces carefully placed in each room could prevent people from popping in out of thin air.

'How exactly was he living in a mansion like this without drawing attention to himself?' K whispered.

I had no idea. Hiding in plain sight was not an easy job. Somebody would eventually notice that you weren't ageing and get suspicious. A while ago, it was easy to simply leave the city for a couple of decades or so and then come back pretending to be your own son. Things had got a lot harder since. Everywhere we went, there was a paper trail. Taxes to pay, funds to procure, utilities, services, identification documents and the like.

By and large, India was still a haven for well over a thousand Celestials, since the red tape, which choked up progress, also worked in our favour. Still, the last thing you should do if you are a Celestial is own a big-ass villa in prime real estate.

We were fortunate to have Sars on our side. She was incredible at this—managing our finances, giving us multiple identity papers, and keeping us off the books. She also had a deft touch when it came to dealing with public servants.

Sars's informant was a policeman who, unsurprisingly, was on the take. He had an oily salesman look about him as he bowed obsequiously at her. K remained invisible, and I stood next to him, cloaked in his aura.

'I can only give you ten minutes with the corpse, you understand. Ten minutes, no more. After that, I have to call my supervisor, and you'll have to be away from here.' He extracted a large blue handkerchief and blew his nose vigorously into it. 'Wear gloves at all times and don't touch the body or pilfer anything from the crime scene.'

'Will do, Mr Sharma. What about the cameras in the front?'

'I'll erase the footage.'

'Thanks.' Sars shook his hand. A tiny bundle of notes was transferred between them. Sars had plenty of experience bribing the judicial system. That little packet she had handed over was more than he would have made in a year of honest work.

The policeman followed her as we walked into the hall, his head bobbing eagerly as he spoke. 'It's an open and shut case, Miss. We have camera footage of the main entrance,' he chuckled. 'He didn't even bother to cover his face. Gave a good stare into the camera as if daring us to catch him. Arrogant sod. We are even better than Scotland Yard at ...'

I tuned him out as I made my way through the room. I had heard this bit about the Mumbai Police before. To their credit, they were actually first-rate at detective work. But politics and corruption plagued every government department across the country, and the Mumbai Police were no exception. If only there was a way to pay them adequately. Or prevent politicians from transferring them when they did their jobs.

But no, that was a ridiculous idea. Might as well wish for trains to run on time.

Sars politely asked him to wait outside, and he happily obliged. Probably wanted a quiet corner to count the money he had been given.

The body was lying face up in the centre of the room. The blood had been absorbed by the white carpet, made maybe of sheep skin or that of a polar bear. His eyes were wide open. It was obvious from the way he looked that he had died in great agony.

'It's Nahusha!' I exclaimed.

'You know him?' asked K in surprise.

'No, I just like saying "It's Nahusha" every time I see a corpse!'

K scowled at me but said nothing further.

Sars stared at the dead man's face.

'I keep a dossier on all Celestials who've been living here. He mostly kept to himself.'

'Don't we all heal very quickly?' asked K. 'If he's a Celestial, how did he die?'

'The same way immortals always die,' I said. 'Very, very surprisingly.'

I pointed at a small silver tattoo of a lightning bolt on his forearm. 'He's not just any Celestial, he is an Indra. Or rather, was an Indra.'

A few hours ago, post our battle with Vritra, I was telling K the conclusion of the mythological battle. Indra had used the bones of sage Dadhichi to kill Vritra. The bones were freely given and used for a good cause, but killing a sage was a grave sin that required penance. The reigning king of the Gods, Indra Vritrahan (Slayer of Vritra) was thus forced to give up his throne and atone for his sin. He chose a secluded lake and lost all sense of time as he got swept away in penance.

In his absence, someone had to look after the throne. In those days, unlike today, the God's role used to be more vital. No Indra meant no monsoon until someone took the throne. That's when the rest of the Gods chose Nahusha.

Nahusha was a king in northern India, part of the Kuru clan and one of the early ancestors of the Pandavas. He was seen as possessing many fine qualities including fearlessness, good character and statesmanship. He was also a devout and pious ruler, and seen as deserving of a place in heaven after his death. The Devas offered him the role of Indra, and he accepted.

Alas, power corrupts. Nahusha grew arrogant and started to abuse his position. The Devas were helpless to stop him since they had placed him above them. Nahusha possessed all the powers of Indra: lightning, thunder, the ability to make it rain. He was also physically stronger than any of the other Devas.

One day, Nahusha saw Indra's wife Sachi and desired to possess her for himself. Knowing that his pride would be his undoing, Sachi agreed to meet him if he agreed to visit her in a palanquin carried by the Saptarishis (the seven most powerful sages) of that era.

The sages were a counter-balance to the Devas because they could accumulate power by tapping directly into the cosmos. It made for a tense and uneasy relationship at get-togethers, since one or the other was usually beset with feelings of insecurity.

Of the seven sages, Agastya was the shortest, so the palanquin did not rest easy on his shoulders. Impatient with the slow movement of the palanquin, Nahusha planted a kick on Agastya's shoulder, leading to the short-tempered sage cursing him—since he had dared to kick a sage, he would lose his legs.

Nahusha immediately turned into a snake and fell from heaven. The curse would last until Nahusha met someone who truly understood dharma. It's rather telling when a supposed cornerstone of your entire civilisation is so baffling that centuries go by before anyone can actually grasp what it means.

Eventually, someone did come along. The Pandavas, in exile in the forest, met Nahusha, still in the body of a snake. He trapped Bhim, the second of the Pandavas, in his coils and threatened to eat him. Yudhishthir, the eldest, begged the snake to release his brother. The two engaged in a long discourse about dharma, a topic nobody prior to this had ever considered debating with a snake. Yudhishthir's answers pleased Nahusha, and the curse on him was broken.

That was pretty much the last I had heard of him until now when I saw him lying in a pool of his own blood.

K peered at the body more closely.

'What's this about the tattoo?'

'All Indras acquire a tattoo when they hold the title. It endows them with the powers of that portfolio, that is, rain, lightning and the rest.' I raised my forearm to show them. Nestled at the back was a similar tiny lightning bolt.

Sars gaped at me. 'You were an Indra too?'

'For a very short time. It's a story for another day.'

'But … But why have I never heard any reference to this before?'

I grinned. 'My life was struck off the official records, remember? I'm an embarrassment to the Gandharva court; they would like to pretend I never existed.' I sobered as a thought occurred to me.

'Sars, we already suspected a Celestial's hand, but this clinches it. Look at the way he was killed.'

Sars clicked a few photos of the body from different angles and then turned to me. What about it?'

'This open wound on his throat, shaped like an X? It's made by two blades simultaneously slashing downwards. It's an extremely skilled murder wound designed to kill Celestials.'

She looked troubled. 'I don't understand.'

'Our bodies start to heal almost immediately from most wounds. The only way to kill us is to cause such catastrophic damage that the Celestial dies faster than they can heal. A wound like this … the killer cut Nahusha's food pipe and windpipe at the same time. The angle of the blow and the way it's done, he managed to asphyxiate him while filling his lungs with blood and drowning him.'

'And you know this how?'

'I've seen this before. During the great war. The more skilled warriors, 'maharathis', were proficient in ways to fend off and fight Celestials.'

There was no need to explain which war I was referring to.

'You think this was done by a maharathi?'

I had to study the scene for a bit. 'No, this has been done with knives, not swords. But it's still somebody with decades of fighting experience, I'm almost certain of it. Most humans would also not have the strength or precision to execute such precise slashes.'

'You may want to take a look at this', K called out. He had lifted one edge of the carpet and was staring at the bottom. We stepped closer to where he was standing and peered at the floor.

A pentagram drawn within a circle stared back at us. There were several glyphs in different positions within the circle.

'Umm, thoughts?' K asked.

'It's a standard pentagram to summon demons,' Sars said. She gave me a quick look. 'Still think the two events aren't related?'

'You remember that saying Shukra is fond of? Once is happenstance, twice is a coincidence, thrice is enemy action.' I held up a hand to forestall K's quips, 'I don't think this is a coincidence. At the same time, something seems off; I can't quite put my finger on it.'

'Sars, you want to ...?'

'On it.' Sars extracted a slim notebook and a pencil from her bag and began sketching the symbols from the circle.

'Did the ritual work?' I asked. 'Is there a demon loose somewhere in the city?'

She shook her head. 'If they did summon a demon, it didn't get out. This is pretty well made.'

'At least the police should be able to catch this guy quickly if they have him on film', K said. He caught us both giving him incredulous looks. 'What did I say?'

Given that he had lived for so long, it was easy to forget that K could sometimes be just a touch clueless. 'They are never going to find the guy, K. Why do you think he stared into the camera?'

Changing your appearance was one of the most basic forms of illusion that any Celestial could perform. If you know there is a camera in the room, you change your appearance into something nondescript, a face that you use once and then discard. It's shapeshifting 101.

It is pretty easy to fool other Celestials by altering your appearance as well. Unless you consciously look at their physical shape on other planes of existence through your third eye, you can be fooled into believing someone was who they claimed to be.

The policeman entered the room. 'Miss, you really need to be going,' he said apologetically.

Sars thanked him for his susceptibility to bribery, and together we headed back out from the main entrance and continued to walk down one of the inside roads which curved to the right and lead to the beach. We sat on a bench below a streetlight and began to plan our next move.

Something occurred to me, 'This problem that I'm facing at the moment with my powers … I am assuming you are all in the same boat? Has it been getting worse for you too?'

'My powers are more passive', Sars said. 'It's not often that I try to use them. I've not encountered any specific instances where they failed.'

Sars could perform all the basic tricks most Celestials could—shapeshifting, turning invisible, etc. Her real power, though, was understanding the hidden paths of learning. She could access higher order insights and decode what people tried to hide. As a young Goddess born less than a few decades ago, her powers were naturally sporadic—sudden flashes of insight rather than omniscience. If they blinked out on occasion, she wouldn't necessarily notice.

K yawned. 'Do you mean if I have suddenly turned visible in public without wanting to? That hasn't happened'. He considered. 'I haven't tried making people fall in love since they learned how to do that themselves, so maybe that power might be failing; I've never bothered to check.'

K's invisibility was unlike that of other Celestials. His was an art form of the highest order. When he walked, there was nary a sound nor a mark of his passing even on sand. His breath did not fog glass, his whisper in your ear could be heard by no one besides yourself. It was the most potent form of invisibility there was; nothing that I knew of could dispel or circumvent it.

It was also a natural extension of himself. To him, it was like breathing. He had acquired it as an unintended gift when Lord Shiva burnt his physical body and brought him back to life. Being invisible was his default state.

Besides that, he had no real powers of consequence. Unless you counted his ability to annoy people and drive them up the wall.

Me, on the other hand? As a Yaksha and a warrior of the Celestial court, battle magic was pretty much my most important skill. Using it in the service of dharma was what I was raised for. I could feel the magic within me, itching to pour forth—I just couldn't reach into my main wellspring of power. All I had was my mini well, the one that held only a little trickle of mana at a time, just enough to keep me alive.

'So, where do we go now?' Sars asked.

In case I haven't mentioned this before, Sars is the youngest of our little clique. There are times when she is like an excitable teenager. Grisly murders and forbidden knowledge were like catnip to her.

'Sars, you aren't coming with us. I'll investigate this with K.'

'What?!' she cried. 'That's ridiculous! I can be much more useful than K, and you know it. All he can do is turn invisible!' She made herself disappear briefly before shimmering back into existence. 'See, I can do that as well!'

'Yeah, but can you make people fall in love?' K drawled as he pulled out and tore open a packet of pistachios.

'You just said you haven't done that in a while.'

K looked sheepish. 'That's true'.

'Sars, you are super valuable to us, much more than K, I admit.'

K made a rude noise and continued munching.

'I can't decide if you are being sexist or just pig-headed,' she groaned. 'Come on, Akran, this isn't fair, and you know it. You tried to pull this macho crap with Deanne last time, and she nearly killed you for suggesting we leave her behind.'

'Sars, I swear to you, this is not a gender thing, alright? Among all of us, you are the only one who can help look at all the angles from a different point of view. Whoever we are up against is far more tech-savvy than me or K. Between the three of us, who do you think could best unravel the digital trail?'

She nodded, mollified but still looking annoyed.

'Hear me out on what we need. Once that is set up, we will take you along. Heck, I give you my word, you can be by our side every step of the friggin' way.'

'Okay, what do you need?'

'The Watcher Programme, you are still updating it?'

A couple of months ago, I had requested Sars to help track any/all Celestials still on Earth—not just from our mythos but from across the world. Given that there were so many of us, there was always a chance something would go wrong somewhere and we would get affected. All Sars had to do was record any sightings of Celestials around the block and keep an up-to-date roster on them. She had labelled it the Watcher Programme, which I guessed was either a reference to a show about a teenage girl who slayed vampires or a middle-aged Scotsman who went about chopping people's heads off with a sword.

She gave me a quizzical look. 'Every chance I get. Why?'

'I want to know if this is recent. Have there been any other Celestial deaths before this, or is it a new development? Do you have some facial recognition algorithm that can do that?'

She nodded. 'I wrote the code for it when we were on the case with the missing girls.'

'Okay. Any murders or disappearances in the last year? Let's check if there were any Celestials. Anyone else with a matching tattoo like the one I just showed you? Or anyone murdered in this fashion. Maybe it's a signature move.'

She nodded briskly, her eyes unblinking.

'The summoning circle in the middle will be connected to some sort of ritual. Check if that matches any prior crime scenes.'

'Shouldn't take longer than a day.'

'One more thing. Look for star charts, planetary alignments, anything that's been mentioned in old texts that indicates why this is happening.'

She gaped at me. 'You want me to study planetary alignments? There could be billions out there. I don't even know what I'm looking for!'

'Start small. Look at every mention of a sacrifice, yagna, ritual in Puranic texts, Vedas conducted because stars aligned. Check if any of those matches with anything that's coming up in the next month or so. You can continue to see Mumbai as the central spatial coordinate for the star chart. It's like finding a needle in a haystack, but if we get lucky, we might know what the agenda behind the next murder is and when it is taking place.'

'I wish it was as clear-cut as a needle. It's actually like looking for a stalk of hay in a city full of haystacks.' She grumbled. 'I'll need to write a whole new programme for this.'

She sounded like she was complaining, but I knew she was pleased. Sars liked these challenges. Like a cat with a ball of string, Sars would play with this problem till she had extracted every scrap of insight from it.

'If anyone can do it, it is you, Sars. Now, do you get why we thought you should stay back?'

She rolled her eyes. 'Spare me. What are you two idiots going to be doing?'

'I'm going to try and find information the old-fashioned way,' I said. 'Banging on doors and seeing what turns up.'

CHAPTER FOUR

Let me introduce you to the universe's most exhausting tropes: Aspects, Avatars, Heroes and Chosen Ones. Each one is a cosmic joke—proof that whoever's running this show has a terrible sense of humour.

Aspects are fractured pieces of divinity walking around in semi-mortal forms. Picture a deity staring into a broken mirror; each shard is an Aspect. When the original God kicks the bucket (yes, even Gods expire), one Aspect gets promoted. The rest vanish like bad tweets. Sars, for example, is an Aspect of Saraswati, a Goddess of Knowledge.

Avatars are divine cheat codes. Gods use them to bend their own rules without technically breaking them. It's like swapping your divine form for a mortal one—suddenly, you can get drunk, fall in love, or even straight up invade their island kingdom and assassinate a troublesome demon. Or interfere in a family feud to ensure one side completely exterminates the other. The catch? Kill an avatar when he *isn't expecting it, and the God dies too. You'd think that'd keep them away, but no—some of them have a death wish.*

Heroes are cosmic accidents. The universe occasionally produces individuals who, through some combination of trauma, circumstance and stubborn refusal to die, become catalysts for change. Parents murdered in a dark alley? Planet exploded? Summoned a demon in Newcastle that ate your friends? If you got through all that with your sanity intact and decided to now 'help' other people, then you're a Hero! The Greeks insisted they needed divine DNA, because apparently, being extraordinary isn't impressive unless Zeus was a deadbeat dad. But truth? Heroes aren't born—they're just survivors history calls 'brave' instead of 'unlucky'.

Finally, Chosen Ones—because when cosmic forces need something done but don't trust the professionals, they grab some poor schmuck and go, 'Tag, you're it!' One incredibly special lad (occasionally a girl, but the world has always been sexist, so it's more often than not a man) upon whom the survival of the species rests. The identifying marks—lightning shaped scars, birthmarks, or prophetic dreams—are less for the Chosen One's benefit and more so everyone else knows who to blame when it all goes tits-up. They've got plot armour thicker than a John Wick movie, but don't get too comfy—your loved ones? Your dog? Your sense of humour? Fair game!

—The Private Journals of Akran (Abridged, Amused and So Over It).

The party was in full swing when we made our entrance. For K, the blaring music, seizure-inducing lights, obnoxiously dressed people and the smoke were completely normal. I, on the other hand, had to grit my teeth and remind myself this wouldn't last very long. It was my fault, really, I still hadn't developed an appreciation for places where the primary goal seemed to be a pointless assault on the senses.

The Garage Pub was the most popular bar on the west side of Mumbai. We were there to meet a man we had heard plenty about but never actually seen. Takshaka, was an information broker and thus, one of the most powerful people in the city.

We found ourselves a booth near the entrance and settled down. K, as he typically did, decided to mingle and immediately vanished. Sars was doing shots at the bar. A bottle of Old Monk and some appetisers kept me entertained.

An hour went by. I was just about to order another Old Monk when someone joined me.

'Narayan?' he said with a raised eyebrow and a beaming smile.

I was in no mood to entertain strangers. 'No. Go away', I said before my mind registered the fact that he hadn't walked over to my booth. One minute the seat opposite me was empty, and the next, he was sitting there, bemused.

'My apologies', he said, his voice rumbling with laughter. 'It's a private joke.'

Celestials and their sense of humour! Nobody else gets their jokes.

He had a pleasant, kind face and smelled strongly of sandalwood. He wore an ash-grey suit with an open-necked shirt and no tie. It was the wrong kind of look for the bar we were in, but somehow, he made it work.

I pushed the Old Monk towards him. Like it or not, he was at my table and in the city I called my home. I would observe the basic courtesies. 'Would you like a drink?'

He beamed at me. 'Is this one of those things where once I drink from your table, I'm not allowed to harm you?'

'Huh? No!'

'Or where I accept and then lose consciousness and you take me to your room and have your way with me?' He leaned forward and gave me a conspiratorial wink. 'I've been watching humans for a long time. I know all the tricks.'

I glared at him. 'It's just a drink. Do you want it or not?'

He shook his head, white teeth shining as he spoke. 'I don't drink. Never touch the stuff. Too vile for my taste.'

'Well, you must be fun at parties,' I muttered as I poured the last remaining dregs into my glass. I wasn't trying to be rude. I had this mild headache for the past couple of hours, which was unusual … Celestials didn't suffer from earthly illnesses.

'What's with the suit?'

'I heard its customary on earth during formal meetings.'

I snorted. 'In Orange County perhaps'. We don't stand on formalities here.

The stranger's eyes twinkled. 'So glad you cleared that up—you are holding a lot of the cards, you know. Literally, I mean.'

The quip was clever, but it was starting to wear thin. I leaned back, letting my silence speak for me.

He straightened, his voice shedding its playful edge. 'Akran Adi Kuru, of the clan Kuru. I've heard much about you.'

Now we were getting somewhere. 'Just Akran,' I said, meeting his gaze. I knew power games—had written the rules for a few myself. He was flexing, dredging up a family name buried for millennia, erased from every record. 'And you're Takshaka, I presume.'

He laughed, a deep, rich sound that felt like a warm baritone inside my head. 'Takshaka? Why would you even want to meet him?'

I opened my mouth to answer and then stopped. For the life of me, I couldn't remember why I wanted to meet Takshaka. More importantly, what was I doing in this pub?

I looked around. Sars was with us? Wasn't she supposed to have gone back home? I recalled us talking on the beach, and then I had found myself here, drinking in a bar waiting for a man who, until a short while ago, I hadn't even heard of.

Add this together with the annoying pain in the back of my head and this stranger grinning smugly at me, and this had decidedly turned into something more insidious.

I slid one hand under the table. A quick flick of my wrist and a card lay between my thumb and index finger, charging up as I studied the stranger.

He was still watching me with an amused look on his face.

'Easy there, friend. I didn't mean to frighten you. You are right. I did nudge you and your friends to meet me, but my intentions were a hundred percent honourable.' He gave a disarming smile. 'Can we please start over?'

'Who are you?'

'I'm not Takshaka. That will have to do for now.'

'Okay, not Takshaka. Why did you bring us here?'

'I needed a place we could talk without being watched.'

His explanation was smooth and well-rehearsed. Like he knew exactly what I was going to ask.

I don't usually find men attractive but this stranger was charm personified. There was something about him that I liked. He seemed like a kindred spirit. I could imagine sharing a drink with him, climbing atop tables and singing lustily, not a care in the world.

Something niggled at the back of my mind. It was not in my nature to like people instinctively like I was doing right now. I was more the 'hate everyone till I get to know them' kind of person, and as I tried to focus on what was different, the pain in the back of my head intensified. Now it was a hammer beating inside my skull. Something was telling me to ignore this stray thought. Don't let it get in the way. Be happy and be loved.

Yeah, fuck that!

I hadn't survived millennia letting random assholes fuck with me. The pain intensified into a keen blade, still stabbing the inner recesses of my mind as I gripped the edge of the table and pushed back against this foreign intrusion.

The man smiled as he watched this play across my face.

'One of my innate talents, Akran, is to defuse situations. I add a sense of calm and tranquillity to my surroundings. Your mind is rebelling because it senses a spell being cast, but I assure you I am not your enemy; stop fighting me, and the pain will go away.'

I shook my head. 'I don't trust anyone who needs spells to make me trust them.'

The man's eyes narrowed. 'You believe you can challenge me and win? I am not like that fool Ashwatthama whom you beat last time around. Throw down with me, and you will find what true power feels like.'

I snorted. 'I don't give a fuck how powerful you are. You think you are the first asshole to tell me to just bend over because he thinks he's got the biggest dick in town?' I leaned forward and snarled into his face. 'Whatever the fuck you are doing to me, quit it NOW! Or face the consequences!'

'With what? That flower in your hand?'

I withdrew my hand from under the table. Sure enough, in it was no longer a card but a bright red flower.

Oddly enough, the sight didn't deter me in the slightest. Quite the opposite, it snapped the leash on my tightly reined anger. As it spilt free in my head, it burnt away the little charm spell. No longer did I think of him as a wonderful person. I could feel hate right under the anger bubbling to the top.

'I invented this move, wanker! It's a great illusion, I'll give you that. I suppose if I was one of your regular rubes, I would just fling it away and be done with it, right?' I shifted my fingers slightly as I prepared to fling the flower onto his face. 'Silly me, this is just a big, harmless flower. Here, let me toss it at you and see what happens.'

The man sighed. 'Akran, stop. If you attack me, I will be forced to kill you. This is completely counterproductive. I did not come here for this.' He raised his hands in a disarming gesture.

Almost instantly, the headache was gone, leaving a dull throbbing sensation; the flower changed back into an ordinary playing card and flickered in my hands, saturated with energy. My fingers itched to throw it across the table. I tapped it lightly, and the glow faded as I absorbed the mana back in.

The man's eyes narrowed slightly as he studied me.

'You are a strange one, I must admit. I had not expected you to be so difficult. At least now, I can see why he was so fond of you.'

He was no longer the handsome man my brain had initially perceived. To be fair, he wasn't bad looking either, just an ordinary man with a nondescript face and dark circles under his eyes.

I placed the card on the table along with the rest of my pack. My hands shook with rage. I clenched my fists to get my anger under control.

There are a lot of things I could let slide but violating my mind was not something I could ignore. Not after all the trauma I had undergone over the last few millennia with my memories locked up.

'You brought me here. You planted the idea in my head that we were supposed to meet Takshaka.' My fingertips brushed across the deck lightly to let him know that just because I had lowered my weapon, I wasn't going to start trusting him yet.

I glanced around and saw Sars and K watching us from the other side of the room. They had sensed something was wrong and were starting to make their way back through the crowd of nubile female bodies and the fat, sweaty men dancing with them.

He gave them a quick glance before turning his attention to me.

'You are right. I apologise for what I did. As you can see, you and your friends are fine. Even now, they are making their way across to us.' He paused. 'And you will need to visit Takshaka anyway so all I've done is nudge you in the right direction.'

I scowled at him but said nothing.

'We seem to have gotten off on the wrong foot, little Yaksha. Could we start again?'

I was getting really tired of this 'little Yaksha' crap. At five feet and eight inches, I was doing pretty decently on the average height for this era. It wasn't my fault most Celestials were at least seven feet, to begin with.

I don't think they even realised that adding a diminutive was offensive. It was like how in some worlds you could just call someone a bastard or a dwarf because that's what they were and expect them to not take offence.

I gave him a glacial smile, one that would freeze even Elsa's socks off. 'You know what they say about people who call others little—they are just overcompensating because of their, you know …' I gave a meaningful glance at his groin in case I was being too subtle.

The man guffawed. 'If you are suggesting we whip them out and indulge in a measuring contest, little Yaksha, all you will find is another reason to feel small in my presence.'

I closed my eyes and counted to ten. He was getting under my skin. Also, it felt like he had come across better in our little snippy game, so I decided not to give him the satisfaction and just pointedly turned my head away to watch my friends.

K and Sars reached our table, sparing us from continuing the pissing contest. K was whispering something, and Sars was giggling. They looked like two happy, normal humans in a bar. Normal, except for the fact that one could make you fall in love with a lamp post if he wanted to, and the other had forgotten more knowledge than most humans would acquire in a dozen lifetimes.

The man gave him a smile that stretched from ear to ear. 'Kama dev,' he said warmly, 'I'll have you know that I have only succumbed once to your influence. Never again. I am humbled by your presence here.'

K accepted the praise with a bemused smile, then gave me a who-the-fuck-is-this-guy look. I shrugged. I had no idea.

The man took Sars's hand and kissed it gently. 'Lady Saraswati, this is an honour.'

Sars looked at him closely, and her eyes widened. 'Lord N ...' she began, but the stranger put his index finger on her lips.

'To say my name is to force my hand. My enemies will know who I am and what I can do. At present, I am free, and I would very much like to remain this way.'

Sars nodded gravely. It was like watching a curtain fall. The happy-go-lucky teenager was gone, leaving behind someone sombre and intense. She muttered a hymn, and I felt a cone of silence descending upon the table. Anything we said here could not be heard outside.

I still had no fucking clue who this guy was. His calm, self-assured manner indicated that he was someone of power, but as far as I could tell, he was neither demon nor Celestial. He seemed human but a long-lived one. I could have glanced at him with my true sight, but alcohol, like most intoxicants, blinds it. In my defence, this was an unexpected situation. He had played us. The whole point of getting us to a bar and making us wait was so that we would have a few drinks and not be able to use our true sight. What he hadn't counted on was Sars's innate abilities kicking in. I saw his eyes widen in surprise when she figured out who he was. Sars and I were going to have words later.

'How can we assist?' she asked politely, casting me a meaningful look.

The stranger spoke slowly. Like every word mattered.

'I came because you'll need my help.'

A brief silence followed his words.

'I believe that if you continue on your present path, you are likely to meet a quick and very nasty end.' He glanced around the table. 'Each and every one of you.'

I cleared my throat. 'Could you be more specific? What is our present path? And why do we matter enough that you have chosen to give us this warning?' From the corner of my eye, I saw Sars glare at me, and I quickly added, 'Not that we aren't grateful for the warning, but it would help to understand what it means.'

The stranger sighed. 'Ever played Chaturanga?'

I had played it on occasion. It was a precursor to chess and immensely popular among Celestials and kings at one time. I shrugged non-committally. Every Celestial I knew played dice, cards and chaturanga. Besides weapons, these were the essentials in a warrior's kit.

'You have unwittingly become a part of a game being played on a cosmic scale. The stakes are immeasurable; they impact the lives of every living thing on this planet.'

'A game?' I repeated, trying hard to keep the scepticism from my voice.

'I call it a game because of what it looks like from the outside peering in. It's not a frivolous activity being indulged in to pass the time. This is a war that started before the birth of man, when the Gods as you know them today were nought but pale imitations of themselves. A battle being fought in secret for millennia but which will explode out of the shadows and into open warfare very soon.'

'You are one of the players in this shadow war?' K hazarded a guess.

The man shook his head. 'No. It's bigger than everything you are thinking of, bigger than the Devas, the trinity, all of it. I am but a tiny piece, forgotten and undeployed in the field of battle.'

'So why aren't you taking a more active role?' I asked.

'Does the king step out and crush his enemies all by himself? Does the queen expose herself too early? Some pieces are on the board, and their time has not yet come. Bringing them out now may win a battle, but they could lose the war. I have either been forgotten, or am in reserve, waiting for the right moment. Either way, it allows me a certain latitude in my movement.'

'You are saying you are not free to act,' K guessed. He had grasped the convoluted ramblings of this guy. I hadn't. Listening to these vague, airy threats felt like he was peddling some pyramid scheme.

'Every piece has free will, but not every piece can see beyond its own nose. There are those of us with self-awareness who choose when to make a play that will have the most impact.' His smile became a bit more brittle. 'And there are some that get swept up by the currents of what's happening around them and sacrifice the long gain for the short win.'

Oh, okay! He had moved from crackpot conspiracy theories to talking about me.

'You have blundered onto a cosmic board, Akran, and your actions have made you a part of the game. You were a non-entity, a nobody, someone who was ignored because you didn't officially exist in the Celestial records. That was Krishna's plan all along, for you to live out your life in ignominy, forgotten and underestimated. You could have, at the right time, dealt a crippling blow when the enemy least expected it. Instead, you chose to expose yourself early and reveal yourself as someone of consequence. Now every move you make will have a counter, every action a reaction.'

He gave me a pointed look, and I met his gaze unflinchingly.

'I suppose you would have preferred that I let Ashwatthama resurrect Narakasura?'

He sighed again, the third time in as many minutes. He had got the disappointed parent routine down pat.

'Don't take offence at my words, but you all are like children playing with fire while drenched in oil.'

Condescending asshole. 'How could we possibly take offence to the lovely picture you've painted of us?' I enquired sweetly. Sars kept giving me warning glances, and I kept pointedly ignoring her.

'Yes, you should have ignored Ashwatthama. Trusted that things would take care of themselves, that you were not the only one out there watching over the fate of the world.'

Maybe, I conceded. 'But I'm pretty damn certain I was the only one watching out for the fate of the kids.'

He sighed.

'They were not your concern. You got lucky with Ashwatthama. The only thing you can do now is play the game to its end, until you fulfil your destiny or are yourself removed from the board.' He looked grim. 'Your current path, this proverbial bull in a china shop approach you have to solving problems, is precisely the behaviour that will get you killed. That's what I have come to warn you about. As a friend, devotee and well-wisher of your patron.'

'Patron?'

'You have neither the strength nor the wit to deal with this on your own'. He looked at my friends. 'Present company included. You need an ally, someone more powerful than you, to assist in this fight. Someone not from our realm who will come to your aid when you call them. They are beneath the notice of the true players.'

'All of this is what? A pitch from you, offering to be our friend to assist us?' I knew I sounded churlish, but I couldn't help myself. He had rubbed me the wrong way, and it was taking me time to move from my mood of severe dislike back to my usual mild indifference.

He smirked. 'I'm afraid I would make a very poor ally. I would gladly sacrifice all of you if it meant gaining a material advantage.'

At least he was honest.

Sars spoke up, 'Tell us more about the shadow war. Who the players are, what you know about their plans ... we can then act accordingly.'

The man said nothing, choosing instead to merely stare at her. A minute passed with both of them sitting there, staring at each other.

I felt a rush of irritation at his behaviour. Admittedly, I was not at my best. I had never been comfortable showing deference to someone more powerful than me, and them being rude to people I cared about was intolerable. Who did this idiot think he was? He had brought us here and was choosing to ignore a perfectly reasonable question to gawk at Sars. I leaned forward to give him a piece of my mind, but at that moment, K grabbed my arm. He too was staring intently at Sars.

She had a dreamy look on her face. I knew that look. It was when she applied her mind to a problem, and her power nudged her towards an answer.

'You cannot tell us because the mere act of explaining the rules draws attention to yourself,' she said softly. 'You would no longer be neutral because you have brought new people on the board.'

K brightened. 'I think I'm starting to understand,' he whispered. 'It's like Fight club. Or how we don't talk about Bruno.'

I gave him a pained look. 'Yes, it is probably exactly like that. Now hush.'

If Sars had heard our whispered exchange, she chose to ignore it. She was still staring at the man, her eyes glittering with excitement.

'The churning of the ocean,' she said, 'that's a likely point when the game, as you call it, began, because only after that event did you have immortals—long lasting pieces that could influence centuries instead of mere decades.' There was a slow and burgeoning confidence as she spoke. 'Which is why the death of Krishna and the age of science beginning was so devastating. It levelled the playing field and overturned the board, forcing everyone to start over.'

The man continued to say nothing. He looked like he was carved of stone.

'We are all given the same information, it's up to us what we can infer from it,' Sars spoke slowly, perhaps unconsciously emulating the man's measured tone. 'If you tell us what to do or what the rules are, or any other details, we would end up becoming a part of the board.' Her tone grew perplexed. 'But why? You claim that you haven't yet made your move, but you have awareness. Which means it's actions that determine what you do, not knowledge.'

She studied him closely. 'Ah! For you, actions and awareness are two entirely different things. But for us … that's not the case. You think we are impulsive. That we will run around putting out little fires instead of looking at the big picture. Like we did by stopping Ashwatthama.'

The stranger finally cracked a smile. 'Lady Saraswati, you are everything I was lead to believe. It has indeed been an honour to meet you.' He reached out and kissed her hand once again, and Sars blushed a deep crimson.

'That's it? You brought us here to tell us a half-baked conspiracy theory about cosmic games, and you think that was helpful?' I couldn't keep the sharpness from my tone. 'How could we have survived without that utterly useless information?'

He gave me a curious look.

'I gave you a warning. Was that not enough?'

'You've told us nothing of consequence except to be careful.'

He gave us another of his infuriating smiles. 'Let me spell it out then. You are reckless, stubborn and ill-tempered. Instead of forging you into a living weapon, your experience among humans has made you soft and weak. You cannot be trusted to do the right thing. Your decisions are clouded by sentiment. In short, Akran, you are a wild card. Taking you off the board entirely to prevent our enemies getting a hold of you and using you against us is a scenario we are seriously considering.' He cocked his head. 'Is that enough, or do you need me to spell it out even further?'

This was what he meant when he said If I attacked him, he would be forced to kill me. If my actions were being studied, an attack by me on anyone would invite scrutiny. And if the victim responded, his actions would draw attention. Damned if you do, damned if you don't. This was what they called the prisoners' dilemma.

I could almost admire the cold-blooded rationality behind it. Almost.

Maybe I should have worked a bit harder on ingratiating myself to him.

I clenched my fists. 'You arrogant little shit! I have always lived by my code. Protect the weak. Help the oppressed. Kill only when there is no other choice. You and your masters, whoever they are, do not know me well enough if you think I can be turned. To act against my nature.'

Sars grabbed my arm in alarm as I started to rise from my seat. Even K looked panic-stricken, but I would not be deterred. I shook my hand free as the anger within my breast now rose to the fore. 'What you are describing with all your fancy-assed euphemisms as a "cosmic game" and whatnot is just big talk for what we encounter on a daily basis. You are just trying to couch it in mystic mumbo jumbo to make it sound like the whole fucking universe is caught up in some giant conspiracy. The choices we make every day define who we are. Good or evil. Light or darkness. And I have always, ALWAYS, done what is right!'

If I had ignited even the tiniest spark of anger, it didn't show. 'I may have gone about this the wrong way,' he murmured. 'I apologise for not handling this very well. Perhaps I could just show you?' He pointed at the deck that was still lying on the table next to me. 'If you permit, I would like to do a reading. May I borrow that for a moment?'

I glanced at the deck and did a double take. These were no longer the playing cards I had sat down with. These looked like a tarot deck, but unlike anything I had seen before. They had hand-drawn illustrations, lifelike in appearance. Of greater concern was that the illustrations were moving. A snake slithered across the branches of a tree bursting with fruit, an old man hung on a tree branch while ravens pecked at his eyes, a massive war chariot flew across the skies as two vast armies of monsters I had only heard legends of collided all around it.

Creation myths. I recognised some but not all. This was not a deck constrained to the mythos of the subcontinent; its origins seemed more primordial, encompassing multiple realms.

Wordlessly, I passed the cards to him.

'You are doing a reading here?' K asked incredulously. 'In the middle of a crowded bar, surrounded by humans?'

The man looked around. 'Crowded?' he asked with a smirk.

He snapped his fingers. Reality … shifted.

I felt my eyes blur for an instant and my ears popped. When my vision cleared, we were all alone. Still at the garage pub, but the lights were out, the people had departed, and the stools were propped up on the bar.

Even the sticky residue of spilled drinks on our table had dried, hours old. The murmur of Mumbai's early morning traffic filtered in from outside, replacing the thumping bass that had filled the space just seconds ago.

The clock struck 5 a.m. We were the only people inside the place. It was pitch dark except for the cards which glowed in front of him.

'I have some control over time, among other things,' the man said. 'We are quite alone now.' He began to shuffle the deck, slowly at first, his hands gathering momentum as the shuffling intensified.

K and I shot each other a quick glance. Manipulating time was an incredibly rare and dangerous skill.

'You may think of yourself as a good person, Akran. I know you believe it with every fibre of your being. I also know my opinion isn't worth much to you at the moment, but that little outburst of yours really moved me. It would be folly for us to dismiss what you could bring to the table.'

Sars looked completely and utterly taken in by the stranger, star-struck as his hands began to blur, and the cards were shuffled faster and faster.

I have seen divinations performed before. It is old magic, often attempted, rarely interpreted properly. The problem, as I understand it, is that divination can only show you potential futures. It is inexact, and a lot depends on the skill of the user. I had no doubt that the man dealing the deck was an expert, yet even he could not predict a future set in stone, could he?

'Didn't you tell us that performing magic would expose you?' I asked.

The man shrugged. 'Divinations are not magic, not really. I'm laying out potential futures, that's all. One could argue that the magic is all in the cards, and I'm just playing with them.' He smiled again. 'Now, if I were to select a particular future for you fine people and make that yours, that's more than just a little trick. That's real magic. It would expose me, yes. And bring the world tumbling down on our heads.'

'You can do that?' Despite Sars's awe for the man, even she must have felt that some of his claims did seem far-fetched.

'This is no ordinary deck, lady. It is one of the most powerful artefacts in existence. A true master of the deck could unmake creation with something like this. Fortunately for all concerned, there has been no true master in over ten thousand years.'

Sars leaned back in stunned silence.

'What I am about to show you, as a journeyman, is what has occurred, what is possibly happening and what may happen. Pay no heed or learn from it, the choice is yours.'

With an almost careless motion, the man tossed the cards on the table. We watched in stunned silence as they came alive, shuffling themselves rapidly.

A pressure began to build in the room as the cards rose from the table.

'Secrets buried, secrets deep.' The man's voice was devoid of the amusement with which it rang until a moment ago. Now he sounded brisk and cold. His hands stayed on the table, but his words seemed to echo. 'From their slumber let them leap.'

The cards began to twirl faster, and the images inside began to reassemble. A blue-skinned warrior fired an arrow that penetrated three shining cities floating in the sky. A half-man, half-lion burst forth from a pillar. A young woman stepped into a massive pyre as all around her, monkeys armed with weapons wailed and screamed.

'Thread of fate, strand of time—show what reason cannot rhyme.'

One of the cards rose higher than the rest. On it was a picture of K. He looked … young. A mendicant seated cross-legged, clad in tiger skin, was immolating him in a fire that was pouring from an eye on his head. The card screamed, and the smell of burning flesh filled the room. K's eyes were wide and frightened as he stared at the card, his whole body drenched in sweat. This was a memory from his past. The card slammed into him, lifting him off his chair and flinging him into the wall behind.

I rose from my chair to lend K a hand. One of the cards caught my eye. A little boy standing barefoot in a forest. Animal skin covered his waist, his hair wild and unshorn. He held a wooden boat and a look of intense longing in his eyes, standing next to a dry river bed. Behind him the sky was overcast, a massive storm was brewing.

The card sparked a memory but I couldn't quite place it. In a second, it was gone, and the card now depicted a vast ocean as far as the eye could see.

'What is woven, what is spun—show the threads that can't be undone.'

A second card rose above the rest—a montage of images flickering rapidly past: an old woman trapped in a hellish prison while a young girl earnestly sought her release; Deanna, my ex-girlfriend, kissing a tall, blonde, muscular Scandinavian holding a hammer; me lying face down on the floor in a pool of blood, eerily similar to the crime scene we had seen earlier that evening.

The last one hadn't actually happened. And the Deanna image was also probably just random, right? I opened my mouth to ask when the card hit me in the face, and I found myself on my hands and knees, dry retching on the floor.

Past and Present. Not the one I had lived through perhaps but a glimpse into a sideways reality. Had I avoided this? Or was it meant to happen?

I looked up and saw the third card, the one that had risen above the rest. This one wasn't for the rest of them; it looked like a future that only I was meant to see.

Sars was front and centre on this card, a quizzical expression on her face. Behind her was another woman with her face masked in shadows. And as I watched, the image moved. The woman grabbed Sars's hair and slashed her throat with a red knife. Blood spurted from her throat as the Sars in the card fell to the floor.

The room felt colder, and I gasped for air. My throat tightened like a vacuum sealed bag had been wrapped around my face.

I gave a hoarse scream as I tried to get up. Blue lightning arced from my outstretched hand and hit the card. I had no idea how I called the magic to me, but it sparked from my fingers and struck the card dead centre.

It didn't do a single bit of good. Five more of the cards rose from the deck and appeared in front of me, each showing a future that I had thought impossible until now.

The first showed an older me, eyes pitch-black, blood pouring from them. I held a dagger in one hand, and a bleeding heart in another. The lifeless body of a woman lay below.

Another had me cradling Sars's body, hunched over in grief. A shadowy hand lay on my shoulder, trying to comfort me. I could hear a sibilant whisper from the person behind me but it was drowned by the noise from the others, so I couldn't hear what was being said.

A third image had a summoning circle with Sars reanimated and floating in the air. She seemed like a marionette jerking to invisible strings as I stood outside the circle, grief and anger evident on my face. K lay dead in one corner, as did Shukra, Mas, Deanne, and every single person I cared about.

A fourth card showed a world burning around me, but the look in my own eyes was empty and past caring.

And finally, the fifth image was of a mountain of skulls. A man sat on a throne that stood atop the skulls. The card moved closer, hovering right in front of my face. I stared at the card and was unsurprised at what I found. Me. On the throne.

Five possible futures. Or maybe one single dystopian future due to a sequence of events that all begin with one of my friends dying.

My limbs felt like lead. I could barely move my neck as I tried to see what was happening to my friends. Sars looked like she had fallen unconscious on the table.

The man walked up to me and crouched on the floor, placing his hand on my head. His touch was gentle, but it did nothing to quell the anguish. He bent low and whispered in my ear.

'And that, little Yaksha, is why I don't believe that you will always, ALWAYS do what is right.'

PART TWO

CHAPTER FIVE

In ancient times, there lived a bandit named Ratnakar. He was notorious for preying on unarmed travellers passing through the forest.

One day, Ratnakar accosted a sage. Far from showing any fear, the sage pointed out that the crimes he was committing now would not earn him any favours in the afterlife. His sins would ensure that he would be reborn again and again in an endless cycle, never able to attain moksha, i.e. liberation from the cycle of death and rebirth.

On principle, Ratnakar should have just chopped this fellow's head off when he began sermonising. But regretfully, he didn't and everything that followed lies on his head.

'Now hold on just one blooming minute!' said Ratnakar. 'I ain't doing this for myself. It's to put food on the table. I feed my family, don't I? They should bloody well take on some of this guilt, innit?'

'Well, that's easily resolved,' said the sage. 'Go ask your family. I'll wait! You can even tie me up, if you want.'

Knowing fully well never to trust a fellow who volunteers to be tied up, Ratnakar added a couple of extra knots and raced home to question his wife.

He was in for a rude shock.

'You chose this line of work! Don't expect me to suffer for your sins!'

'B-But, what happened to "Till death do us part?"'

'You were a thief before you married me, buddy!'

His son was also a disappointment—'Look Dad, I love you to bits, but not enough to risk my immortal soul.'

'I did what was necessary for survival.'

*'Those were choices **you** made!'*

Filled with grief, Ratnakar returned to the sage and released him, weeping and asking him how he could redeem himself. Days of cheerfully murdering people in this life hadn't really bothered him all this while, but something imperilling his soul?—That was deeply troubling as far as he was concerned.

The sage advised him to meditate on the name of the Lord Ram—because complex theological problems could often be resolved with single word solutions.

The bandit took the sage's advice. He threw away his weapons of mass abduction, sat in meditation and lost all sense of time. He did not desire food or water as he sunk deep into his trance. Years of austere penance followed. The forest became a peaceful place. An anthill grew all around him, but his penance was so deep that he didn't notice it. When he finally emerged from his trance, the bandit became known as Valmiki ('Anthill Guy'), proving that all you needed for credibility was to stand very still and let nature cover you in dirt. (It also explains why India still has so many godmen— the bar was set astonishingly low.)

Valmiki was the author of the epic poem 'Ramayana', the second most important piece of literature from Ancient

India (the first being the Mahabharata). It tells the story of Prince Ram, the seventh avatar of Lord Vishnu, and his triumph over the evil demon king Ravana who kidnaps his wife. It is one of the largest ancient epics of world literature (24,000 verses) and possibly history's most verbose way of saying 'Crime doesn't pay. Get your hands off my wife!' Or to put it even more succinctly ... FAFO.

The sage who kick-started Ratnakar's transformation? I have a sneaky suspicion that he was the stranger in the ash-grey suit I met last evening.

—The Private Journals of Akran

I rose out of bed, eyes bleary and head feeling like someone had been hitting it repeatedly with a hammer as they recited bad poetry—the kind that didn't rhyme. It had been a while since I had experienced a true hangover, that sensation of your brain trying to escape through your eye sockets.

K and Sars had both stayed over last night, or technically, the morning. Sars had taken one of the spare rooms while K had fallen asleep on the couch. It was now nearly 4 p.m., we had slept through most of the day.

I made myself a pot of elaichi chai with extra sugar and sipped it on the balcony. It helped me focus. I kept my eyes shut as I tried to recall last evening's events.

Within the last twenty-four hours, we had fought a demon, visited a crime scene, had our minds manipulated by a pompous immortal, received his cryptic warnings, watched a divination and then ...

This was the blurry part. How did we end up at my place? When did the stranger leave us?

Even as I probed the inner recesses of my mind, I knew what I would find. There were a few carefully constructed gaps in my memory. I remembered two parts of the divination—the past and the present. After that, things seemed to go dark. I knew the stranger had shown me something that had upset me. Every time I tried to recall what it was, I felt a profound sense of sadness and loss. He had deleted the memory but not the emotion associated with it.

I would need to ask K and Sars if they remembered what happened, but I wasn't holding out hope. This was not some alcohol-induced fog, this was magic; and he wouldn't have wiped only my memories.

This wasn't something I could politely ignore. Like discovering a mystery bra hanging from your ceiling fan, it demanded investigation—regardless of how uncomfortable the answers might prove to be.

I had my suspicions already. Narada, if that was who it was, believed I would go over to the 'dark side'. That would probably entail cutting my anchors, killing my friends, and burning the tethers of my normal life.

I knew stories of men from ancient myths—Raja Harishchandra, Daniel, Job—people whose faith was so strong that they shrugged off anything life threw at them and just kept on believing.

I wasn't one of those. For one, they were fictional. Even if they weren't, I lacked the noble, self-abasing, fervent zealousness that these people felt for their Gods. Having been on the other side of the fence, I knew how the sausage was made. Nobody deserves blind adherence. Not even Gods.

I would crack under pressure. The big question was if I would take the whole world down with my hatred or if I would just self-destruct alone in a corner.

A while back, I had threatened a gang of hoodlums while on a kidnapping case, by showing them what their futures would look like if they continued down that road. The cards had wailed and screamed as they tore themselves apart and frightened the gang out of their wits. It looked fancy, but those were just illusions. Sars, being the smart, methodical, and sensible one, had tracked the gang members down to see what the long-term ramifications of their interacting with someone like me were. She ran a dozen such projects, and this one was about testing on a small scale how people would react to knowing that Celestials walked amongst them.

Nearly all the hoodlums had decided to go straight. On the flip side, nearly all of them had nightmares, difficulty sleeping, elevated blood pressure, and several other stress-related ailments; their leader was currently in a mental hospital, raving about monsters.

Any Celestial or even a human with a modicum of talent would have laughed at the pathetic little illusions I had conjured, because that's all they were: Illusions. I wouldn't call what Narada had done malevolent since that would imply that he had sought to harm. Using an artefact of such power, if you were an amateur, would end your existence. There are some objects that are so far above your ability to grasp, they could turn you into a gibbering husk before you even realised it.

What he had performed was a true divination, which meant what he showed me were several likely futures. I might end up making completely different choices, and none of what I had seen might come to pass. Or, because I was running away from that future I dreaded, I could end up being pushed towards just that future. That was the whole problem with divinations—knowledge of what could happen could create a self-fulfilling prophecy.

Guess that's why he wiped my memories.

Still, the evening had not been a complete waste. For all his posturing, he had given us a few clues. For one, this cosmic game he was talking about.

I tried to recall everything he said. What would a truly cosmic game look like?

I would imagine it as one played over millennia by two or more sides. Pieces being brought into play and then discarded once they achieved their goals. Every villain who rose to become a major player countered by one of Vishnu's avatars. Synchronised steps, each one acting in tandem, serving as a check and balance for each other's abilities. A cosmic dance. Or a game. Or a shadow war, depending on how you looked at it.

Or there was no vast underlying conspiracy, and these were all the paranoid theories of a crackpot.

The most annoying part of that whole conversation? It rang true. Sage Narada (I'm sure it was him) was a shit stirrer and a pain in the ass, but he was a devout follower of Vishnu. There were plenty of stories of him going from place to place, singing the Lord's name and dropping truth bombs.

Would the trinity be players in the game? Would they even know if they were being manipulated by a cosmic entity greater than them?

Any further musings on the subject were abruptly ended when K sauntered in. He had made himself a cup of elaichi chai and was making appreciative noises and smacking his lips as he sipped it.

'Slept well?' I asked.

K nodded. He looked surprisingly okay for someone who was forced to watch one of the most traumatic events from his past in full 4D last evening.

'Do you know who that guy was from last evening?'

K stopped to consider. 'The Buddha?'

I glared at him. 'Why the fuck would we find Buddha in a bar?'

K shrugged. 'He is an old monk. Where else would you find him?'

There was no appropriate response to that. I counted to ten in my head.

'In fact,' K continued, warming to this line of reasoning, 'have you ever been to the Buddha Bar?'

'Forget about the Buddha for a moment. Any chance you remember what happened during that last divination?'

K gave me a blank look. 'What divination?'

So … some of us had even less recollection than others.

'What is the last thing you remember?'

A confused look came over his face as he tried to recall. 'You were shouting at him and then …' his voice trailed away as he realised what had happened.

'Yes. Exactly.' I caught him up on all that I remembered, including the bits before Sars and K joined us at the table, and everything I could remember from the divination.

K had known me long enough to recognise the particular pattern of stupidity I was thinking of embarking upon. 'Akran, whatever you are thinking, this guy is out of your power class.'

'Did you get a look at his aura?'

'I didn't. We were all a few drinks down. He was probably counting on it, which is why he set up the meeting at a bar and arrived fashionably late.' He hesitated. 'From what I understand, he does not appear to be one of the bad guys.'

'I'm not going looking for trouble but you heard what he said. There is a possibility that he, and whoever his friends are, might decide I'm a liability. If that happens, I need to give myself a fighting chance. He's not a Celestial, so he is prolonging his life with his own power? Or perhaps a boon of some kind? Maybe I should reach out to Mas to check if there is something new he could help design for me.'

Sars, who had woken up and silently made her way behind my chair, spoke up. 'Maybe we could think of ways to keep you safe that don't involve attacking the guy who warned us?'

I gave her a sheepish smile. I hadn't noticed her.

She pulled up a seat next to us. 'K's right, you know. He is definitely out of your power class.'

'I figured as much, with the time dilation, divination and memory manipulation.'

'Let's not forget how he calmly and coolly threatened to kill you if you attacked him', K added unhelpfully.

'Yes, that too. Which reminds me, he didn't want us to say his name. Sars, what was that about?'

She shrugged. 'From what we hinted at yesterday, there are some pretty powerful "pieces" in this so-called game. If someone is out there keeping tabs on you, there's no harm in being careful.' She raised an eyebrow. 'I believe we can speak freely here, though.'

She was right. I had lived here in this very house for many years now. The building had several layers of defensive spells and enchantments laid into its foundations. Nothing short of an asteroid could harm it. It would also not show up on a map through scrying or other magical means, and any attempts to eavesdrop through the protective charms would result in an ear-splitting headache.

How had I managed it? Pretty simple, really. I owned the building. I rented out multiple flats through a shell company and a real estate agent who asked no questions. This allowed me to be selective about my neighbours. More importantly, I had all kinds of mystical wards scattered through the building, making this place an impregnable fortress. It made me feel like Tony Stark. I certainly wasn't the only Celestial living well. Let's face it, if you are alive for as long as I've been and are still dirt poor, you probably deserve to off yourself. Compound interest alone should make every immortal a billionaire. It's Immortality 101, right after 'Don't get attached to mortals' and 'Avoid getting your picture taken'.

'So, Sars, I'm betting it was Sage Narada who paid us a visit last night?' She nodded. 'Was he always such a ...' I tried to think of a suitable expletive.

'Wanker?' K suggested.

'I was gonna go with douchebag, but that works.'

Sars stayed silent for a long minute. 'From what I recall, Narada's behaviour is like a mirror to the people he meets. He shows them how they came across when they interact with people. In other words, Akran, if you found him rude and obnoxious ...'

Ouch!

'Fair point. We got off on the wrong foot with him trying to to make me like him and the whole planting of suggestions in our mind about meeting Takshaka.'

'Actually, he did mention that us visiting Takshaka may be the right thing to do,' K said.

I gave Sars my most innocent look. It was what I could imagine using when rescuing puppies stuck in burning buildings.

'So, Sars, I'm really interested in knowing more about him. Does he have any particular strengths or weaknesses that you know of?'

'I've said it once already, and I'll say it again. Let it go. Narada is one of the most powerful sages on the planet. Making an enemy out of him is just plain stupid.'

'But he is human, right?' I persisted.

'Human and has been alive for thousands of years. Shouldn't that tell you something?'

'I'm not saying he is weak. I'm just saying, if he is human, then he is presumably alive through his own powers, yes? If he were to accidentally get bound and thrown into a magically sealed vacuum without his powers, he would just fall apart, correct?'

K chortled. 'You think adding "accidentally" in that sentence is going to fool anyone?'

'Besides,' Sars said, 'we don't know anything about why he is long-lived. Maybe one of his parents was a divine being. Maybe he got a boon. Maybe it's his own yogic powers. Maybe he's got a magical amulet around his neck, and it's never been mentioned so far. What I mean is, when you are dealing with people as powerful as him, being human is not a factor, he has transcended the limitations of being human.'

She had a point. Grumbling, I leaned back into my chair to think.

Sars softened as she watched the worry lines on my face. 'Why is this so difficult for you? Why can't you just accept that there are people out there who are tougher than you and get on with your life? You don't need to step into his orbit, and you may never even see him again.'

I gave a mirthless chuckle. 'Sars, this is not a fragile ego crisis, if that's what you think. I have no problem with accepting there are bigger, badder fish in the ocean. It's just ...' I shrugged helplessly. 'Something about the vision he showed me. I have no idea what it was, but it scared me. It feels like we are walking down a dangerous path and I need to do something to keep us safe. I just don't know what it is.'

'Picking a fight with someone like that may be exactly what your brain should be warning you not to do,' said Sars.

'You both know me pretty well by now. I'm not going to roll over and let nature run its course. If you have other ideas, I'm happy to hear them.'

'I had a suggestion,' Sars said. 'I was going to tell you about it yesterday. Remember what we were speaking about? When the demon Vritra got resurrected? You said the only way to do that was through the Sanjivani mantra?'

I nodded. 'What about it?'

'There's one more way, apparently. It's not publicly known or referenced anywhere except in one text, a treatise for alternative healing written by the royal physician of the kingdom of Manalura.' Sars looked quite pleased with herself. 'I transcribed it myself. It was written in Pali, but a lot of the etymological roots were from Odia and once I ran them through a neural net using a combination of LLMs, and vectorised the shared latent spaces ...'

'Sars,' I interrupted gently.

She looked embarrassed. 'Right, right. So, there is a story of how the Celestial brothers of Bhishma were angry with Arjuna for his role in killing Bhishma through treachery in the Kurukshetra war. You know it?'

I did. Bhishma had sworn never to harm a woman, and so Arjun rode his chariot into battle, hiding behind Shikhandi, and shot Bhishma with arrows. Bhishma refused to shoot back, and that's how he was eventually defeated.

'Okay, so the Vasus decided that this way of killing Bhishma was dishonourable and so Arjun would die and be sent to hell. Uloopi was a Naga princess who was deeply in love with Arjun. She heard about the curse and pleaded for a way for it to be lifted. The curse was then modified so that Arjun would die at the hands of his own son Babruvahana. This eventually came to pass during an Ashwamedha yagna.'

I nodded. An Ashvamedha yagna was one where the king performing the yagna let a horse loose to wander where it chose to for a year. Anyone who disputed the sovereignty of the king performing the yagna could seize or kill the horse and defeat the warriors accompanying it. After one year, if no enemy had managed to kill or capture the horse, the animal would be guided back to the king's capital. The horse was then sacrificed, and the king would be declared an undisputed sovereign.

Royal legitimacy, it turned out, could be measured by one's ability to successfully babysit a wandering horse for twelve months. The entire empire would watch as their mighty ruler dedicated a year of military resources to what was essentially an elaborate game of follow-the-leader with livestock. Should the horse survive its leisurely tour of the kingdom—dodging the occasional enemy who fancied themselves horse-killers—it would earn the privilege of being butchered as proof of the king's unquestionable greatness.

In my opinion, it was just another pointless dick-swinging contest.

'So, after the war, Yudhishthir conducted an Ashwamedha yagna. Arjun was the one guarding the horse. It wandered into the territory of his son Babruvahana, and the two battled despite the fact that Babruvahana didn't really want to fight his own father and even told Arjun so. Instead of taking the win, Arjun admonished his son for failing to perform his duty as a Kshatriya, protector of the honour of his kingdom. So Babruvahana seized the horse, the two fought, and one of Babruvahana's arrows pierced Arjun's heart, ending his life and fulfilling the curse. At that moment, Uloopi stepped in and used the magical gem of the Nagas to bring him back to life.'

I hadn't heard this tale before.

'The gem,' continued Sars, 'was a closely guarded Naga secret, and its use on anyone besides Nagas was strictly forbidden. Uloopi being a princess, got away with it.'

I nodded slowly. 'You think this gem might be the one being used to resurrect demons?'

'It's possible. I know the evidence is thin …'

'But it's better than anything else we have got at the moment. Alright, Sars, good work. Any thoughts on how we could go about tracing that gem?'

She just stared at me, and I felt foolish as the import of her words struck me.

'Never mind, I should speak to a Naga who is also an information broker. That's what Sage Narada meant when he hinted that we should meet Takshaka.'

She rose. 'I'm going to work the murder angle and all those references for star charts, summonings, etc.' She yawned. 'I'll get started today, probably take a quick nap around midnight and work through the day tomorrow. It should not take me more than seventy-two hours, four days tops.' She headed out. 'Let me know what happens. I'll see myself out.'

K lingered for a while.

'You know where we can find Takshaka?' I asked.

'He runs a fairly exclusive club called the Lair. Invitation only. I'll see if I can get us in. We might need a few days for me to wrangle an invitation. Probably by the weekend.'

'Works for me.' I paused. 'K, you might want to dress for dinner.'

His face broke out into a huge grin. 'I was just thinking the same thing.'

'Dress for dinner' was a code we had invented a while ago. K's invisibility allowed him to carry an astonishing amount of contraband on his person. He had gotten himself a trench coat filled with hidden pockets which included everything from guns with silver bullets to wooden stakes, garlic, holy water and even a miniature flamethrower. Apparently, he'd prepared for a vampire apocalypse while we were facing demons.

'I have the perfect joke to go with that coat. Want to hear it?'

'No. I did have another thought, K. Wanted your opinion on it.'

He pouted. 'Fine. Just so you know, it's a really good joke. But never mind, what did you want to ask?'

'Narada mentioned we might need to take help from a powerful ally. I was wondering how you might feel about that.'

His face sobered up immediately. He knew who I was thinking of.

A month ago, we'd made some new friends the old-fashioned way—by nearly dying together in a Victorian mansion while battling the Daoine Sidhe: a race of immortals from Irish folklore. Lasting friendship is pretty much guaranteed when you experience shared trauma and a host of very determined killers trying to murder you.

By and large, Celestials all tend to stick within their own lanes—the reason why vampires don't cross an ocean and choose to feed on the denizens of Mumbai is that they don't hold the same dread here. Most beings of magic are strengthened by the mythos surrounding them—the whispered tales in the night about what they can do—the feeling of awe, or helplessness or desire that sustains them, yadda yadda.

That's one theory. Another, less romantic one, is that we're just spectacularly set in our ways. Not lazy, per se—just immortal and deeply disinterested in self-improvement. Immortality and innovation rarely share the same residence. When you've lived for several centuries, you develop what polite society calls 'preferences' and what everyone else calls 'being insufferably stuck in your ways.'

But, despite the fact that we were all a bit out of our comfort zone, we found ourselves halfway across the world and banding together in a Victorian mansion, battling faerie elementals from another realm. Victorian architecture, it turns out, is surprisingly resilient to otherworldly combat. The garden, however, was beyond saving.

It's a tale I will need to record in my journals someday in full and excruciating detail, but for now the following should suffice—a young girl named Tamara had been kidnapped by a group of rogue English magicians.

A motley crew of adventurers, including K and myself, decided to rescue her. We looked like the setup to a particularly questionable joke. 'A dreamwalker, a ghost and a dog walk into a magical confrontation ...'

It was one of those epic battles poets should have been singing ballads about. We won against a group of smug, insufferable pricks who were not used to losing. We also made many enemies in the process—the immortal kind who would hold a grudge until the stars turned cold, but what mattered was that we all walked away, unharmed.

It was one of the most bizarre adventures we had undertaken, but completely in line with the circus my life had turned into in the past year. We made some solid allies that day and swore to support one another in case another crisis of epic proportions would ever turn up. But more importantly, we ended up getting to know the riddle wrapped in a mystery inside an enigma that was Tamara Blackwater. Nothing builds friendship quite like violently extracting someone from a kidnapping. Conventional wisdom suggests coffee first, but we've never been conventional.

Tamara was a young Haitian girl with a unique power set. Imagine puberty with the added bonus of being able to bend reality to your will. We had become friends, of sorts, after our last encounter.

There's a reason why the group of magicians kidnapped her in the first place—she happened to be the main star of a 'Chosen One' prophecy, and I cannot for the life of me emphasise how bloody much I hate those. Those prophecies are like weather forecasts—vague enough to never be entirely wrong, yet specific enough that someone will inevitably get wet. They pop up every century or so, and every sensitive, psychic or para-normal expert out there collectively goes into a mad feeding frenzy when they imagine they've found that special someone.

I personally think the whole idea of a 'Chosen One' is a load of BS. Me not believing in them is particularly ironic since I believe in avatars—avatars behave fundamentally in a very similar fashion as Chosen Ones—born to fulfil a singular destiny that only they could untangle and resolve, to the eternal gratitude of the adoring masses.

But here's a key difference—the avatars are Gods themselves, only in human form. Their claim to divinity was never in doubt. A Chosen One has all the credibility of a Nigerian prince asking for a loan.

And I can honestly say none of the avatars I knew personally were assholes. Even Parashuram was a sulky, temperamental little bitch at the best of times, but you try living with a dad who asks you to cut off your mom's head just to test you—that kind of shit is likely to cause PTSD. The fact that he went along and did it also speaks volumes about him by the way.

So why do I dislike Chosen Ones? For one, the whole fervour and weight of expectations that are put onto the person in general can be intimidating.

But besides that, the whole idea that you need to wait for someone special to come along to clean up your messes is stupid. Humans have incredible potential—for mass destruction, great creativity, inspired brilliance, petty malice, everything you can think of, in spades. What most of them cannot abide by, however, is the lack of a safety net—a belief in themselves, as it were.

The narrative of a 'Chosen One' holds them back. People need to get off their asses, roll up their sleeves and do their own dirty work. Their brains are still wired as prey animals in the wild—huddle together, don't stand out in the crowd, wait for someone else to make the next move. They'll spend decades developing technologies to avoid face-to-face conversation, then risk their lives to save a stranger. They are also the only species that built nuclear weapons and meditation apps in the same century. Contradiction is their most consistent quality. You would be amazed to see how far a little hard work and grit will take them, if they just muster up the courage to do it themselves.

But I digress. According to the cabal we encountered, Tamara was destined to either be the greatest magician of our age or the one who would likely destroy magic forever. Seeking to control that which they had no business getting involved in, the bumbling amateurs got themselves killed, and the rest of us got involved in this whole mission of rescuing her.

'She's Ta'veren,' K observed.

'She's what now?'

He scowled. 'It wouldn't kill you to open a book occasionally.'

'And How many pages is this book of yours?'

He mumbled something inaudible.

'Speak up.'

'Twelve thousand pages. About 4.3 million words over Fourteen books. But it's worth—'

'Not for all the tea in China.'

'People like her turn our lives into side quests,' he continued, undeterred. 'We become NPCs. The expendable kind wearing red shirts, dying tragically to fuel her character development.'

'You're mixing TV metaphors with video games.'

'You get the point.'

I threw my hands up. 'No, I have no idea what your point is.' My question remains, 'What do you think of us calling in Tamara?'

He pursed his lips thoughtfully. 'I don't understand her powers. Voodoo's like a completely different school of magic. Remember when Darth Maul showed up with that double-bladed lightsaber? Total game-changer.'

I waited as K rambled on. Being friends with him forced you to learn patience. It even built character. Or so I've heard.

'On the other hand, that's what makes her completely unpredictable,' K continued. 'Anyone who comes up against her wouldn't even know how to fight her. Her powers are too alien, too foreign to counter. She's like a Mary Sue, but one who is in our corner. I mean, who wouldn't want a Mary Sue.'

There's a limit to how much character development through suffering I was willing to endure in one conversation.

'K!' I growled. 'I don't have time for this rambling word salad of yours. Go with your gut. Should I call her to help us or not?'

K gave me a grudging nod. 'Let's reach out to her. I think she can help.'

I had reluctantly come to the same conclusion and was half-hoping K would talk me out of it. 'That's settled then. I'll go make a call.'

INTERLUDE 1

(2 Months ago)

K thinks I dislike all religions. That isn't true. I'm actually quite fond of some of them.

See, religions are nothing but an evolutionary trick to ensure the survival of the species. Without it, humans would have wiped each other out a long time ago. They were always too short-sighted, too violent and too given to acting out of emotion.

Someone once said, 'You could never convince a monkey to give you a banana by promising him limitless bananas in monkey heaven.' That's a pretty astute observation. Religion kept the lunatics in check. Over time, these religions became more and more complicated. Today, it's a vestigial organ, like your appendix—useful for nothing except the occasional painful inflammation.

Gods just want to be worshipped. They don't want to be co-opted into your wars, or constantly needled for favours, or blamed for your screwups.

If you happen to be one of the 'smart Gods', you leverage your influence to increase the size of your worshipper base. Peaceful methods don't give quick results, so yes, bloodshed is preferred. It's why you cultivate a few rabid idiots in every religion.

If you are even smarter, you diversify. Spread your followers all over the globe so they don't get wiped out by a war or a plague, leaving behind nothing more than a bad memory. That's the reason so many of you were moved out of the Steppes in the first place—though don't blame us for the 'Aryan superiority BS'—that's all a human invention.

But the genius Gods? They don't bother with logistics. They invent religions, each one a Venus flytrap for human devotion. One venerates virgins, another dangles them in the afterlife. One blesses booze, another bans it. One bans religious icons and pictures of God, the other conveniently drops the middle Eastern roots and pictures them like a white hippie with lustrous golden hair.

On the surface, they're oil and water, sparking wars as followers slaughter each other over whose fairy tale is the truest. Yet every prayer—screamed by zealots, whispered by sinners, sobbed by the dying—funnels back to one entity. That's not just your usual run of the mill clever, that's fiendish, diabolical poetry in motion.

Which brings me to the angel I was here to meet, standing on a bridge, preaching peace while his bosses schemed. Gods and their games—the tune never changes, only the puppets dangling at the end of the string.

—The Private Journals of Akran

The Atal Setu bridge was one of a kind. It had been built to so much hope and fanfare right before the recent elections and started showing signs of decay right after the results. In many ways, it was an accurate representation of the past decade of government rule—flashy inauguration, structural defects and a concerning tendency to crumble under pressure.

Micah stood in the middle of the bridge, arms held politely behind his back. He was dressed, like always, in a trench coat. Over the centuries, every time we met, he had always maintained the same look. Dark haired, clean shaven, impeccably dressed, lithe physique. He nodded amicably as I stepped closer.

'The peace of the lord be with you always, Akran.'

'And also with you,' I said automatically. I had known him a long time. We had an easy, familiar relationship of mutual trust and respect—like Sisyphus and his lesser-known twin, each pushing our own boulder up separate hills, nodding to each other in passing as the rocks rolled back down.

'You are looking a little sleep deprived,' he said, polite concern on his face.

I was actually finally getting some decent sleep. But it felt like it was never enough. I had a couple of thousand years of sleepless nights to shake off.

None of this, of course was going to be of interest to Micah. He would listen and make sympathetic noises at all the right places. If I needed that, I would just get myself a dog.

'Aren't you a little far from home?'

He smiled. 'Isn't the whole world our home?'

From any other archangel, a statement like this would get me bristling. Not because of the truth of his words, but because they made such statements with smug condescension, as if to imply that was but the natural order of things. Micah never did that, he always had this bemused, tempered way of speaking that somehow didn't rile me up.

Besides, he wasn't wrong. The cult of the one God used to generate much amusement each time it materialised, for all other religions at the time were polytheistic. It failed many times, over and over, before it finally took root in a beleaguered tribe of slaves in Egypt when a tired and hungry man encountered a burning bush in the desert.

It began to catch on again when, a few centuries later, another man fasting for forty days in the desert encountered the devil and refused to be tempted. That tiny sect became the default religion of the Roman empire and spread across half the civilised world.

And it expanded again when a merchant fleeing across the desert between Mecca and Medina encountered an angel who spoke to him in God's own language. He became the founder of a third monotheistic religion that spread its roots across much of Asia and Africa.

Three gigantic, civilisation-defining religions that turned polytheism on its head.

Nobody was laughing anymore.

Surely, there was nothing common about them besides monotheism, geographical proximity, burning deserts and each of it's founders being close to starvation at the time, was there?

Well, maybe there was one more detail that might be relevant. It's so insignificant really, that I hesitate to even mention it.

This thousand square mile area that served as the birthplace of these three religions is populated with a bunch of plants unique to arid climates. Like the acacia tree and the Peganum harmala shrub. What's special about those plants, you ask? For one thing, and this may be a coincidence, both these plants contain psychoactive compounds that when ingested can cause hallucinations. Like say … a burning bush?

A devil that tempts you?

An angel that suggests that you are special?

What are the odds? Really?

All of this ran through my mind as I listened to him.

I smiled to show Micah that I had not taken offence.

'Right. So, seriously, why are you here?'

His face took on a sombre expression. 'There's something we need to talk about.' His eyes slid sideways for a moment, taking in the few other people on the bridge. A couple had parked their car on one side and were talking in hushed tones, and a man in a scruffy blue suit on the other end was staring aimlessly at the sky.

'It's about Tamara.'

'What about her?'

He gave me a reproachful look. 'Akran, this is beneath you. You know the rules!'

'She's just an ordinary girl, Micah. Maybe not ordinary-ordinary but certainly not enough to get everyone all worked up.'

He shook his head. 'We can't take that chance and you know it!'

And there, lay the crux of it all. Tamara wasn't just the latest in a long line of voodoo priestesses. She was one of the most powerful mages I had ever met. Despite her youth, she had vanquished a Loa (a powerful Haitian spirit), performed several exorcisms, and even rescued her grandmother in a daring raid on one of the inner circles of hell. She had immense power but very little training. Her abilities were terrifying, and still growing. I was glad to call her a friend but I wasn't too thrilled about spending time with her.

'You are suggesting we get her to bat for your team?'

A look of pain crossed his face. Micah found human metaphors hard to deal with, though not from lack of trying.

It was a challenge for all Celestials who chose not to spend time on earth.

'I am suggesting we speak to her, that's all. Assess how dangerous or not, she is.'

'And if you think she is too powerful?'

'We keep her in the Loft.'

The Loft was a high security prison for Celestials like myself. Cronus, Set, Loki and all manners of other beings deemed too dangerous to be out in the world. It was established after the Celestial Accords, made millennia ago, when different pantheons had gotten together to tackle the most dangerous of our kind, those who possessed the power to end all of existence.

Given that we were essentially immortal and had pretty long memories, the Loft wasn't like a Russian gulag—far from it. It was more likely to be like a second-tier Airbnb of sorts, just with no WIFI and a bit more security.

How did I never grace those hallowed halls? Quite simply because despite all the hate directed my way, I was deemed very much a local problem. The Loft was not for the hoi polloi. You need to be regarded as a world ending concern before the powers that be—across pantheons, I should add—decide to intervene.

'She doesn't deserve to be locked away. Not when she's done nothing wrong.'

'We can't wait for something to go wrong,' he pointed out. 'And it's not like she'll be doing hard time on a diet of watery gruel. She'll be treated well. With some of my people supervising and training her.'

'With a little indoctrination between lessons?' I suggested mildly.

He sighed. 'Would that really be so bad? Look, Akran, I'm trying to do the right thing. We don't plan to use her in any nefarious plots, we simply want her off the board!'

Something about what he said bothered me. I was a bit distracted so I hadn't put it together fast enough. But the furtive look and the use of the possessive 'We' when he spoke gave me an unpleasant feeling in the pit of my stomach.

Micah was more of a solo player. He was also incapable of lying—every word he spoke was the literal definitive truth as he knew it. It was part of his being an archangel. So when he said 'We' …

Slowly, I looked at my surroundings. There was nothing that looked out of the ordinary—just one sad little fellow looking gloomily out at the water and another fellow who was sad in his own unique way, having made absolutely no progress beyond first base.

So why were the hairs on my neck standing up?

'We've known each other a long time, Micah,' I said softly. 'Did you really need to bring the goon squad along?'

He shook his head. 'Their orders come from much higher than my pay grade.' His brow furrowed. 'Did I get that right? I wasn't sure since we don't actually get paid.'

I nodded. 'A for effort, C for Creativity.' I picked up a cigarette butt that had been carelessly tossed to the side, lit it with a smidgen of my power, aimed it at the couple, and sent it flying through the air at the man with a snap of my fingers. It struck him squarely on his nose, and he blinked, bewildered.

'I need to get back,' I called. 'Can we drop the act and get to the end of whatever this tamasha is?'

The man and woman glanced up from their hushed conversations, blank looks on their faces. With a flicker of light, their human forms dropped away, revealing what they actually were.

Seraphim.

The Seraphim were the enforcers of the Shining City. Counterparts of the Yakshas but prone to more flashy appearances with trumpets and heavenly light.

For the most part they still looked human, aside from the luminescent skin, and the feather wings that had sprouted on each of their backs. Both were dressed in flowing white, their traditional garb when they visited the earth. The woman appeared to be wearing a white bodysuit which, despite looking like a bollywood sari in a downpour, made her look sexless. Their unsmiling faces and hostile demeanour were very much in keeping with their usual attitude towards people like me.

Two seraphs. I could handle them.

'I'm here to observe. Not to intervene,' Micah said, as though reading my mind.

Which was worrying. Because angels only ever 'observed' things right before the whole place went to hell.

'Who is in charge?'

'I am.'

The fifth person on the bridge, the man who was fishing alone, rose to face us. Unlike the rest, he hadn't bothered to even look like he was from the subcontinent. He had the blonde hair, white skin, and blue eyes that the '88s' would have loved. This chap wasn't even trying to blend in.

'Hello, Akran.'

'Uriah,' I said flatly. There was no love lost between us—a fact of which we were mutually aware.

Quite frankly, Uriah was a dick. He represented the smug, condescending assholes convinced of their own superiority, and always willing and quick to display it.

He was an archangel, in the same league as Micah. This made him an extremely dangerous enemy. I could have handled him when I was at the height of my powers. But at this point, a one-on-one confrontation would only get my ass kicked.

'I heard you gained your powers back. Is this really all of it?'

'What do you want, Uriah?'

His eyes narrowed. 'The girl. Hand her over!'

'No. Are we done?'

He sneered. 'I wasn't asking permission.'

'Just like your dating life, I suppose. The answer is still no. You want her? Molon Labe!'

He frowned. His people claimed they spoke all the languages of mankind yet here he was, struggling to grasp a simple enough concept.

Uriah's eyes glinted dangerously. 'Maybe we could go for a walk. I'm betting you would be more willing to talk once we spend some time together.'

'Maybe you should offer to buy me dinner first.'

He sneered again. 'I was hoping you would resist.'

'Uriah, for fuck's sake, are you not getting it? Every dialogue of yours is straight from an incel playbook. Didn't they teach you anything before setting you loose on the world? Besides, are you sure you want to start a fight, here, in my home territory, on a ground of my choosing?'

Uriah chuckled. 'We've got you outnumbered, outgunned and out planned, you old fossil. Give up already and quit embarrassing yourself!'

'Outnumbered? Sure. Outgunned? Perhaps.' I let my gaze drift to a spot right behind Uriah. 'Out-planned? Really? What gave you that idea?'

Uriah opened his mouth to speak but choked on his words as an arm snaked around his neck and grasped it. A gleaming metal blade lay on his jugular, pricking ever so slightly into his skin.

'Is this a private party?' K asked cheerfully as he materialised out of thin air. 'Or can anyone crash?'

The other angels all stood frozen in shock. Pretty stupid of them to have tried this black ops BS without factoring in my invisible friend who is always with me.

Then again, he is invisible, so never mind. It's understandable they forgot about him.

I hadn't actually invited K, but I knew there was a good chance he would be around.

K was like herpes—mostly dormant, always inconvenient, and guaranteed to flare up at the worst possible moment. And he knew how to make an entrance!

'Hey, Mikey!' Kama grinned. 'How's it hangin'?'

Micah gravely tilted his head in K's direction. 'Greetings, Kamdev. I'm afraid I don't quite understand what you mean.'

K chuckled. 'Always so formal. Tell me, what's your return policy on a defective angel with his wings clipped?'

'You wouldn't dare!' began Uriah hotly, before Kama pressed the edge of the blade lightly across his cheek.

'Aah, ah, little cherub. The grown-ups are talking. Be a good boy and let them finish!'

I don't think K has ever killed anyone before and I didn't think he would start today. Part of being a love God was that he was very good at peacocking—strutting around, pretending to be a sigma when he was trying to impress someone, or switching to his usual happy-go-lucky self when he was hanging out with us.

Of course, the fact that he was a love God also meant that occasionally, when someone he cared about was threatened, he would bristle and posture like a she-bear protecting her cubs. All in all, it was safe to say Uriah would be stupid to antagonise K in any way.

Micah shook his head. 'I would be disappointed if you were to harm him, Kamdev. He is zealous, yes, but it is something he is working on.'

K frowned. 'Is he someone important? He looks like a dime store Leonardo.'

Knowing K, he wasn't referring to the renaissance inventor. Once again, I was annoyed at how much useless trivia he had burnt into my head.

'The name's Uriah,' the angel spat out, eyes blazing, his fists tightly clenched as he spoke.

'If you were to harm him, I would be obligated to step in,' Micah said softly.

Kama shot me a look and I shook my head ever so slightly. Micah was the embodiment of politeness and courtesy but even he wouldn't stand back and do nothing when one of his compatriots was being harmed. We needed to de-escalate this situation.

'So, let's work this out then,' K offered cheerfully. 'First off, these two don't need to be here, do they?'

The two angels looked in mute appeal at Micah, then at Uriah.

Most Celestials were vulnerable to silver and iron. The Shining Host were immune to silver for some reason. They took it as a sign of God's favour. Their realm was even called the Silver City. I personally took it as just one of those random quirks that nobody had really figured out yet; I wasn't going to assign any divine meanings to it.

K tutted. 'In case you guys were under the impression that this is an ordinary knife, let me disabuse you of that notion.' He drove the knife a millimetre into Uriah's skin, and Uriah arched his back and shrieked and hissed like a scalded cat. 'See what I mean'?

A thin trickle of blood oozed out—barely a paper cut. For those who believed they were cloaked in some invulnerable divine armour, this was a rude wake-up call.

Something must have shown in Uriah's eyes, for the two seraphim bowed and disappeared.

'Micah,' I said, as I watched both of them. 'We don't need to escalate this, do we?'

Micah nodded. 'Set him free and you have my word we will leave you alone for the next forty-eight hours.'

'How about I leave Tamara alone and you folks come calling with your pointy sticks only if I contact her again?'

Micah nodded. 'So be it!'

I shot a quick glance at Uriah who nodded sullenly.

'I trust you, Mike,' said K, grinning. 'But are you sure about this guy?'

Uriah's face flushed purple. 'The word of an angel, you low-born gutter-snipe ...'

'... is worth diddly-squat, buddy. Don't live up to the stereotype at least.' He withdrew the knife and stepped back.

Uriah glared at K, his face scarlet with rage. 'I will not forget this,' he snarled.

K pointed at his neck. 'In case you ever do, I've left a little reminder.'

I cleared my throat.

'Uriah,' I said in the most polite tone I could muster. 'Do yourself a favour and kindly fuck off! You've lost this round!'

I half expected him to unsheathe his flaming sword and come at me. In case you are wondering, it's not a euphemism for his penis—the heavenly host all did possess white-hot flaming swords they could call at will. And they don't really have penises, which is a whole different story. Explains a lot about their temperament, if you ask me. Celestial blue balls spanning millennia would make anyone a bit testy.

Uriah didn't do anything foolish. He stared at Kama for a bit, as if committing his face to memory, and then disappeared.

Micah stepped forward. 'I'll take your leave, Akran. Thank you for your restraint.'

'There's a better way this could have been handled, Micah. This wasn't it.'

He shrugged. 'Perhaps. But this was necessary. Not all of us are in agreement on how things are to be handled.'

That, sadly, came as no surprise. Even here on earth, we had people garlanding rapists and bragging about murdering babies because somehow, they had justified that behaviour as 'in service of the greater good'. Dehumanising those who were different had ironically turned them into what they feared the most.

'His faction will lie low for a while after this setback.' He hesitated. 'If you end up working with her again, I don't think I can keep Uriah and his hounds away.'

'I wasn't planning on it. But if I do decide to get in touch, I wouldn't really bother with what Uriah thinks about it.'

'A word to the wise—Uriah is not a good enemy to have.'

I shrugged. 'Neither am I.'

He smiled. 'I admire your confidence.'

'He needs to pick a number and wait in line.'

Micah frowned. 'Another earth saying?'

'Yeah. Doesn't matter.'

There was a flicker of light, and soon K and I were the only ones left on the bridge.

'I'm pretty hungry,' K said brightly. 'How do you feel about Chinese?'

'Sounds good,' I said lightly, as we headed back. I didn't have any plans of getting in touch with Tamara again.

CHAPTER SIX

Takshaka appears to be one of those who stood on the wrong side of history, though in fairness, the 'right side' set an entire forest ablaze, charring its inhabitants, so moral clarity wasn't exactly abundant. This spawned a personal vendetta against the Kuru clan, particularly the Pandavas.

So how did this vendetta start? During their quest for a capital city, Arjun (acting on the advice of Krishna) destroyed the Khandava forest with arrows that rained fire; Takshaka's wife was killed in that blaze. Naturally, this was filed under 'divine will' and not arson or murder—a distinction that tends to be made exclusively by the victorious.

Arjun's grandson, Parikshit (whom Ashwatthama tried to kill in the womb), grew up to be a king of some renown. However, exhibiting the impeccable judgment for which royalty is so often trusted, he decided that harassing meditating sages was an appropriate pastime for a monarch of his stature. One fine day, annoyed by a sage who was *meditating, he decided to place a dead snake in the man's hair. The sage's son cursed him to die of a snakebite. Takshaka, displaying the patience and dramatic flair that makes for excellent villainy, disguised himself as a worm inside a fruit. When the fruit was brought to the king, Takshaka leapt out and sunk his fangs into the king, killing him instantly.*

One might have hoped that would be the end of the story. But no. The king's son decided simply killing Takshaka wasn't enough—he went full Netanyahu, vowing to wipe the Naga people off the map entirely.

Fortunately, cooler heads intervened and Takshaka survived.

Hopefully, I can get through this evening without burning his house down.

—The Private Journals of Akran

Saturday evening, 9 p.m.

I had never met Takshaka. We had fought on opposite sides in the great war, but that was not something we were likely to hold against each other. At least I didn't. War's an ugly business, and while the stories make it sound like all the good guys lined up on one end, the bad guys on the other, and good eventually triumphed, the reality is always murkier. When the war began, there were several political alliances, petty feuds, grievances, and complex schemes in play, so everyone had their own agenda for choosing their sides. Takshaka, for his part, had no interest in seeing the Kauravas succeed, but he hated Arjun for killing his wife. I wasn't going to judge someone in the present for their motivations from millennia in the past.

So what were K and I doing this evening? Well, Takshaka owned a massive underground nightclub called the Lair.

Among its two levels, the upper was entirely for his legitimate business, the nightclub. There was plenty of noise, loud music and flashing strobe lights, and at any point in time, it looked like all the teenagers in Mumbai had crammed themselves into that one floor.

The lower level was a very exclusive, highly illegal casino he had been running for some time. This was where most of his illicit money came from and also where he acquired his reputation as an information broker. Our plan was to find out more about the fabled gem that could restore the dead, when it was last used, and maybe who had it at the moment. Based on my own experience dealing with Nagas, I wouldn't be getting this information for free. Most Nagas had a good head for business and had accumulated significant wealth over the years. They were the first Celestials to assimilate among humans and several large, family-run businesses belonged to them. Takshaka would probably want to trade something for information about the gem.

We had landed up at the Lair promptly at 9 p.m. K had wrangled us an invite (courtesy of one of his many star-struck lovers—details I wisely avoided asking, else he would reveal them in every intimate detail). He strutted in wearing his infamous trench coat, looking absurdly pleased with himself. The fact that he was the only one dressed like a noir detective in a Mumbai nightclub didn't faze him.

A young hostess escorted us to the lower level. The mood in here was decidedly more sober. The clientele was the upper crust of Mumbai, used to sipping scotch and smoking cigars while making million-dollar deals as they played. There were a few slot machines, a couple of roulette wheels and the like, but that was not the main attraction this evening. Poker fever had gripped the city a year ago; overnight, hundreds of card dens had opened up. Takshaka had no less than thirty high-stakes games running in that room.

'Remember the other day you were asking about our powers?' K said abruptly.

I nodded.

'Well, I noticed something today. My powers also appear to be getting weaker. I can stay invisible but I can no longer include others in my aura.'

'Sorry to hear that,' I muttered. Really, what else was there for me to say? I had gotten used to being a shadow of my former self, but I had thousands of years to get used to it. Waking up one morning and discovering that you are not half the Celestial you used to be can be discomfiting.

K shrugged. 'It'll work out eventually. Meanwhile ... have you called Tamara?'

'I did.' Despite our conversation a few days ago, I kept putting off calling her. It sounded foolish to say it out loud, but I couldn't help thinking that inviting her was like bringing a rocket launcher to a knife fight. It was an escalation in hostilities and could complicate things further in the long run.

At the end of our last encounter, one of the fay made a rather spectacular announcement: if we were to get involved with her again, someone close to me would die. As he put it, 'the fates are vague about many things, but not this one.'

It might have been sour grapes after we sent them packing with their tails between their legs—they were known to be malicious tricksters at the best of times. Still, that grim pronouncement at the end had left me with a bad taste in my mouth.

Eventually though, I did call her. The conversation with Narada had spooked me a bit. I sent her a message an hour before getting here. I kept it brief: we were in trouble and could use her support. I specified it was not an emergency and this was one of those 'come if you can make it, but if you are busy, I totally understand' messages. This way, I was not tempting fate when she did arrive, I was just leaving it all to chance. I skipped details about assassination contracts etc., because that would tip the balance towards her getting on the next plane here. Hopefully, if she was free to make it, we would see her by mid–next week.

'You know, Akran, I was thinking about something in the shower just this evening,' K said suddenly, a thoughtful, melancholic look on his face.

'Uh huh,' I grunted non-committally. Knowing K, conversations that started like this could turn awkward very soon.

'It's horrible not to be the star in your own story. Never the protagonist, only the side actor, occasionally providing comic relief, only experiencing life in the shadows of those who are mightier than you.'

This was a surprisingly profound thought from K. He was not given to introspection, or even dealing with most emotions. The last time I mentioned that I missed Deanne, his response was that the best way to get over someone was to get under someone else.

I patted him on his shoulder.

'K,' I began awkwardly, 'You will always be the hero of your own stories. You've played an integral role in every one of them.' I trailed away because K was giving me a bewildered look.

'You aren't talking about yourself, are you?'

'Me?' K exclaimed. 'I am definitely the hero of my own stories. I meant you!'

'What on earth are you talking about?'

'Well, last time you had Deanne helping you, this time we are calling Tamara … seems like a sitcom that constantly needs guest stars to help it survive.'

I've often suspected that K's much vaunted invisibility is just his secondary power. His real talent is in driving people insane. If he didn't get under everyone's skin there would be fewer people trying to actively kill him.

I glared at him, trying to convey what an annoyance I thought he was. Somehow, he interpreted this as me needing a hug. Our hostess appeared at that moment, sparing him from a bleeding nose. She had stepped away to inform Takshaka we had arrived, and was now ready to lead us to his table.

K kept up a steady stream of chatter as we walked.

'Don't worry, Akran; I don't think you are weak.'

'That's a relief.'

'I mean it. You are defanged, cantankerous, a bit of a sour puss, mildly overweight, but weak? Pfft. Don't ever believe that.'

'I am not overweight!'

'Not at all,' K assured me in a voice that made me want to smack him. 'Shall we say, a tad plump perhaps?'

'We aren't saying anything of the sort.'

'Honestly, Akran, it's no big deal. Bollywood Zumba's and haute yoga can only take you so far!!

"I have never done, or plan to do Bollywood Zumba."

'Sure,' he said, ignoring me entirely. 'Anyway, certainly nothing a few crunches wouldn't solve.' He gave me a critical glance. 'A couple of hundred thousand to start with.'

'Great pep talk. Just what I needed.'

The hostess had lead us to a small private room at the back. It screamed luxury, with plush red carpets and garish but expensive-looking paintings on the walls. One wall had television screens showing the goings-on inside the club.

When we entered, Takshaka rose from the large L-shaped sofa in the centre of a room. He was a fashionably dressed, tall, lanky man. Most Nagas I know like to flaunt their jewellery. But not Takshaka. His style hummed quiet luxury.

Beside him sat a girl dressed in plain black slacks and a white sleeveless top. Like Takshaka, she wore almost no jewellery except an emerald choker that matched her eyes.

'Lord Akran, Lord Kama,' Takshaka greeted us warmly, though his voice was strained. 'Welcome to the most exclusive haven for people like us. Allow me to introduce you to my daughter, Lyla.'

'I just remembered something,' K whispered. 'Apparently snakes have two penises.'

I ignored him and looked at Lyla with more interest. There had been a gradual decline in our procreation abilities since the Kali Yuga began. The only Celestials being born were those with one human parent.

She was quite good-looking, and it was evident she got her looks from her mother. Takshaka looked a bit lumpy next to her.

The girl rose smoothly. 'It's a pleasure to meet such distinguished guests,' she murmured as she shook hands with us. Though she appeared to be in her early twenties, I had no doubt that she was essentially several hundreds of years old, like other Nagas. Her arms were lean and lightly muscled—definitely an athlete, or proficient in martial arts, if I had to guess.

We nodded politely and sat down. Takshaka appeared nervous. His eyes kept darting across the room even as he made small talk.

'Lord Kama,' he said. 'I love your book. When will you be writing a sequel?'

It took effort not to roll my eyes.

K gets a lot of praise for things he often had nothing to do with. For instance, the wildly popular brand of contraceptives in Asia. Or the most popular book about sex in the world, the *Kamasutra*.

By and large, the text written in the fourth century BCE is less about sex and more about the art of living well, the nature of love and finding a life partner. Yes, it includes methods for courtship, seduction, sexual positions, and dozens of other topics. Humans, being who they are, tend to focus primarily on the sexual bits. Most of the book is about the philosophy and theory of love, what triggers desire and what sustains it.

K gets credit even though all he actually did was share a name with the book. I remember asking him what its gist was once.

'Let me put it this way,' he said with a straight face. I waited.

Apparently, that was the answer to my question.

If I haven't mentioned it before, celestial humour is the worst kind! Most of the jokes are ten thousand years old, if not more, and usually only the person who cracks it finds it funny.

Anyway, K was on his best behaviour tonight. He thanked Takshaka, did not immediately attempt to seduce Lyla, and generally did not make an ass of himself.

I am reasonably taciturn, so having someone like K keep up the inane, pointless chatter before we got down to business was a good idea. While K rambled on, I studied the room, noting entrances and exits, discrete cameras in the ceiling, and a couple of armed security guards roaming amongst the club's patrons.

I pulled my eyes away from the décor and found Lyla staring straight at me.

Like Takshaka, she too possessed a nervous energy, like a coiled spring ready to release. There was something catlike about her as she watched me closely, and I had the distinct impression she thought of me as a mouse.

'Have we met before?' I asked. People who dislike me usually have had at least one prior meeting with me.

She shook her head. 'I've heard a lot about you,' she murmured. 'The protector of Mumbai, first among the Yakshas.' Her voice turned low and husky. 'If even half the rumours about you are true …'

Okay, maybe I was reading this wrong.

By my side, K snorted his drink out of his nose. His face was impassive, but his body shook with laughter. I was going to have words with him later.

'They are not,' I said. 'True, I mean. I stopped paying attention to any rumours about me a while back.'

'I'd love to hear some of your stories,' she sighed.

It was one of those semi-ecstatic noises you expect from a repressed woman on the sets of Bridgerton. I was conscious of K's grin beside me and that her father was sitting right there, so all Lyla did was make me uncomfortable.

Takshaka cleared his throat. 'While I appreciate your patronage,' he said, 'I assume this is not merely a social visit.'

Reluctantly, I turned my eyes away from Lyla to focus on Takshaka. 'I've heard about a gem that the Nagas possess. I believe it's called the Nagamani. I had some questions about it.'

Takshaka's expression changed. If anything, he looked even more sour. 'The gem and everything to do with it is a secret known only to the Nagas. Where did you hear about this?'

Aah. I was about to struggle with one of the most challenging enemies I have ever dealt with. Diplomacy.

Sometime in the late 60s, a young plucky Celestial with dreams to change the world had been aghast to discover that most Indian kids didn't even know the name of Ram's mother. Determined to rectify this, he setup a small publishing house with comics for kids, telling them stories from the Celestial Archives. It turned out to be a huge success.

Of course, not everyone was happy to discover all the skeletons they thought had been forgotten were now in the public domain as immortal picture stories.

'It's really not as secret as one might imagine. Not since it was used by Uloopi to bring Arjun back to life.'

Takshaka's face paled. Lyla caught hold of his arm and whispered urgently in his ear. I was struck once again by how unlike each other they looked. I wouldn't have taken her for his daughter. She seemed more in control of the situation than he was.

'Forgive my father, he's been unwell lately,' she murmured.

Takshaka composed his face into a mask, supressing the momentary panic he had displayed. 'Forgive my reaction. Just like you were in charge of the sacred weapons for the Devas, one of my responsibilities involves looking after magical objects and items for the Nagas.' He grimaced. 'The gem, in particular, has been a bone of contention between our people for years.'

'How so?'

'We have received many requests over the years for using the gem to bring the dead back to life. It's been a source of friction amongst us as we have debated among the Naga council whether to rent it out to paying customers or reserve its use exclusively for the Nagas.'

'Hang on,' K said, as he scratched the nape of his neck. 'You just said it was a closely guarded Naga secret. And you are receiving requests and gifts for its usage. How are those two statements not contradictory?'

Takshaka gave him a tight-lipped frown. 'I cannot answer that,' he said stiffly.

The obvious answer was that the people asking for it were friends of the Nagas. The implication of course was that neither K nor I were on that exclusive list.

'Is the gem on loan right now?' I asked.

An uncomfortable silence greeted my words. Takshaka refused to meet my eyes. He was hiding something. I didn't care about the petty Naga politics Takshaka was embroiled in but this was starting to piss me off.

'Takshaka, someone has been resurrecting demons. We fought one called Vritra recently. He was …'

'Killed by Indra using the bones of Dadhichi,' said Lyla. She looked awed, impressed even. 'He was almost impossible to kill back then. You defeated him?'

'Well, yes.' I frowned at the interruption. 'He was definitely dead after the first time which meant he was brought back to life.'

'What does this have to do with us?' Takshaka demanded.

I chose my words carefully. 'A few months ago, I unravelled a plot to end the Kali Yuga. It involved resurrecting a demon which would trigger an avatar being born to stop him and would have millions, possibly even billions of innocent people getting killed in the crossfire.

'There are only two ways that a resurrection is possible. One is through the Sanjivani mantra—something only Shukracharya knows—and the second, as I've recently learned, is through this jewel. I believe that Ashwatthama, who was planning to raise the demon, was not working alone. He was working with someone else. If my hunch is correct, it's the same person who resurrected Vritra. He may, at this very moment, be resurrecting other demons. We need to stop him.'

'That is not our concern,' he began, but my patience had stretched thin by this point.

'Raising demons violates the First Law, Takshaka,' I said. My voice had grown colder as I spoke. It was a voice the people around me knew all too well. I was one hair's breadth away from grabbing him by the scruff of his neck, which would have been properly intimidating if I still had the power to hurl him through several walls. As it stood, I might manage to wrinkle his undoubtedly expensive suit.

'You are an exile,' he began. 'You have no right.'

'Anything that reveals our existence is a threat. This isn't something that impacts only you, it affects all of us. The Celestial Council has allowed places like this to operate right under their noses because you have respected the rules. You have been a model citizen. Do you really want to throw it all away because some fool with an agenda decides he wants to have demons running around in the street?'

Takshaka wiped the sweat from his forehead and rubbed his palms on the side of his pants. 'I don't know how you think we can help.'

'Tell us who has the gem. For now, we only want to speak to him.'

Lyla once again grabbed Takshaka's arm and whispered urgently in his ear. I couldn't hear what was being said, but she looked as stressed and worried as him.

K also appeared clueless. His low-level telepathic abilities seemed to have failed him completely. Which left me with one final option.

It was considered terribly crass to use your true sight on another Celestial without express permission—the equivalent of peeking up someone's skirt. The logic was simple. Celestials took pains to look a certain way on the mortal plane, the only one they could actually manipulate to make themselves look younger and sharper or older and uglier (if that was what they were going for). Trying to see what they looked like was just bad manners.

In my case though, things weren't as clear-cut. Previously, I had lacked the power to do this, so it never even occurred to me but now, given that I was frequently encountering murderous demons, cryptic strangers with dire warnings, and the like, and had a contract out on my head, it didn't seem like a big deal.

I gave them both a quick discrete glance. On the higher planes, Takshaka looked exactly as I expected: a giant cobra with a large diamond on his hood. He lay atop a massive pile of treasure—gold bars, precious stone-encrusted goblets, etc. I never knew a Naga who wasn't inordinately fond of shiny things.

Lyla, on the other hand, was … blank. No aura at all.

I frowned as I tried to make sense of this. Lyla noticed my scrutiny and gave a tight-lipped smile as she tapped the emerald studded choker around her neck. The emeralds on it briefly shimmered and changed colour from green to midnight blue and then green again.

Magical concealment jewellery. Charming. In my experience, people who wear accessories that hide their true nature usually have excellent reasons for doing so. None of those reasons have ever worked out well for me.

Takshaka cleared his throat, 'I have many enemies, Yaksha. Some of them are indiscriminate in who they harm to get to me. My daughter suffered some nasty first-degree burns in the last attempt on her life. Until they heal fully, she does not wish people to see what she looks like. I would ask that you respect her wishes.'

Okay, yes. Bad form, Akran.

I bowed to her. 'My apologies. I recently learned about an imminent threat to my life, and I tend to be suspicious.'

Takshaka frowned. 'Forgive me if I have missed something. I was told you had recovered the cache of Celestial weapons. And you had regained your lost powers? Surely there are no significant threats out there that should concern you.'

The cache was gone, my powers trickled like a leaky faucet. I'd gone from nuclear warhead to water pistol in the Celestial arsenal, and the timing couldn't have been worse. I could sense that my tank was full but the pipe trickled mana at a pitiful rate. As K would put it, 'a tactile dysfunction.'

I had no intention of revealing just how vulnerable I truly was. So I improvised.

'I am unwell.'

His frown became more pronounced. 'Unwell?'

'Like a cold.' I waved my hand around at the players across the gambling tables. 'I am currently experiencing a few setbacks. So, I'm being cautious. That's all.'

Takshaka and his daughter exchanged a loaded look, full of meaning yet inscrutable to the rest of us.

'Maybe we could help each other,' Takshaka looked at his daughter, who gave a silent nod. 'As it turns out, I need a favour, and you might be uniquely able to assist me.'

There it was. I knew there would be a price for the information I sought.

'There has been a rift among my people. A series of disagreements around many things, including the use of the jewel. Within the Naga Council exists a splinter faction that has taken to more violent means to get what they want.'

My phone buzzed and I ignored it. I had a feeling I knew where this was going.

'Of late, this faction has escalated their attacks against me. I fear for my daughter's life.'

Yup, it was going exactly where I thought it would go.

'I need a few days to root out the conspirators and end this threat. In that time, I need someone to keep my daughter safe.'

'I'm sure the protector of Mumbai would have no trouble keeping one girl safe,' Lyla said demurely with eyes cast downwards. She gave me a coy smile. 'I would be very grateful for his help.'

Okay, a blind man could have picked up on the sexual tension. I'm not celibate, not by a long shot, but this somehow didn't work for me. She was unbelievably attractive and several hundred years younger than me, judging by how perky everything about her was, but you don't throw yourself at someone when your father is in the room, sitting right next to you. That just makes the guy feel like he is a pawn in some warped 'daddy issues' which will ultimately bite him in the ass.

Takshaka just looked uncomfortable. Or maybe constipated. I couldn't quite tell. For the most part, he looked fidgety before we had even sat down and Lyla seemed to have made that significantly worse with her last statement.

I hated to get involved in problems like this. The last girl I had gone to rescue had turned out to be just one part of a whole series of kidnappings. Unravelling that conspiracy and getting involved had nearly killed me and my friends. That girl was a minor. Lyla, on the other hand, was a completely different case. She kept making bedroom eyes at me, which was flattering, but also awkward. Not to mention suspicious. The last thing I wanted was to take her home and then have her murder me in my sleep.

'Here's what I propose,' Takshaka said. 'Keep her safe for three days. After that, I give you my word, I will tell you who currently has the gem.'

'What will change in three days?' K asked.

'It will give me time to root out the conspirators. Until then, her safety is all that matters.'

'You have nobody in your own organisation you trust?' K asked.

Takshaka spread his hands. 'Not with someone so important to me. I know that there is at least one highly placed traitor in my organisation. That's why I need Akran. He has no connection to me or my people.'

'I'll do it,' I said heavily. I had lead divine armies into battle. Babysitting sounded like a similar skill set.

Takshaka gave me a beaming smile. 'Excellent. One more thing though. I …'

What he was going to say was interrupted by an ear-splitting sound from my phone. It was Sars. She had sent a couple of attachments and a message in all caps: 'PICK UP YOUR DAMN PHONE.'

Something was not right.

K had also gotten her message. With photos from a pair of surveillance cameras outside the club timestamped 11:05, roughly seven minutes ago. They showed six men stepping out of a parked vehicle, all dressed identically with bulging jackets and waist pockets, which I was pretty sure wasn't because they were excited to meet me. What was slightly more disturbing were their facial features. I knew it was not a trick of the light. They were identical, right down to the sub-atomic level.

K made a disgusted sound as he looked at the pictures. 'RBs,' he said, waving the phone at us.

The RBs were a paramilitary outfit operating in South Mumbai, all literally the same person. The original progenitor was a demon named Raktabija, who had an extraordinary gift. Each drop of his blood that fell on the ground resulted in a new demon springing forth from him, identical in every way. In battle, he would deliberately slash his arm and create hundreds of copies.

The original Raktabija had died in a battle with the Goddess Kali. Everyone assumed that he had tricked the Goddess, left one of his clones to die and gone into hiding.

The RBs had been around for at least a few years; they had a couple of chapter houses in the city, and all the proper paperwork in place. They were a legitimate investigative agency with rates so high that most humans couldn't afford them. By and large, we stayed out of each other's business.

Most demons are agents of chaos, seeking destruction and revelling in the pain of others. Several higher-order demons are also fiendishly intelligent. And dangerous. You didn't survive thousands of years by being stupid.

Arriving en masse at a public place armed to the teeth was extremely reckless behaviour for generally smart demons. Maybe they were being paid exceptionally well to do something so colossally stupid.

'I bet they are here looking for you,' K whispered.

I wasn't planning on taking him up on it. We saw on the screens that the first of the RBs had already stepped onto our floor. He had his hand on his ear as he spoke while scanning the room. They were all in communication with each other. It would not take them too long to converge on our location.

K and I both rose from our seats.

'Is there another exit?' I asked. I didn't want to get into a full-fledged battle in close quarters with civilians nearby.

Takshaka shook his head. 'There's an exit that leads to an alley behind the building. To reach it, you must go across the room to the red door and up the stairs.'

Lyla looked outraged. 'You are planning on running away without a fight?'

'Easy there, princess. We are not running away! I'd like to get you to safety. Battling demons in a room crowded with humans is bad for all of us!'

'But, but …' she sputtered, still indignant.

'They are right,' Takshaka said heavily. 'Too many humans here, Lyla. Our first priority is to keep you safe.'

From what little I knew of Nagas, he was probably more concerned about the loss of revenue from paying customers if a shootout forced him to shut the place down.

Lyla shot him a venomous look. I ignored their family drama for the moment.

'I'm going to circle around. If they are after me, this will confirm it. If they are here for you, I will cause a distraction and hit them from behind.'

She sidled closer to me, her eyes locked onto mine, her heady perfume intoxicating as she leaned towards me. Her gaze conveyed unspoken promises that would make a courtesan blush. I'd met enough Nagas to know their idea of afterglow often involved someone's bones being digested. Hard pass.

Her left hand squeezed my shoulder, and I felt her fingernails cut into my skin.

'Stay safe!' she whispered, and there was something frighteningly intense about the way she gazed at me. There were wicked intimate rewards in her eyes, sensuous pleasures that would be generously provided if I survived this. 'I am very much looking forward to getting to know you better after this!'

For fuck's sake! Going into a fight with an erection is not only uncomfortable, it also presents a big fat target for them to pound on. I needed my blood in my head, so I could focus.

I freed my shoulder from her grasp and withdrew a pack of cards from my back pocket. 'K, you ready?'

'Almost,' he replied. He had nearly reached the end of his drink and was sipping noisily through the straw to suck the final dregs of alcohol. Four thousand years of existence, and his crisis response protocol still prioritised not wasting alcohol.

I flicked one card from the deck to my right hand, the familiar motion as automatic as breathing. Then I froze.

The card felt … ordinary. Paper and ink, nothing more. I'd been handling powered cards for millennia—they had weight to them, presence, like holding a small thunderstorm. This felt like holding a grocery receipt.

Slowly, I examined the card. It was definitely one of mine, complete with the small mark I made on each deck. Except I couldn't feel the power within.

The power that should have been there.

The power that was always there.

Being cut off from the wellspring of mana was not a new experience for me. Being cut off so completely that I didn't have even the barest trickle? That was new.

'Akran?' K asked, sensing my discomfort.

K's powers had chosen a wonderful day to fritz. If only they could have lasted through the night, we might have all been able to escape under cover of his aura.

'K, you have anything useful in your trench coat?' I asked, not holding too much hope.

'Garlic, wooden stakes, a mirror.'

I gave him a disgusted look. 'Anything we can actually use today?'

'We can break the mirror into two parts, and you and I can each clutch one piece in a handkerchief and … oh, never mind, you are in one of those moods,' he muttered as he kept digging. 'Nope. A handkerchief, flashlight, sneezing powder, an old deck of cards, a Swiss knife, a can opener …'

'Wait, back up.' I was going to have a serious talk about the junk he carried with him but not right now. 'Did you say a pack of cards?'

He brightened. 'Oh, yes, here you go.' He passed me a deck of plastic cards. Probably swiped from an airline because there was a bright picture of a plane on each one.

I slid my thumb across the edge of the deck, savouring the smooth feel of a new deck that had been opened for the first time. Having used hundreds of decks, I could tell by touch how well the cards would spin through the air or how far they could be flung. Fully charged, they would be a potent weapon. These had no power. I didn't mean 'no power' as in I couldn't access the power within. I meant 'no power' as they had never felt mana poured into them.

'What was your plan with these exactly? Invite our enemies to a game of poker?' I asked as I thumbed through the deck.

K had the gall to grin. 'I thought a day would come when we had to go on a stake-out, and then we would be like, oh, if only we had a pack of regular cards to play with, and I would go voila!'

His face sobered. 'Can't you charge them?'

I didn't want to tell him in front of Takshaka and his daughter that my powers were acting up. 'These will do for now.' I shoved my powered deck—the one I couldn't use right now—into my pocket. I'd deal with that later.

'K, take Lyla and go left. Head straight for the staircase, and don't look back; I'll meet you in the alley.'

K's eyes gleamed with mischief. 'What he really means is "Come with me if you want to live."'

She rolled her eyes but nodded and followed him. I ignored him. I had a bad feeling about this.

Takshaka was on his phone, berating someone. It sounded like his security chief would be out of a job the next day.

I wasn't certain they were here for me. I had acquired a reputation, and it was a little ridiculous to send only half a dozen when you could make a hundred copies. Maybe they were here for Lyla.

'Our window of opportunity is closing. On three … Go!'

I stepped out of the room with K and Lyla following close behind. All six RBs were now on the same floor as us, heading from table to table, looking closely at each player, searching for someone.

While they had identical faces, they had each tried to carve out their own distinct personalities. One had a goatee, another a ponytail, one even had a snarling grizzly tattooed on his face. He had probably misunderstood the discussion about how when given a choice, women would choose the bear.

I suppose if they did need to make a public appearance, a club like this was a pretty good choice—low light, most patrons drunk and ogling the hostesses. Not many people would give them a second look. Besides, this crowd—the one percent of the one percent of Mumbai's elite—was known to be discrete.

The first to spot me was a bespectacled RB with a crew cut and a goatee. He uttered an oath and whispered frantically into his headpiece. Within a few seconds, his friends converged around me. Six identical ruffians surrounding me in an upscale casino. This wasn't even the strangest Saturday night I'd had this month.

They spread out, giving me breathing space, yet fanning around and behind me. Good execution but a bit sloppy in tactics. They really should have left one guy closer to the door.

From the corner of my eye, I could see K and Lyla making their way around the edge of one of the tables on the far right.

I had watched enough action films to surmise that filmmakers are idiots. Nobody survives an actual fight with six or more people all by themselves. The only way this works is if they attack one at a time.

One of them moved into my peripheral vision. I caught the gleam of metal on his fingers and spun to face him. He had spiked knuckles on his fist. I caught his arm and twisted until I heard the sharp sound of bone cracking masked by his screams.

In the pin-drop silence that followed, I felt the weight of everyone's eyes on me. It was a lull in the storm—that split second before everyone shook themselves out of the spell of inactivity and reacted.

I needed to seize that moment. Sustain this attention on me a few seconds longer.

I threw my hands up in the air and yelled like I was a rockstar at a concert and the RBs nothing but my groupies for the after-party.

'ARE YOU NOT ENTERTAINED?'

Maximus Decimus Meridius, at his finest. If I was going to die in this gaudy casino, surrounded by demons in knockoff suits, at least I'd go out yelling. Which is pretty much exactly how I imagined I would go.

Warily, a couple of them inched a few steps back. They had come prepared to intimidate someone into submission, not deal with a madman. Demons and humans alike had a healthy respect for insanity. We know it's not contagious, unlike the frenzy of a mob, but there is something primal about it that tickles your lizard brain.

One of them whipped out a gun and the fragile silence suddenly turned brittle. More poignant, yet loaded with meaning. Waving guns around might be perfectly normal behaviour in American high schools or the wilder parts of Bihar, but this was Mumbai—a place where people solved their problems with 'Kem Cho' and absconding to UK, instead of violence.

A woman screamed a high-pitched shriek of terror that cut off abruptly. People were staring at me, a mixture of shock and horror in their eyes.

The silence stretched.

Mexican stand-offs, as it turns out, have a finite shelf life. Any moment now, this would end. Messily and with a whole lot of blood.

That's when I felt it—a singular pair of eyes, more consequential than the rest. Boring into my back, willing me to turn around and look.

I knew who it was even before I spotted him. At the bar, sat the last person I wanted to see in a room full of demons with guns.

He was dressed in blue jeans and a bright red sweater this time around but there was no doubt in my mind it was him. After having obsessed over how I could take him in a fight and letting my imagination run wild about what he had shown me that night, I would have recognised him if he was in full drag and a clown costume. I had a feeling that I was seeing him because he chose to let me see him.

Narada grinned as he raised his glass in a mock salute. I recalled him saying he doesn't drink. The glass had orange juice in it.

The well-shuffled but completely unpowered deck I was holding?

Narada's smile widened, and he raised his glass a fraction higher.

Those cards in my hands grew warm. I felt something like the buzz of a generator in my ears.

As if they'd suddenly remembered what they were supposed to be, a few of those cards rose up and floated in the air.

I heard gasps and cries of delight. The 'normals' in the room thought it was an act. The alternative was just too bizarre ... a bunch of gun toting hoodlums in the most prestigious nightclub in town? It had to be staged.

The gun pointing at me jerked out of the RB's hands and joined the spinning cards. As did the baton and a few other items that had gotten caught up in the current ... lighters, knives, a couple of wallets. All of them spinning around with me at the centre.

One of the cards exploded, filling the room with a massive riot of colours and sound. It was like a flash-bang grenade had ignited directly in front of my face.

And then shit really hit the fan.

Something hard slammed me to the floor, pushing me down. I heard a few screams but by and large everything was muted. My ears felt warm, like a bomb had exploded right next to them.

I tried to stand up but an overwhelming dizziness overtook me.

The Celestial court had one fucking rule. The First Law. Our Prime Directive. No revealing ourselves to the mortals. I had a pretty good idea who had broken it and I also knew that somehow, I was going to get blamed. Celestial justice at its finest—why investigate when you can just blame the nearest Yaksha?

In that moment, it didn't matter. My arms and legs felt leaden and exhausted. A pleasant cloud of sleep descended on my brain and I felt myself sink into its embrace.

'NOT YOU!'

The voice in my ear was sharp and urgent. There was strong disapproval in the tone and I felt myself snapping awake.

I rose up and looked around. My vision had gone from 20/20 to something resembling swimming in murky water. I clutched my ears as I staggered in the direction I thought the staircase would be.

Dark silhouettes lay sprawled across the room, none of them moving. The ringing in my ears prevented me from thinking clearly. I made it to the red door behind which lay the staircase. Grabbing the handrail for support, I climbed a few stairs and waited, trying to catch my breath. My heart felt like it would explode out of my chest, like I had just run a marathon.

I squeezed my eyes shut and listened as the minutes ticked by. After about two minutes had passed, I opened my eyes again. My vision had returned but everything was blurry. I glanced back at the room. It was not a pretty sight.

The chap who was trying to sneakily blow my brains out? He lay on the floor in a pool of his own blood, a playing card sticking out of the tip of his head. The first RB who had identified me and whipped his gun out had fallen where he stood, his throat slashed to ribbons, another playing card stuck in there.

Around the room, all the demons lay dead, each with a playing card stuck in them. All the rest of the humans—customers, hostesses, dealers—were asleep, slumped in their seats or, in some cases, slipped to the floor and snoozing there.

Narada was missing. Honestly, I hadn't expected him to stick around, but I was hoping for some answers.

I looked down at my hands. In the chaos of the moment, someone's blood had splattered my right hand. My left still clutched the remainder of the deck. Narada had used precisely seven cards—one to stun the room, and one to kill each of the six demons.

I sighed and took stock of the situation. The RBs had gotten what was coming to them but at what cost? The Celestial court's First Law was clear: never reveal ourselves to mortals. And now this massacre at the nightclub with playing cards sticking out of every demon's corpse was a clear sign of magic, of the supernatural. The mortals may have been unharmed, but it wouldn't take long for whispers to spread. I needed to get out of here. I rose, my muscles protesting, and made my way out of the club.

I could hear K above me. 'Akran, this way.'

'I'm coming,' I answered as I slipped the powered deck into my pocket. I was outclassed in every way. All I could do now was get Lyla to safety, find who was using the gem and see if I could stop them. Hopefully, that would be easier to execute.

CHAPTER SEVEN

According to scripture, Narada and Kama had crossed paths before. It was clearly more memorable for one than the other. But here's the tale in all its cosmic absurdity.

Narada once immersed himself in an intense yogic trance. The reigning Indra at the time, suffering from chronic insecurity issues, decided to disrupt his trance just in case it resulted in the sage gaining too much power. He dispatched his finest Celestial dancers. They failed. He sent his most charming Devas. They failed too. Finally, he sent Kama himself, the God of desire. Naturally, this also failed. Indra then considered addressing his own insecurities, but decided that was too much work.

Narada emerged from his trance bursting with new powers, but with an ego to match. Seeing this, Vishnu, being a prankster at heart, decided to burst his bubble.

A few days later, Narada 'coincidentally' heard about King Silnidhi organising a swayamvar for his daughter.

The suitors would line up in a row and the princess would walk past each of them, garland in hand, and choose one, because nothing says happy marriage quite like choosing your husband in public and rubbing the faces of all other suitors into how inadequate they were in comparison.

Narada laid eyes on the princess and fell head over heels for her. His fourteen thousand years of spiritual practice proved ineffectual against thirty seconds of batting eyelashes.

The king suggested Narada join the line-up of suitors during the swayamvar, helpfully adding that the princess was already in love with someone named Hari, so his chances were non-existent but at least it made his daughter seem more in demand. It was always a shame when you were putting your daughter up for marriage and no suitors turned up.

The lovesick sage decided to play the system. Instead of upping his charisma, he reasoned he could just trick the princess into marrying him. So he went to Vishnu with a request: turn him into Hari. What fun it was to have magical powers and no morals!

Vishnu, Lord of Righteousness, carefully considered the ethics of this ask and decided it was a very reasonable request.

Unfortunately for Narada, Hari has two meanings. First, and this might be a total shocker, it's one of Vishnu's many names. So, yes, the Hari the princess was in love with was none other than Vishnu himself. But Hari also means 'monkey'—a linguistic nuance Narada somehow missed despite his supposed omniscience. And naturally, the Hari Vishnu turned him into was the tail swinging, dung flinging version, instead of the handsome suave Hari. The sage stood proudly among the suitors, blissfully unaware of his simian appearance until he heard the poorly concealed laughter rippling through the assembly.

Furious, Narada assumed Vishnu had orchestrated this humiliation as part of some divine love triangle. In a rare moment of rashness, he cursed Vishnu: someday he would lose his wife and would require the assistance of monkeys to rescue her. Vishnu, thrilled at the success of the prank, decided that the appropriate response to Narada's tantrum wasn't to turn him into something even less appealing than a monkey. Divine restraint at its finest.

Vishnu then revealed that the entire scenario—the king, princess and swayamvar—was an elaborate illusion. There was no princess to win, no competition to lose, just a divine teaching moment crafted to demonstrate that Narada was still vulnerable to Kama's influence. The god of love was easy to underestimate—but his powers were so potent and pervasive that no one really escaped their influence. Not even the gods themselves, much less uppity sages.

Embarrassed, Narada begged forgiveness. Amused at the potential for future narrative symmetry, Vishnu accepted the apology but allowed the curse to stand, knowing he could repurpose it for the greater cosmic good.

And so, centuries later, when Ram needed monkeys to rescue Sita, the universe nodded sagely. 'Ah yes,' it said. 'Narada's curse. How convenient.' Meanwhile, Vishnu smiled and nodded sagely to himself, whispering so that only he could hear …

'Worth it.'

—The Private Journals of Akran

K met me at the top, a huge grin on his face. 'Why didn't you tell me your powers were back?' he said, a delighted expression on his face. 'If you can do stuff like that, why are we even calling Tamara?'

'You mean you didn't see him?'

K frowned. 'See whom?'

Lyla was staring at me with wonder and fear on her face.

'How were you able to do that?' she whispered.

'Later,' I said brusquely. I had to figure out where we could stash her before making our next move.

Sars picked up on the second ring. Her terse, clipped tone was an indicator of how anxious she was. Briefly, I recounted what had happened.

'Any idea what brought the RBs to me?' I asked. 'We've not crossed paths with each other in a while.'

'I guess the hit has been sub-contracted, but I'll need to confirm. The thing I am more concerned about is how they knew you were there.'

I had this niggling sense of worry in my gut. 'Sars, maybe Narada did this. Followed us to where we were, called the RBs and then had them killed. That would be a good way to win our trust.'

I could feel the weight of her disdain through the phone. 'If he wanted to kill you, he wouldn't go through this elaborate scheme. He's had a chance to do it already.'

She was right but I wasn't fully convinced.

'He said he didn't want to reveal himself or his powers. Why would he do so now?'

'I don't think he has revealed his powers in any way. From what you told me, he used your signature move. A deck of cards that you were holding in your hands. Anyone who saw that probably thinks you did it.' Sars grew thoughtful. 'That actually makes sense. Set you up as a straw man that enemies will take pot shots at. He can stay in the background, learn who they are and eliminate anyone without revealing his hand.'

I had arrived at the same conclusion. It didn't make things better, but I could see the logic of it.

'Whatever his plan, he has violated the First Law, Sars. The RBs could explain away their presence as some kind of gang rivalry. He used magic in front of a lot of Normals. And everyone's going to assume it was me.'

'Not your concern for the moment,' Sars said firmly. 'Get out of there so we can figure out the next steps. Do you know where you can take her to keep her safe?'

'I have a safe house in Juhu. A place called Sangeeta apartments.'

I could hear her voice change over the phone. 'Would that be B2, Sangeeta Apartments?'

'Yes, why?'

She sighed. 'The moment I spotted the RBs at the Lair, I checked where else they were sighted tonight. Three apartments were firebombed this evening.' She rattled off the names as I listened quietly. This was going to be an expensive night.

'All three belonged to me.' My knuckles were white as I gripped the phone. 'Anyone hurt?'

'No, all of them were evacuated through anonymous phone calls made in advance. An old lady dislocated her hip running down the stairs, but that's it.'

That was good. I wasn't worried about the money. Or that this put me at risk with the human authorities. You could kill half a dozen homeless people by running over them with your car and you wouldn't serve a day in jail. The only time they sat up and took notice was if you were a comedian cracking jokes at the ruling government—then they really threw the book at you.

Still, this usually meant some sort of legal hassle—an endless, mindless back and forth between government clerks getting you to fill forms in triplicate.

'I've changed the names on the listings and other details in the digital records, so nothing gets traced to you.'

That was a relief. 'Thanks, Sars. What about my place in Bandra?'

'That one's okay.'

'I'll take Lyla there tonight.'

'Okay,' Sars sounded unhappy. 'We shouldn't keep her there for too long. I don't like having anyone we haven't fully vetted inside the building.'

As mentioned earlier, Sars had undertaken a massive Celestial tracking programme. Every Celestial sighting, every interaction with humans that might reveal our existence, and every display of our abilities was being recorded by her. The sub-basement of the building was the nerve centre of the project, her primary data centre, and she spent most of her time there.

My last encounter with a handful of 'powered' individuals had made me realise that if I was serious about protecting my city, I needed to take a more proactive approach. Somewhere along the way, I got too caught up in stomping out the fires and less focused on the arsonists. Sars had taken the haphazard gathering of intelligence I was doing and reorganised it into something I doubt even the CIA could replicate. It was now wholly her baby, and she took her responsibilities very seriously. 'It's just for tonight. I'll ensure we find another place for her tomorrow.'

'I'll meet you there. I am already en route but need to check a few security logs. If you aren't too tired, then wait for me. I want to discuss what happened.'

'Sounds good. See you soon.'

I ended the call and headed back to K and Lyla. Lyla was pestering K about who I was speaking with and what could be more important than getting her to a safe place.

Quickly I told K what had happened. He took it in stride.

So ... we taking her to our fortress of solid dudes?

I'm going to point out that I would never call it that ... he decided to make it weird all by himself.

'Lyla, let's get you out of here. I'm taking you to my place. Tomorrow we will pick up a change of clothes, toiletries and anything else you may need for a few days. I know your father said three days but let's assume a week in case of any unforeseen problems. After that, you can lie low for a few days till your father does whatever he needs to do.'

Lyla looked withdrawn and subdued. Her disappointment hung in the air like a deflated balloon at a toddler's birthday party. She probably expected more chest-thumping from the 'legendary Yaksha protector' and less 'middle-aged guy who hides in alleys'.

I could see whatever fantasy she had of me was crumbling. I wasn't the gallant shirtless knight on a horse she had been picturing in her head. I was the gutter crawling blade in the dark, more likely to hide and stab someone in the back to get the job done.

She remained silent throughout the cab ride. K, on the other hand, was his usual chatty self.

Now that I thought about it, hadn't K been mentioning a horse a while ago? Maybe I could get him to turn on the charm.

'You ready to hear my joke now?'

'No.'

He pouted. 'In that case, it's your turn to keep the conversation going. Tell me a bit more about Raktabija. Is he the Jamie Madrox of our world?'

K honestly was the weirdest person I knew. He read a shit tonne of stuff on random topics and had opinions on everything, but the stuff we had literally lived through often just flew over his head. It wasn't that he had no interest—he seemed interested in everything—he just forgot every second word.

For my part, I knew most of the lore I had lived through. There were bits that I had missed, such as Uloopi's gem, but mostly, I had a fairly good grasp on the historical side of things.

'It goes back to a story of Durga, the main Aspect of the primordial mother Goddess. Two demon brothers, Sumbha and Nisumbha, received a boon from Brahma that no man, God, or demon could defeat them. They hadn't considered Goddesses.'

K snorted. 'You've told me a dozen variations of this tale, and there's invariably a loophole that the demons forgot.'

'I don't think it's a loophole that demons forgot. You gained immortality through the nectar from the churning of the ocean. Once that was used by the Devas, there was no more to spare. Even the chiranjeevis (immortals) aren't truly immortal; their life spans extend to the end of the Kali Yuga. Besides, if the Gods *could* dish out the nectar, they certainly wouldn't do so just because someone prayed to them. So, what the demons really needed to do was ask for something as close to immortality as they could manage without making it look like they were asking for immortality.'

Lyla finally spoke up, her dark green eyes boring into me. 'How is it that you have lived for so long then? Nagas avoid conflict, yet our numbers have dwindled over time. Yakshas seem to thrive on it, yet there are plenty of you.'

The age-old question: Why do the annoying ones live forever?

'Nagas avoid conflict, yes. But they also choose to live among humans in their crowded cities, seeking to earn wealth and emulate them. Yakshas used to be warriors, but once the age of science began, many of them disbanded and flitted away to stay apart from the world; they lived in uninhabited spots like deserts and mountains deep in the forests. They have no desire to get involved in the ways of humans. They certainly aren't immortal.'

'Isn't the primary role of a yaksha to play pranks on humans?'

I sighed. 'That's just a stereotype. Like saying all ghosts moan "wooo" or all Gods have perfect hair. Hardly a life goal for warriors.'

She looked like she didn't quite believe me.

'I thought Yakshas were meant to be air and nature spirits.'

'Some of them are. But most were bred for war. Legions of us, at one time. I don't think there are even a handful of us still around now.'

Lyla nodded. She went back to staring out of the window, lost in thought.

'Back to what I was saying. The two brothers had several fearsome warriors, and Raktabija was one of them. The Goddess was baffled by his ability to create multiple copies, so another Aspect of her, Kali, emerged.'

'She's the one with four arms and a necklace of skulls?'

'That's the one. Also, don't forget the skirt of severed hands and the bloody sword. She pounced on Raktabija and began to suck his blood before it reached the ground, and ate each clone. She kept that up, whittling away his forces until there were none left.'

K had this huge shit-eating grin, and I groaned inwardly, knowing what was running through his mind.

'So … I'm not judging,' he began, 'but you can see how this can be interpreted in a more … naughty way, yes? Taking a little break in between the battle to …'

'She wasn't taking a break. It was necessary.'

'Of course it was … A very hands-on approach, wouldn't you say?'

'K …' I warned.

'It is always important to stay hydrated,' he said with a straight face.

'It was his blood'

'Sure, his blood.' He smirked as he said it and made air quotes with his fingers. I showed him one of my fingers as well.

I shot Lyla a quick glance, but she just sat and stared out of the window.

'So nobody thought to question how she pulled it off? Fighting multiple demons while trying to ensure no drops fell on the ground?'

'She had multiple heads.'

'That doesn't help at all. She still had just one neck, yes?' Horror dawned on his face. 'Wait. Could the heads detach and run around by themselves? That would explain a lot!'

I squeezed my eyes shut to get rid of the ghastly image. 'Can we move on? I don't claim every legend is accurate. There is always something added or lost in the retelling.'

'Well, I hope you know you are on your own if there's ever any blood-sucking.' K gave a little shudder of disgust. 'Knowing demons, it'll also be fatty and full of cholesterol.'

The taxi pulled up outside my building. The private elevator carried us to the penthouse level. The familiar space felt different now, less secure than it had this morning. Lyla appeared sullen and withdrawn. I guess watching someone murder a bunch of demons in cold blood might dampen one's ardour.

I showed her to her room. K dawdled in the hall while I stepped into my room and changed. I was feeling … different. My clothes were damp with sweat, and I was exhausted.

I peered at my shoulder in the mirror, the one which Lyla had grabbed when she was telling me to stay safe. Four tiny scratches were clearly visible, the skin around them flushed an angry red. Her nails had drawn blood—tiny ruby beads that gleamed in the light.

I healed much faster than humans. Our bodies pulled themselves together and looked none the worse after a trying battle. Flesh mended, splintered bones healed, and skin scarred and stitched itself together in very little time. I had suffered plenty of cuts and scrapes in my life. Most were a lot more severe than this; wounds from being cut right to the bone that healed the next day.

These hadn't healed. They still looked fresh, like it had happened a few seconds ago.

I took the cards out of my back pocket and tried once again. No luck. I could sense the energy in the deck, but somehow my hand couldn't quite grasp it. Like I was trying to wolf down soup with a noodle instead of a spoon.

That wasn't even my biggest worry. I was more concerned that this was just the beginning.

A few months ago, Sars had theorised what would happen if the magic in our world disappeared. People like myself who were cut off from our mana or had very little to spare daily would be the first to feel its effects. We would lose our longevity and our healing abilities, eventually becoming fully human, or worse, fading away into the ether.

We knew that Ashwatthama's yagna had created a rift in our dimension, a tear in the fabric of space and time. Those who could sense it could feel it like a perpetual whistle at the edge of hearing, a wrongness that made teeth ache and skin prickle when you reached out for the source. We also knew the magic was leaking, and our best efforts so far hadn't been able to stop it. We didn't know how big the rift was, how fast the magic was leaking or even the long-term consequences for our world. Like many other really smart people, Sars was working on the problem. It was one of a dozen different challenges she had on her plate.

I resolved to tell her what had happened once she came up. She was in the building already. For now, I poured some alcohol on the wound, hissing as it bit into my flesh, before changing my shirt. If I was losing my healing abilities, I had to ensure my wounds didn't get infected. I gave it a minute before walking back to the hall, and handed the rest of the bottle to K. We headed out onto the balcony for a nightcap.

'This is a two-hundred-year-old Japanese whisky. Don't tell me you wasted it on your shoulder?' K asked as he sipped his drink.

I grimaced. The pain had faded into a dull throb. I didn't know how long this would last, but I needed my invulnerability back. I wouldn't survive without it.

'Are you thinking what I am thinking?' K asked.

'That your stupid trench coat is holding a bunch of junk instead of useful things that might save our lives? Yes, that is what I am thinking!'

K gave me a hurt look. 'You don't even know half the stuff in there.'

'If it's like the half you showed me already, I don't even want to know.'

'Wait, you'll change your mind soon!' He reached in and extracted two black cylindrical bands. 'See?'

'For the last time, I'm not interested in friendship bracelets!'

K smirked. 'After we fought Vritra and I nearly got electrocuted by those falling wires, I dug through some of the stuff Mas had kept in one of his storage lockers. I thought these were interesting.'

Mas was Mayasura, architect for the Asuras and a genius beyond compare at building epic shit. He was a close personal friend and one of the few people I knew who did not turn their backs on me when the Celestial court accused me of killing Krishna and starting the Kali Yuga. He had designed a set of knives that could kill Celestials. I had used them a few times, defending myself against overzealous attackers who had a score to settle; or those who wanted to make a name for themselves; or were filled with righteous indignation that I was walked free; or who just liked murder and mayhem. His knives had saved my life many times over. Knowing these were designed by him made me look at them with new respect, though I still wasn't clear what they were.

'Here, catch.' He tossed one of the bands to me. I grabbed it with my left hand, and the band reacted with a life of its own, snaking around my wrist before the tiny clasp on the side snapped shut.

And with that, my magical senses went blind. The tiny throbbing pulse of magic I could still access folded in on itself and disappeared. I was now completely cut off from my powers.

'K, what the fuck is this?' I fumbled trying to get the damn thing off my wrist. It looked like one smooth, unbroken piece of metal, the clasp having seemingly disappeared.

Meagre as they were, there was a comfort I took in the limited powers I had. This was like a curtain had fallen across the sun.

K chortled. 'From what I understand, these were used to bind Celestial prisoners. You can't see the clasp once it's on you, but you can feel it. Here, look.' He took my thumb and rubbed it on the edge of the band, and I could feel a tiny indentation.

'Once you feel it, it can be easily removed, but the band blocks access to your powers while it's on.'

I studied the band with interest. 'So the next time we meet someone like Vritra, we need to find a way to wrap this around his arm?'

'Not necessarily. I think Mas intended it so that the person bound with this cannot be persecuted by someone with powers. It works by creating a dead zone of sorts around you. Not only are your powers useless, but anyone trying to attack you magically will not be able to do so. So

Vritra can throw fireballs at you, but you will be completely immune.'

I handed the metal band back. It was easy to unclasp, so maybe there was more to it; we would need to investigate.

'If it comes down to a fist fight, a demon like Vritra can still pound me to a pulp.'

'True,' K conceded as he dropped the bands back into one of the coat's many pockets. 'But with the state of your powers at the moment, I'd say a fistfight gives you slightly better odds.'

He wasn't wrong.

'Incidentally, that's not what I meant when I asked if you knew what I was thinking. I was talking about Raktabija.'

I nodded. 'We assumed that the original Raktabija escaped Kali during the battle and was hiding all this while. But now, with all these resurrected demons popping up … He might have been the first one resurrected by whoever our mystery villain is. We didn't think it was suspicious because his powers naturally support the idea that he had snuck away.'

'It never bothered you that they were demons?' K asked.

I gave him a quizzical look. 'Why would it bother me?'

'Well, I'm a God of Love, so Asura, Deva, human distinctions never bother me. But Yakshas were bred for war, weren't they? Isn't that your whole purpose of being?'

I took a long swig before I answered. 'I was that way once. Now … I think who am I to begrudge someone looking for redemption or second chances? As far as I'm concerned, their slate is wiped clean when they die. I'm not going to judge them for the mistakes they made in their previous life.'

'At least you finally have the power to back that up, huh?'

'Not quite.' I quickly briefed K on what had really taken place at the Lair. K sat back with a thoughtful look on his face.

'Why didn't you mention this before?'

I grimaced,'You don't think Lyla is a bit odd?'

'Aside from the part where she was coming onto you when the God of Love was sitting right next to her, you mean?' K pretended to think. 'Clearly she has terrible taste in men, but I'm guessing that's not what you mean.'

'It isn't. I think she had a very different set of expectations from me and she's disappointed that I don't match up. I don't want her to have some sort of meltdown if she thinks we can't keep her safe.'

K arched an eyebrow. 'So, your plan is to pretend you have your powers and can protect her for the next three days?'

'For now, I need to do whatever it takes for us to get the name of whoever has that damn jewel. Until then, I'm not telling her about my lack of abilities, the crazy sages with insane powers, the psychopathic murders, contract killers, mind wipes, and God knows what else. By the time three days are over, Tamara will hopefully be here, and then the real work can begin.'

K started to speak but at that moment the intercom buzzed. I had a visitor.

I couldn't remember the last time I had someone buzz my intercom. K and Sars both had their own spare access cards. I thumbed the button, giving whoever was out there access, and a split second after I did so, K shot out of his chair like a scalded cat.

'What happened to you?' I asked, puzzled.

'Uh, you aren't going to believe me if I tell you.' He rubbed his head gingerly. 'Now I know what that feels like.'

'Like what feels like?'

'When someone talks to you in your head.' Seeing my look of incomprehension, he clarified, 'The person coming up right now? That's Tamara!'

CHAPTER EIGHT

According to the Ramayana, Ram spends fourteen years in exile along with his wife Sita and his brother Lakshman. When the demon king Ravana kidnaps Sita, Ram recruits the vanara king Sugreeva to his cause by helping him depose his brother Vali.

Some people today believe the vanaras were a different species of half-man, half-monkey. They point to that as an example of evolution.

To clarify, those people are idiots.

The term Vanara comes from 2 words. Vana (forest). Nara (man).

While vanaras are depicted as monkeys in popular art, their exact identity is unclear. They were a tribe living in the jungles of southern India, (in a region around the Tungabhadra River near Hampi in present-day Vijayanagar district, Karnataka. They were shorter and darker than the Kshatriya princes from Ayodhya. Their appearance and *possibly their worship of monkeys led them to be referred, either unintentionally or in a derogatory form, as monkey-men. Which is a shame because they were incredibly brave Heroes and were nearly exterminated by the end of the war.*

—The Private Journals of Akran

'Huh?' I gave him an incredulous look.

'That's not possible! I asked her to assist us less than twelve hours ago. Even if she dropped everything and came here, it would still take at least …' I did a few mental calculations for the distance between Haiti and India '… a lot more time than this.'

'Maybe she hopped onto her broomstick and flew here.' K suggested with a smirk.

'Comments like that are why you have no other friends!'

K raised an eyebrow, 'Coming from you, the expert on friendship?' he scoffed. 'I'll go let Sars know that Tamara has arrived.'

It had been a few months since we last saw Tamara. At the time, she had been kidnapped, beaten and malnourished, so I expected there to be some difference between the image in my head and the girl at my door.

Tamara was a half-Haitian, half-British slim fourteen-year-old teenager with coffee-brown skin and incredibly curly hair. The person standing before us was a full-grown woman, no less than thirty years of age, and Indian. Not the kind with casinos on reservations. The sub-continental type—southern Indian, to be more precise.

'Akran,' she said, smiling, 'it's really good to see you.' She held her arms out, expecting a hug.

I took a step back. The woman sounded genuinely happy to see me but there was no fucking way I was hugging whoever this rando was before I got a handle on what was going on.

She gave a theatrical sigh as she saw my reaction and gave K a look. 'You didn't tell him?'

K made this pointless shrugging gesture that made no sense whatsoever.

The woman claiming to be Tamara smiled. 'Akran, relax. It's me all right? You needed me here, which would have taken way too long by conventional means, so I took a shortcut. It's a little unorthodox, but it worked.'

'What shortcut?' I wasn't sensing any danger from this woman, but I couldn't help feeling anxious.

'Okay, the name sounds worse than it is, but it's not as big a deal. It's quite a common practice in Haitian voodoo.'

'Just spit it out,' I growled.

'It would take too long to get here through normal channels. Did you know there's no direct flight from Haiti to India? With layovers and whatnot, it would've taken at least thirty-six hours or more of sitting all cramped up in a flight or waiting at airport terminals.' She shook her head in disapproval. 'No, this is better. My body is back in Haiti, in a deep meditative trance. And when I am not confined to it, I can get here super quick.'

She said that very matter-of-factly. Like she was talking about the weather.

'So you know this woman? The one whose body you are inhabiting?'

'I've never met her before,' she said cheerfully. 'She happened to be in the neighbourhood.'

'She is trapped in there with you?' I asked. I had an image in my head of this young woman minding her own business when out of the blue, her body got hijacked by this passenger who was now operating it while she sat inside like a mute, passive prisoner witnessing events unfold.

Tamara gave me an odd look. 'Of course not. I guided her spirit into my body as a temporary waypoint for her to stay anchored. It would be messy if two of us occupied the same body.'

I couldn't decide which was worse: finding your body hijacked or finding yourself in another woman's body halfway across the world.

K apparently had a similar thought.

'Couldn't you let her float away instead of sending her to your body? Maybe she could find her way back once you finish.' He caught my glare and amended hastily. 'Not that I condone this method of travel, by the way.'

Tamara's face turned sombre. 'That's too dangerous. If her spirit isn't tethered, it might wander for years, trying to find its way back. It's a lot like what happens to people in comas. Or when they have dementia.'

'So let me get this straight. You essentially hijacked some poor woman's body, sent her spirit on a vacation, and now she's stuck taking care of chickens and goats in Haiti while you gallivant around halfway across the world in her body?'

Tamara smirked. 'Oh, relax. She won't remember a thing when she wakes up.'

'Exactly what someone might say before they wake up in a bathtub full of ice,' muttered K.

'Besides,' she continued blithely, 'it's not like I'm using her body for anything nefarious. When she wakes up, she'll be back in her own body, good as new. Plus, most women would happily trade an older body for a younger one, even if it's only for a few days.'

I shook my head in disbelief. 'I'm not getting warm, fuzzy feelings about your mental health right now.'

Tamara just grinned. 'You always know how to make a girl feel appreciated.'

I looked at K, who winced in sympathy. This was wrong on so many levels I didn't even know where to fucking start.

'I've read about this before,' said Sars as she entered the room with a wave and a smile at Tamara. 'Body snatching. It's fairly common in Voodoo.'

'Technically, it's body swapping,' corrected Tamara. She smiled warmly as she walked towards Sars, hands outstretched. 'You must be Sars. I've heard so much about you.'

Before Sars could respond, Tamara had swept her into a hug. Sars gave a startled squawk of surprise. Much like me, she wasn't a hugger. This bubbling, warm personality we had in front of us was a bit overwhelming.

'I've been so looking forward to meeting you. It's so exciting. I've never been to India. And Akran tells me you are the smartest person he knows.' She seemed oblivious that the rest of us weren't as comfortable with this body snatching/swapping business.

This was precisely why I had hesitated so long before reaching out to her. Her heart might be in the right place, but she was a teenager at the end of the day. They believed the universe revolved around their good intentions rather than the actual laws of physics and ethics. When you are someone with reality-bending powers, a sense of what is morally right or wrong becomes essential.

'If we could get back to the matter at hand … Tamara … for fuck's sake.' I didn't mean to swear but I couldn't help myself. I had to rub my temple as I felt the start of a headache behind my eyes. 'You can't do this.' How could I even couch it in terms she would understand? 'We can't just swap bodies like it's a game of musical chairs. It's not just a violation of someone's privacy, it's dangerous. We don't know what kind of psychological damage it could cause to her mind.'

Tamara rolled her eyes. 'Oh, please. I've swapped bodies dozens of times. It's like changing clothes. Except with less heartache and confusion.'

I pinched the bridge of my nose. 'That's … not helping.'

'Well … I found her passed out at a bar three blocks away. Someone had spiked her drink. I might have saved her from a lot more than a violation of her "mind".' She punctuated 'mind' with actual air quotes and gave me an insufferable look. 'If you know what I mean.'

Gah! I hate teenagers. So smug and insufferable when they score on a verbal jab.

'Are you sure you will be able to swap back after this is over?' Sars asked mildly. She seemed the least bothered by the whole thing.

Tamara waved her hand. 'Can I swap back? Of course! Would I want to swap back? Hmm …' She caught the expression on my face and raised her hands as if in surrender. 'That was a joke, alright. Yes, I will swap back. Jeez!' Her gaze swept the room. 'This is a nice place, Akran! It's so bright and vibrant.'

I wasn't quite sure what I could say to that. She had already moved on, and I was still beating a dead horse. 'Tamara, I'm really glad you are here, but why did you not catch a flight or something?'

She gave me a pained look. 'I told you this already!'

I exchanged a bewildered look with K. 'You really didn't!'

Her brow furrowed. 'Didn't I? I forget. Sometimes, I see things that have already happened, only they haven't happened yet.'

Sars made a sharp, appreciative sound of delight. That last sentence must've made sense to her.

'Well, at the risk of repeating myself,' Tamara continued, 'Akran, you should have called me three nights ago. You dithered while you made up your mind and now it's nearly too late. If I didn't come now, it wouldn't have mattered.'

'What wouldn't have mattered?'

She waved her arms. 'This! All of this! Your whole existence! It would all be for naught. Futures would collapse, and the only path left would be a dark tunnel with no light at the end.'

'Did you know she can see the future?' Sars said to K in a loud whisper.

'I don't think she can even see the present,' K whispered back. 'Like that vein bulging on Akran's neck the more she talks about futures and whatnot.'

I tried to tune them out to focus on Tamara's words.

'You are saying that something is definitely going to happen, and I would need your help?' I asked slowly.

'It has already begun, and I hope we are not too late. The future will be decided in the next three days.'

Three days? I knew without a doubt this was connected to Lyla. It could mean a major attempt on her life, and her living or dying might bring the dark future to pass. Or it could mean that keeping her safe would let me know who held the Naga gem and that battle might end up being the confrontation where we would need Tamara's help.

Like always, visions about the future and those who claimed to see them were frustrating and vague. Why couldn't they just draw a bloody map and leave clear instructions on the best path ahead?

Lyla chose that moment to enter the room. Her eyes were bright and sharp, though heavy with sleep. The choker was still around her neck. She had a wary, hostile look as she studied Tamara and Sars.

K jumped in to make introductions.

'Lyla, this is Sars. She's the one who discovered the legend of the Naga gem and brought us to your father's club. She's also helping us find more about the RBs, you know, the people who attacked us at the club today.'

'The club attack happened today?' Tamara's voice dropped to a whisper. 'I should have come earlier.'

'And this is Tamara,' K continued, a bit flustered by her reaction. 'She's a close friend and will be staying here with us. You'll be safe with her around.'

Lyla gave Sars a nod, an almost imperceptible tilt of her head, in acknowledgement. Maybe a sign of respect or that she considered her an equal. Her look at Tamara, however, was a lot cooler.

'You brought a demon to assist?'

Aah, I had forgotten about that.

'Tamara isn't a demon,' K interjected. 'She just looks like one. I mean, not physically, but deep down inside. Not like you know … he gestured to show horns above his head and stuck out his tongue, while making a growling sound like a mad chihuahua. It was embarrassing just watching him.

I had expressed similar doubts when I had first heard this story. A lone human girl walking into hell to rescue her grandmother, tricking millennia-old demons and escaping unscathed isn't just unlikely, it's flat out insane. Even I wouldn't have been able to pull that off. That she did so was a testament to her will. Or her abilities. It was impressive.

Lyla wasn't impressed.

'My father thought you would be good enough to do the job by yourselves. The fact that you need so many people makes me feel he made a poor choice!'

I raised an eyebrow. 'Your father thought we were good enough to handle this task on our own,' I said, my voice cool and measured. 'But it seems that he may have overestimated your ability to conduct yourself in a group.'

She bristled at my words, but I continued, 'If you're not happy with the arrangement, we can take you back to your father tomorrow. But I won't tolerate your disrespect towards Tamara. She stays, and that's final.'

The girl glared at me. 'I will not stay under the same roof as this … this thing!' she spat.

I felt my temper beginning to flare. 'I trust her with my life,' I growled. 'More than I trust you, in fact. So either deal with it or leave.'

There was a moment of tense silence, and then Lyla spun on her heel and marched back inside, slamming the door behind her.

'Tamara,' I said, my voice softening. 'It's been a long night for all of us. Let's get you settled in the spare room down the hall. And Sars, if you have any spare clothes that might fit her, bring them along.'

Sars nodded, leading Tamara away. I watched them go, feeling a pang of apprehension.

This was harder than I expected. Two more days of keeping the brat safe. My head, back, and stomach all hurt from the stress and exertion of the evening.

'Akran, you okay?' I had never heard K sound so worried.

'I'm fine,' I muttered as I clutched my head. The floor rushed towards me as something shut down inside my brain, and I plunged into darkness.

***

When I woke up it was either morning or dusk, I couldn't tell. The light filtering through the windows was soft and grey. I was still sprawled on the hallway carpet, but someone had slid a cushion under my head and draped a blanket over me. It smelled faintly of lavender, probably pulled fresh from a closet.

'You're awake. How are you feeling?'

I groaned as I propped myself up. If you've ever done a hundred burpees just because one of your idiot friends challenged you, you'll know exactly what I was feeling at that moment. 'Like I got hit by a truck,' I muttered, rubbing my eyes.

Sars chuckled. 'You hit the floor pretty hard last night. K and I took care of you. We even made you a nice little nest.' There was even a soft toy placed near my head: a sad-looking pig holding a heart. I squeezed and it let out a loud oink.

'K?'

She grimaced. 'When he said he was getting you something from his personal toy chest ... that wasn't quite what I imagined.'

I didn't blame her. Nobody really knew what to expect when you put K and a toy chest in the same sentence.

She leaned in closer, her voice dropping to a whisper. 'I checked on the club and last night's incident. The official story is that there was a gas leak. People just had some mild hallucinations.'

I sighed. Nothing screams innocence quite like the old hallucination-inducing gas leak excuse.

'Are people buying it?'

She shrugged. 'All the Normals at the event made it home last night with no memory of what really happened. Narada must have wiped their minds clean. Which means he didn't break the First Law. Or at least there's no way to prove it.'

I felt a headache creeping in. 'Great. One less thing to worry about.'

Sars patted my shoulder. 'Don't stress. We'll figure this out.'

Honestly, I didn't care. I'd grudgingly decided Narada was way out of my league, and obsessing over him was just giving me ulcers. I would just ignore him and hope to never meet him again.

I was also famished, and a delicious aroma was already tickling my nostrils. Butter, spices, and something warm.

'You've made enough for both of us?'

She grinned. 'I made enough to feed six of us. Sit.' She loaded two bowls with steaming hot Maggi noodles, golden with butter and sprinkled with just the right amount of spice. We grabbed forks and dug in.

It was the most amazing meal I had eaten in a while. The secret to good Maggi was to drown it in enough butter to give an elephant a heart attack. And to keep K away from the kitchen, else he would insist on adding Nutella or some other nonsense to it.

We spent ten pleasant minutes in companionable silence. I loved that about Sars. She could sit with you and say nothing for hours without being uncomfortable. Those are the kind of people I needed more in my life. K, on the other hand, felt the need to fill every conversation with some titbit he found interesting or pester us with questions about things no one ever cared about.

'So,' Sars said as she dabbed her lips with a napkin, pushing the plate away. 'Last evening, you weren't quite yourself.'

'Yeah, I guess.' I was a bit embarrassed at my outburst. The pain in my head had made me irascible. More than usual, I mean. 'I'll probably go apologise to Lyla.'

She blinked. 'That? Oh, I didn't mean your tantrum. We expect that from you. I meant the tipping over and falling. What happened to you?'

I had no idea. I told her how my powers had conked off almost completely last night and with it had come headaches, nausea and this weird fainting spell.

'I have a few thoughts, but let me check with Tamara.'

I frowned. I had forgotten about everyone else. 'Where are Lyla and Tamara?'

'Lyla stormed out this morning after a heated conversation over the phone.'

I sighed. 'Great! We've lost our chance to find out who has the gem.'

'I wouldn't worry about her, for the moment.' Sars seemed unperturbed. 'You offered to keep her safe. If she can't deal with our methods, then that really is her problem. Besides, I have a feeling Lyla will come back.' She paused. 'I am more interested in talking about Tamara.'

'Where is Tamara?'

'She's out shopping. I lent her your credit card.'

'Okay, sure.' Sars handled our finances and had made us enough wealth to last several generations. She was one of the early buyers of cryptocurrency, and had used it successfully to avoid a paper trail on most of our purchases. I have never quibbled when she chose to spend some of that money.

'Are you worried about Uriah and his guys now that you've brought her here?'

I recalled that I had told Sars about the incident on the bridge a while back.

'Hopefully, this body-swapping thingy she has done will keep them from noticing. Short of me lighting a beacon to the heavens, I don't think they will even know she is here!'

'In that case, why were you reluctant to ask for her help?'

I stared at her. 'Are you really asking me that after what she did yesterday?'

'No, I get it. You don't trust her judgement. She seems like a nice girl though. And her abilities are amazing, to say the least.'

'I have no doubts whatsoever that she is a wonderful person. But you know what they say ... If you need to kill a roach in your home, a slipper should do the trick. You don't need to drop a nuclear bomb on it.'

Sars made a face.

'Tamara is the nuclear bomb.'

'I got that. But it's a terrible analogy because the one thing you shouldn't do to kill a roach is use a nuclear bomb. They are known to survive those.'

'My point being …'

'I get what you mean. But … Tamara may be exactly what you need right now.'

I frowned. 'What do you mean?'

'In case you've forgotten, there is still a contract out on you. Whoever these assassins are … she is a wildcard and they would have no idea how to deal with her.'

That reminded me! 'That woman Tamara took over …?'

'I checked on her. Gita Rajkumari. An aspiring actress, twenty-nine years old, came to Mumbai a week or so ago to try her luck in films. No friends or family here. She won't be missed.'

'Hopefully, she won't remember this incident. She'll wonder where she was for two days or so, but there should be no long-term consequence of this.'

'Tamara did suggest this morning that she could instead swap to someone else every six hours or so, so collectively, no single person would lose too much time,' Sars said.

'Gods, no! Let's not get her to traumatise any more people. And the next time she thinks she is needed, I'll tell her to get here immediately.'

'That's actually what I wanted to talk about.'

'Okay'. Sars wasn't known for being melodramatic or stretching her stories out. 'Did something happen?'

'She woke up this morning and asked me to drive her to the post office. She had sent a package by courier and needed to get it picked up.'

'What was in it?'

'An amulet. It practically reeks of demonic energy. I asked her about it. Apparently, she had it picked up from the bowels of hell. I'm not being metaphorical here.'

'Wait! She got it today? How is that possible?'

Sars gave me a grim nod. 'That's my point. She had it couriered two days ago! Before you even reached out to her!'

I frowned. It's cute when you have a movie character tell you he's scanned fourteen million futures and seen the one which leads to victory, but reality is a bit more nuanced.

'I'm not too familiar with divination,' I began. 'But ...'

She shook her head. 'This isn't mere divination. The accurate term is quantum states but leave that aside for a moment. Akran, her powers are like nothing we have ever seen. That body-swapping thing she did? That's clearly voodoo. She's shown us divination. She can dream walk, do runic magic—pretty much any magical tradition that she encounters, she seems to be familiar with.'

'Okay ...' I still wasn't sure where she was going with this.

'Look at it this way. She's not a Celestial, not like us, I mean. She's definitely human. What does that tell us?'

'Maybe one of her ancestors slept with a human?' I suggested weakly. Because that was always the explanation in our circles. Unexpected powers? Ancient deity got frisky. Weird birthmark? DemiGod had a wild weekend. Kid randomly starts speaking the language of snakes? Maybe someone tried to kill that kid as a baby and part of their soul got transferred to that kid. Stuff like that is completely normal among us.

'That would explain one of her abilities. But she's able to do many different things. Who knows what else she can do? Maybe she can help us close the tear in the universe.'

I hadn't considered that. 'That's an amazing idea,' I said slowly. 'If she can peer into the future and figure out who has the gem, for instance, we could even pay them a visit.'

Sars's expression soured like she had bitten into rotten fruit. 'I thought about that already. As she describes it, the problem is that she is afraid of gazing into the abyss because sometimes the abyss stares back.'

I had no idea what that meant. It sounded like a movie reference, so I continued to chew my food and pretended those were words with great meaning.

'If she keeps looking into the future, sooner or later, one of the futures will crystallise into the path forward, and it may not be a future we want.' Seeing my puzzled expression, she clarified. 'She said it's like shining a spotlight in a dark room. Different parts of the room get illuminated, highlighting possibilities. If she looks for too long at one future, or too far ahead, that future "wakes up".'

'Wakes up?' I had seen one nature show where an Australian chap in a home-made alligator costume made his way into a dried-up river bed chock full of alligators and began to prod them with a stick. The image Sars had conjured in my head was similar—giant sentient sleeping monsters prodded by Tamara.

'If she sees a future in which an extinction-level event wipes out the world, staring at that future might make it come true.' She paused. 'I've never heard of something like this before. Do you think it's possible?'

'I … I don't know.' It was frankly a terrifying idea. 'The amount of power one would need to exhibit to push away or collapse other futures to make way for a single inevitable one is … mind-boggling.'

'I agree,' said Sars. 'I don't think a human body can take that much power flowing through it without suffering some sort of catastrophic breakdown.'

'I don't think even the Trinity would have the power to do that. She is saying she isn't merely viewing possible futures, she can bend reality to make this happen. Without wilful action on her part.' I frowned as the implications of what that meant sunk in.

'Sars, we need to get her out of here.'

She looked at me, puzzled.

'If the Celestial court hears of something or someone like this, they will execute her. They can't risk an unknown, untrained sorceress who can unmake reality walking around.'

'Let's not be too hasty. She can't see much into the future since the more permutations and combinations of possibilities exist, the worse the headache she gets. She usually looks for only a few hours or days ahead in time.'

'So?'

'So maybe she isn't really impacting the future. She sees many possibilities, then latches on to the one most likely to happen. She's not influencing it, only spotting it.'

'I'm not seeing your point, Sars.'

'My point is that we don't know if she can impact reality in that way. She thinks she can. There's a big difference.'

'I doubt the Celestial court will appreciate the nuance. They are not very good at investigations, I can tell you from personal experience. Neither are they overly concerned about an innocent verdict. They won't bother verifying anything. They are more likely to eliminate her and ask questions later.'

The expression of distaste on Sars's face deepened.

'Maybe they will ignore her since she is a guest in our lands. Isn't it none of their business?'

'Guest or not, they can't let something like this slide. I didn't realise until this moment the scale of the power we are talking about. There's clear precedent for an unnecessary execution.'

'What sort of precedent?'

There were a lot of things I didn't talk about. Stuff that had happened or I knew about from a long time ago, because it wasn't supposed to matter anymore. But this ... this was different.

'Sars, you are too young to remember this, but you've heard of the great flood?'

She frowned. 'The one where the first man Manu built a boat, rescued all the animals and was pulled to safety by a giant fish? I thought that was a myth.'

'The very same. Except it's not a myth.' I leaned forward, my voice dropping. 'Every culture remembers it differently, but the story echoes across the entire world. You'll find it everywhere, in the Bible and Quran, in ancient Chinese texts about the Gun-Yu, in Greek stories passed down through generations. The Mayans carved it into their stones, Polynesian elders whispered it around fires, and it's etched into the Epic of Gilgamesh. Even the Cheyenne tribes in

North America and the aboriginal peoples of Australia tell tales of when the waters rose.'

'Very few people know that the flood was an accident. Everyone tends to attribute it to the might of the Gods and their wrath against humans. It's a convenient explanation I had no reason to disbelieve until I took charge of the Celestial archives. They have texts in there that precede any known historical records.

'Back then, magic was different—wild and raw, like lightning in a bottle. You could move mountains with just a whisper, using powers that would barely light a candle today. And in this world of untamed magic lived a boy. His name has been lost to time, but his power … his power was something else. He was one of these wild sparks, someone who could shape and alter reality. Like Tamara. No training, no guidance, just pure, instinctive power that would let him cast spells sages twice his age had difficulty performing.

'One day, when the boy had just passed his eleventh summer, he saved the life of a hunter. In gratitude, the hunter gave the boy a bronze knife. The hunter's gift was precious. A bronze knife back when metal was still rare enough to make people gasp. The boy spent days carefully carving a toy boat, his small hands working the wood until it was perfect. One day, as he stood at the dried-up river bed near his home, staring at the cracked earth, disappointment welled up inside him. All he wanted was somewhere to float his little boat.'

'NO,' Sars mouthed in horror.

I nodded wearily. 'He caused the great flood, Sars. Keep in mind he was a child at the time. I don't know the details of how he did it. Maybe he moved the moon. Maybe he emptied the water from the heavens. He may even have regretted his actions afterwards. What is known is that the flood covered the earth, cleansing it of all humans, except a chosen few who managed to escape because they had a premonition, a divine warning that allowed them to survive in a boat.'

'What happened to the boy?' Sars asked.

'He was executed. It was too late to undo the damage though. It was an extinction-level event that could have been avoided if the boy had been trained or killed.' I paused. 'Do you know what the truly frightening thing was? Nobody was entirely sure who warned the survivors to build a boat.'

Sars frowned. 'What do you mean?'

'Everyone who survived owed their lives to a divine voice urging them to build a boat. But building one large enough to save civilisation? That isn't something that can happen overnight. These weren't just quick rafts thrown together in panic. These were massive vessels, built carefully over time. Someone—or something—made sure humanity would survive. But who whispered those warnings? Who set those plans in motion? Because anyone powerful enough to see the flood coming could have stopped one small boy.

'We still don't know all the details. Maybe the boy didn't make his boat right away. He may have worked on it for many weeks. He was playing a game where a boat full of survivors escaped a flood. Maybe he or his powers nudged Noah, Manu, or Nuh to build that boat that saved mankind. The whole thing was a child's version of a game—except it was a game that nearly destroyed everything.

'That is why the celestial court will not tolerate an untrained, powerful magic user. An accord was reached by

Celestials across the world. It doesn't matter which mythos they are a part of or which geographic location they spring from. A "wild spark" can ruin everything for everyone. If they suspect she has powers like this, they will hunt her to the ends of the earth.' Nearly drowning an entire planet tends to make everyone touchy about proper magical supervision.

Sars had turned pale. 'You've never mentioned this before.'

'I never had to. It's one of several stories that comprise the hidden histories of our world.' Something nudged at the back of my mind. 'Actually, that's not true. I saw this just a few days ago.'

'When?'

'When we met Narada! One of the cards showed me the boy! It looked familiar at the time, but I dismissed it.' I felt my suspicions flare up again. 'Sars, you think that was his plan? Narada was manipulating us in some manner.'

Sars shook her head. 'Your paranoia about Narada is getting tedious.'

I sighed. She was right. I was chasing shadows. Then again, it's only paranoia if it isn't true. And in my long, exhausting experience, it usually is. I should really get that printed on a t-shirt.

'Until such time as the council discovers her, let's get a sense of what she can and can't do. Tell me more about your adventure in London, where you first met her. What powers did she exhibit then? What are her limits? You told me the gist, but I want to know the details. Can you tell me the whole story again? I want to be sure I didn't miss anything.'

The whole story? Maybe not. There were some bits that I wasn't planning on sharing with anyone. Like the warning from the fay that if she got involved in our lives again, one of my closest friends would die.

Still, I could tell her most of it.

I had met Tamara about six months after the Ashwatthama incident. It was an entry I hadn't fully catalogued in my journal. One of those things that I knew I needed to put down on paper at some point, but just hadn't had the time.

'From what I know, Tamara is a mimic, someone whose abilities are so rare, there's only one born every thousand years or so. She can spend time in the company of a powered individual, sometimes as little as a few minutes, and is then able to pick up their abilities.'

'Pick up, as in taking for herself?'

I shrugged. 'I don't think she is stealing their powers. It's like her mind unlocks how a powered individual's abilities work, and she can replicate them.'

'But how does she do it without mana?'

I shrugged. 'This I can't say. I used to think everyone needed mana, but neither the dreamwalker nor the others used it.'

'So her powers keep stacking indefinitely?'

'I don't think she retains all the powers she absorbs permanently. Some of them remain for longer, and some dissipate in a short while. But somewhere in the past, she probably met a seer, and now she can see the future. That ability is now quite natural to her. When fighting the fay, she could read his mind, just like he could read ours.' I snapped my fingers as I remembered something. 'There was a ghost kid with us who could set things on fire. We were trapped by a hedge, and she set the whole thing ablaze.'

Sars gave a low whistle. 'Have you considered bringing Tamara here might give her even more abilities? If she meets someone like Narada …'

'That thought had crossed my mind.' It was why I had been reluctant to talk about it in the first place. 'On one hand, I think, don't feed the monster. Isolate her from everyone and everything so that she doesn't become impossible to stop if we have to.'

Sars opened her mouth to speak, but I wanted to say my piece, and so I plodded on.

'On the other hand, ignoring her and assuming she will remain stuck on her little island is a mistake. You've seen how she got here. Left to herself, sooner or later, she will choose to test the limits of her powers. She will gain abilities but also meet other powered individuals—people of questionable morals. I'd rather she learn from people who won't corrupt her first instincts. People like you.'

Sars blushed, pleased at the compliment.

'You, me, K, we are elementals. Born and shaped into who we are right from birth. We have free will, but our nature is intrinsic. A hundred years from now, Sars, you will still be reading books, absorbing knowledge, and solving the thorniest problems we can put in front of you. K will still be trying to hump anything that moves. I will still be railing against injustice, standing up for the underdog and taking on lost causes.

'Tamara, by most standards, is a child. A human child. Her personality, values, behaviours, and attitudes will be shaped by how people behave around her. If we stay in touch with her, be good role models, people she could turn to for advice when needed, I don't believe the future where she turns into a monster will ever come to pass.'

Sars took a moment to reply.

'Before your name was struck from the celestial records, did you have a portfolio of your own?'

I shrugged. 'All demi Gods do—little things that are too insignificant for the big Gods to ever worry about.'

'What were you?'

'The God of lost causes.'

A smile tugged at the corner of her lips. 'There's a God for that?'

'There's a God for everything. Mine was the most insignificant of all. Forlorn hopes. Wretched despair. When humans, at the lowest point in their lives, prayed desperately for someone, anyone, to hear them, I was the one those prayers reached out to.'

'And do you think,' she asked with all the subtlety of a hangman measuring your neck for the gallows, 'you still end up championing lost causes because of what you once were?'

'Not a lost cause,' I protested.

'No? You have assassins on your trail, your powers are fritzing, the heavenly host is watching you, you are still itching to pick a fight with Narada, you've taken on the responsibility to keep Lyla safe and now, on top of that, you plan to hide Tamara from the Celestial Council when you already know that they will react harshly. Have I missed anything?'

'No,' I said sheepishly, 'you've covered pretty much everything. You think I should turn her over?'

She shook her head. 'No. Especially since she came all the way here because you called her.'

I nodded, relieved. I trusted her judgement.

Sars stepped closer and gave me a hug.

'I don't begrudge your knight-in-shining-armour syndrome,' she murmured. 'It's what I've come to expect from you anyways. I just wish you had better sense of timing. And knew how to pick your battles.'

I opened my mouth to respond when I felt another pair of arms encircle me from behind, pinning my arms to the sides.

'I love group hugs,' muttered K sleepily. Somehow, he had snuck up on us without either of us noticing. 'Why are we doing this one?'

Firmly, I disengaged from his grasp. The intercom buzzed right at that moment.

'I'll get that,' said K as he sauntered off.

'There's something else we need to talk about, Akran,' Sars said as she pulled up her laptop. She spoke as she showed me pictures from last evening.

I listened attentively, my mind churning as I processed everything she said.

'It's all circumstantial, of course, but it's a plausible theory.' Sars concluded.

'I agree,' I said. It certainly explains some bits. 'Have you told anyone else yet?'

Tamara sauntered in right at that moment, followed by K. She had shopped a bit, and was now dressed in a white top and black jeans. Seeing this stranger display mannerisms exactly like the girl I knew still jarred a bit, but that little coma I had been in was, oddly enough, getting me used to the idea.

She sat down beside K, concern writ large over her face. 'How are you feeling?'

'Much better, thanks.'

She cocked her head in this odd, pigeon-like gesture. 'Really? Because I could have sworn the cause of your troubles hasn't gone away.'

'Well, about that.' I shifted uncomfortably in my seat on the floor. 'The rift that's draining magic from our world … Sars and you should …'

'Not that,' she interrupted with a frown. 'I mean the hex that's been put on you.'

CHAPTER NINE

When wishing misfortune on one of your enemies, there are two handy choices for a powered being: curses and hexes.

Curses are fairly straightforward. You find a person you dislike, state the nature of the desired effect and imbibe your words with power. The hapless victim feels the curse like a physical noose around their neck. Curses were the weapon of choice for most sages when they were angered—because nothing said spiritual enlightenment quite like throwing your power around on people who couldn't defend themselves against magic. They are a bludgeoning tool—the more power you have, the more powerful your curse can be. Since the victim knows who is cursing them, there is something almost honourable about curses. They're the supernatural equivalent of leaving a one-star review with your real name attached.

Hexes are a different breed of spells. They use less mana or yogic power but are often a more complex weave requiring *plenty of patience and hate. The practitioners of hexes are often highly skilled and strive to remain undetected; it is a very passive aggressive response to conflict. Hexes are designed to keep your victim unwary of the spells' true origins, and with good reason. Kill the person who hexed you, and the hex will fall apart, making it the only scenario where murder actually solves your problem completely.*

—The Private Journals of Akran

The room fell silent. Behind us, I could hear the clock ticking. Even K, who normally couldn't shut up for more than a minute, looked gobsmacked.

I glanced down at myself. I didn't doubt her, but it was strange being told something was hanging around my neck that I couldn't quite feel.

'A hex?'

Tamara looked unsure of herself. 'Are you not feeling unwell? Maybe short of breath, more impatient, a little less control on your powers than usual, perhaps?'

'Yes!' I yelled. 'Are you saying this is a hex?' I wasn't quite sure if it was good news or bad. Good if it meant this was not due to the rift. It meant I had a solution! Find the person who had hexed me and kill them. Bad because I would still need to find the person.

Sars was shaking her head. 'A hex! I didn't even think about the possibility.'

'To be fair, we wouldn't really have known if he was being "less patient" than usual,' K interjected.

I resisted the urge to prove his point by throwing something at his head.

Tamara nodded slowly. 'That's why I was sending you the amulet. It works as a ward against different kinds of spells.

I thought you might need it. Unfortunately, the post was delayed and only arrived today.'

'Aren't hexes harmless?' asked K. 'Thought nobody uses them because of how weak they are.'

'They aren't weak,' I said slowly. 'There's more preparation involved, especially in masking the identity of the person casting it, to make it undetectable. It's easier to curse someone. Hexes rarely cause as much damage as curses, but you can get fiendishly inventive with them.'

K's ears perked up. 'Tell me more.'

'There was a king in Magadha who had a hex on him that he would always feel like there was a grain of sand in his right eye. He didn't realise he was hexed, and all the court physicians could do nothing. He eventually clawed his eye out in desperation but the magical, invisible grain of sand continued to give him a maddening itch in his hollow eye socket. It was only when his wife accidentally took a tumble from a parapet and broke her neck that the itch in his eye suddenly stopped.'

K whistled. 'Wow! She must have really hated him.'

'That's what all the best hexes have going for them—a great deal of hate.'

'Don't you need to be physically touching the victim for hexes?' K asked.

'Not necessarily,' Sars answered. 'Really potent hexes sometimes use blood, or sweat, or skin. But usually, they need a strong connection between the person casting the hex and the victim.'

'A strong connection like …'

'Like Akran said, hate is usually the main emotion. Could be envy or malice, but usually, it's a connection with a strong passion behind it that sustains the hex, giving it a life, if you will.'

'Does that narrow it down?' Tamara enquired in a timid voice.

'If we get one of those big old phone books and open to a page at random, chances are there will be at least three people on that page who hate him,' said K.

A gross exaggeration since most of the people who disliked me weren't listed in any phone book. His point was valid though. I was not a popular Celestial.

The intercom buzzed. It was Lyla. I sighed as I buzzed her in.

Sars followed me to stand near the lift as she came in, but I waved her back. Lyla and I would probably have an awkward conversation, and it would be best done alone.

Sars stood there looking uncertain. 'Are you sure you don't want me here?'

'I'm sure.' I gestured at K and Tamara. 'When you can get him alone, tell K what you told me.'

'Done.' She walked back to them as Lyla stepped out of the lift.

She clearly hadn't gotten much sleep the previous night. Her face still had that stern, cold, marble-like quality, but there was also something less abrasive in her manner.

She was carrying a bag, presumably with clothes and toiletries.

I gave her a tentative smile. She stiffened when she saw me. I could see she was nervous from the way she held her hands close to her body, fists clenching and unclenching as she spoke.

'I wanted to apologise for last night,' she began. 'It was not my place to judge who you chose to invite to your apartment to keep me safe.'

'I'm the one who should be apologising,' I said. 'I tend to react harshly when people criticise my friends. I meant what I told your father. I will keep you safe for the next couple of days. Longer, if needed.'

Her posture, which was stiff and awkward when she had arrived, now relaxed slightly. 'Thank you,' she said softly. 'My father hasn't been himself these past few weeks. He has been unwell, nervous and paranoid, constantly jumping at shadows. Knowing that I am safe would keep one worry off his mind and allow him to focus on the threat from within.'

I felt a tiny prickle of unease upon hearing her words. 'Lyla, these symptoms you are describing, when did they start?'

She gave me a puzzled look. 'About two months ago. Why?'

'I'll explain. Let's go inside. This time you and Tamara can get properly introduced.'

I lead her in. Lyla was gracious and apologetic. Briefly, while she and Tamara spoke, I told Sars what she had said about Takshaka.

Sars had a curious look on her face, not exactly like she was tapping into a mental insight but more like she had swallowed a bitter pill of some sort. 'Akran, I really need to talk to you about something, but not right away. When we get a chance later, I need to have a word with you and K.'

I nodded. 'Sure.' Tamara was telling Lyla and K how she could cast hexes using voodoo through a straw doll and pins. The subject was macabre, but K was guffawing away, so maybe it was the way she was telling it.

I noticed a chunky bracelet on Tamara's wrist. It looked just a little loose for her hand but she didn't seem too bothered by it. What was odd is that a few days ago, I had seen Sars walking around with that same bracelet.

'Did you give her that?' I asked, puzzled. 'I could swear I saw you fiddling with that a day or so ago.'

Sars punched me in the arm. 'See! This is what I mean! Don't say anything, just listen. Don't draw attention to anything you notice. Stay quiet and simply observe. I'll explain later.'

I could wait. Still rubbing my arm, I followed Sars into the living room.

'Lyla, Tamara here thinks I might be under a hex. From the symptoms you described, your father might also be under one.'

'How do you know?' Lyla asked, her voice barely rising above a whisper.

'I can see the hex,' said Tamara. 'It's around his aura. It's shaped like a chain coiled around his neck.'

'I can't see it,' K announced.

'Neither can I,' confirmed Sars.

Lyla gave Tamara a thoughtful look. I knew this look. Wheels were turning in her head as someone she had previously dismissed as inconsequential suddenly became relevant.

'If what you are saying is true, we should get you to my father.'

'Before we go there,' Sars interrupted. 'Tamara, if you can see the hex, can you perhaps disable it?'

Tamara frowned. 'I don't know if I can. It's entangled around his head, his shoulders and his neck. It will likely kill him if I try to disable the hex.'

I didn't know hexes could be disabled at all, so this was a new thing I learnt today.

'Can you tell us what it does?' Sars asked.

'Oh, that's easy. It's a complex weave, so plenty is going on in there. I'd guess it's doing at least two different things. The first is emotional—heightening certain feelings like paranoia, anger, irritability, that sort of thing.'

'It sounds like this hex has been on him ever since we first met,' K muttered.

'The second is simpler. It's meant to track wherever you go.'

I stared at her. 'You are saying this spell can track where I am at any time?'

Tamara nodded.

'Okay, that's it! I'll take the risk. Tamara, do what you must but get this off me!'

K raised one neatly plucked eyebrow. 'Are you serious? You don't care about the other effects, but this is where you draw the line?'

'I'd love to help, but I don't think I can do that.' Tamara massaged her forehead with two fingers. 'I'm sorry. I can't see too far ahead, but I know I can be of help. I just haven't figured out how yet.'

Lyla leaned forward, intense hunger on her face. 'You can see the future?' she asked.

'Sometimes,' Tamara said wearily. 'It comes and goes. Wait, that's it. She snapped her fingers with excitement. 'I can pull one of these threads.'

'I don't know what that means.'

'Whoever is watching you … I can follow the thread back to where he or she is!'

INTERLUDE 2

The Ramayana—A Different Perspective

Let me set the record straight about the Ramayana—another epic that's been thoroughly sanitised by centuries of retelling. You know the story: perfect prince gets exiled, wife gets kidnapped, epic war ensues, good prevails over evil. The end. Roll credits. Cue the moral lessons about duty, righteousness and the triumph of dharma.

Yeah, well ... not quite.

So, there's no ambiguity here—I have nothing against Ram. Nice guy, mostly. Always willing to lend you an extra arrow during a hunt or pay for another round of drinks when it's his turn. But the whole 'perfect hero' narrative? That's some serious PR work by later generations who needed a squeaky-clean role model. Beneath the myth lies a far messier and more human story that I personally find a lot more interesting.

The story begins with Dasharath, a king whose idea of romance was to bring his wife with him onto the frontline during a war—kinda like how Kama sometimes takes his dates to horror movies just so he could put his arm around them. Seated in his chariot, with arrows flying all around, the young queen decides that gasping with admiration and quivering with fear at appropriate points in the battle are beneath her. Instead, she contributes to the outcome by fixing his broken chariot wheel and consequently saving his life. Dasharath, feeling grateful, offers her two blank checks. Kaikeyi saves these royal IOUs for a rainy day, knowing that a bird in her bush will in the long run be worth far more than one in her hand.

A couple of decades later, her rainy day finally arrives. She cashes them in for one son on the throne and another banished into the woods. And of course, the son banished to the woods is the hero of the tale, Ram, her stepson. (Fun fact: If you actually know the name of Ram's mom without googling it, you are pretty much far ahead of most other people around you.)

Now, any sensible king would've said, 'Listen, sweetie, I made those promises when I was tripping on battle adrenaline and grateful to be alive. Let's renegotiate.' But Dasharatha was old school. A promise was a promise, and a promise that you make, was a promise you can't break. Even if in this case, it meant destroying his kingdom and breaking his heart. He did make the obligatory attempts to weasel out of the deal with a lot of pleading and wailing but Kaikeyi held firm. Ram, being a paragon of virtue, immediately offers to spare his dad this grief and go to the forest voluntarily. His newly married wife, Sita, a role model of duty, virtue and other expectations hoisted on women through the ages, decides that her place is by her husband's side and not in the palace with a spineless king and a hostile mother-in-law. She offers to tag along, and after some token protests, Ram agrees. Royal princes were not really known for their skills at doing laundry or even cooking, so having her along dramatically improved their odds of survival. Sita didn't really mind trading silks for bark while spending years in exile by her husband's side. She probably envisioned this like a longish honeymoon—frolicking among the deer and what not.

But then, his brother Lakshman decided to come along.

There are bits to this story that don't quite fit. Ignore the flying chariots, leaping monkeys, sleeping giants and other fantasy bits as exaggerations if you must. But thinking about it as a story set in a society with rigid social codes, how dense does his brother have to be to not give a newly married couple some space? Not only did Lakshman accompany them, he also got a boon that would allow him forgo sleep for fourteen years, just so he could watch over them. The man voluntarily chooses to give up his life as a prince and spend fourteen years watching his brother and sister-in-law in the forest.

Every.

Single.

Night.

The epic calls this devotion and sacrifice. Modern psychology might have a few other terms for it. The whole arrangement has an uncomfortable undertone that nobody talks about but everyone has probably thought about. It's the kind of 'devotion' that would get you a restraining order today, but in ancient times, it got you called a model brother.

Fast forward to the forest years. Ram, Sita and Lakshman are living the jungle life, building huts, eating roots and berries, and generally having a jolly good time in an Indianised version of a Tarzan and Jane adventure—with Kerchak, the silverback, always watching them in the background.

Everything's going swimmingly, until a demoness named Shurpanakha shows up.

Now, Shurpanakha was Ravana's sister, which nobody knew at the time. She saw Ram, thought he was quite the catch, and decided to skip the running-around-trees and singing-songs phase of courtship. Ram tells her he isn't interested, then quickly deflects her attention with, 'Haaaave you met Lakshman?'

Lakshman, irritable from lack of sleep and in general being a grouch, also rejects her.

Spurned by both brothers, the demoness decides her best shot at improving her odds is by eliminating the competition. Sita, who until then was simply minding her own business, suddenly finds a demoness attempting to kill her. At this point, Lakshman intervenes. His idea of gallantry was to save Sita by cutting off the demoness's nose and ears.

Now, this wasn't random violence—not sleeping for a while can make anyone cranky, but the nose and ears being cut off symbolises the permanent marking of someone who has violated social and moral codes. In the Tamil version of the epic by Kambar, Lakshman goes one step further and even cuts off her nipples. But the escalation is telling. A romantic rejection turned into attempted homicide, which then turned into disfigurement. Nobody in this story believed in proportional responses.

This act of violence is what sets the entire tragic chain of events in motion. Shurpanakha, understandably furious and humiliated, goes crying to her brother Ravana. And Ravana, despite being a noble, revered king who feared no humans, decides that his best course of action is to skulk in the forest and kidnap Ram's wife like a common thief, instead of dealing with him in a more regal fashion.

It might be worth mentioning at this point that Ravana was well known as a lusty king. He even had a curse on him that said his head would explode into a million pieces if he forced himself upon a woman against her will—something he was fully aware of. And despite knowing this, he decided to implement the kidnapping plan. What gives?

Well. For one thing, the story would have been considerably shorter if that had happened. But let's skip that minor plot detail for now. Ravana kidnaps Sita and takes her to his island after fighting off a talking eagle. The eagle, conveniently, lives just long enough to tell Ram who kidnapped her and where to go to get an army.

You might be forgiven at this point of time for thinking that if you have a kidnapper on one side and a grieving husband on the other, there would be no morally grey areas. But no.

The army in question belonged to King Vali from Kishkindha. Ram doesn't go to Vali directly. Instead, he allies with Vali's exiled brother Sugriva, hears his side of the story, decides he doesn't need to listen to Vali's version of what happened, and shoots Vali from behind a tree while Vali is fighting Sugriva in single combat.

This was spectacularly dishonourable per the warrior codes of the time—you don't ambush someone, especially not while they're engaged in single combat with someone else. When Vali calls him out on this, one of Ram's justifications is 'you're a monkey, so normal rules don't apply.' Not exactly the moral high ground you'd expect from the perfect prince.

Then there's Hanuman's little adventure in Lanka. While he was on a reconnaissance mission to find Sita, he ended up burning down half the city. Granted, he was captured and they set his tail on fire first, but turning that into a full-scale arson spree that destroyed homes and probably killed innocent civilians? The parallels to certain contemporary conflicts in the Middle East are hard to ignore—playing the victim card no longer works when the moral high ground is lost.

After threatening to evaporate the sea with a fire arrow and eventually using that arrow to create a vast desert (a place where, once again, there were civilians), the engineering wing of the Vanara army built a bridge, and the troops invaded Lanka. A fierce battle ensued—Ram once again allied with the younger brother, killed Ravana, rescued his wife and went home. The epics describe a peaceful transition of power in Lanka, though if history is any judge, violent invasions and regime changes rarely lead to lasting peace.

Ravana, for all his faults, actually treated Sita with respect during her captivity. He didn't force himself on her (which would have been a pretty bad idea anyway, given the curse), didn't harm her and even gave her a year to make up her mind about marrying him (most men wouldn't have waited half that long). Compare that to how female prisoners of war were typically treated in ancient times, and Ravana starts looking almost gentlemanly.

Don't get me wrong—kidnapping is kidnapping, and Ravana was definitely the aggressor. But the black-and-white morality that's been painted over this story doesn't quite match the nuanced reality of the situation.

The tragedy isn't just confined to the war; it's also what happens after. Ram rescues Sita, but then subjects her to a trial by fire to prove her purity. Fire has always been seen as an excellent judge of character—much better than taking your wife's word for it. It was basically medieval #MeToo—blame the victim and make her prove her innocence. It subtly reinforces the idea that a woman's worth is tied to her sexual purity, and that this purity is always suspect, always needed to be proven. Even after she passes this test, he later exiles her again because the opinion of a random washerman besmirched his honour. The perfect husband, the ideal king, essentially abandons his pregnant wife because of what people might think.

The Ramayana, at its core, is a story about the impossible standards we set for our heroes and the human cost of trying to live up to them. It's about how rigid adherence to duty can sometimes be more destructive than pragmatic flexibility. And it's about how the 'perfect' ending—good defeating evil—often comes at a price that makes you question whether it was worth it.

But there's more. It's also a story about how we mythologise toxic masculinity and call it honour. Ram's treatment of Sita—testing her purity, exiling her based on public opinion—isn't noble leadership; it's a man choosing his reputation over his wife's dignity. The epic celebrates this as dharma, but it's really about a society that values appearances over relationships.

It romanticises co-dependency and calls it loyalty. Lakshman's obsessive devotion to Ram, Sita's insistence on following him into exile, Bharata's refusal to actually rule in Ram's absence—these aren't healthy relationships. They're people who've lost their individual identities in the service of an ideal.

Sita's character gets systematically erased throughout the story until she becomes nothing more than a symbol of purity to be protected, tested and ultimately discarded. She starts as a woman with the pluck to choose exile with her husband, but ends up as a prop in everyone else's moral drama. Her final act— disappearing into the earth—isn't transcendence; it's her throwing her hands up in the air and saying, 'stop involving me in whatever hare-brained twist is going to happen next.'

Perhaps most tellingly, it's about how we sanitise our stories to create the heroes we need, rather than learning from the humans we actually were. The Ramayana we tell children is a fairy tale. It presents social rules as if they're natural laws—like gravity or thermodynamics. Ram must honour his father's word, wives must prove their purity, younger brothers must serve older ones. These aren't presented as cultural choices that humans made up, but as cosmic truths that reflect the fundamental order of reality.

The problem with this is that it makes the questioning of these rules seem not just wrong, but also impossible. When Sita suffers due to the purity tests, or when Ram abandons his pregnant wife, the story frames this as tragic but necessary— like casualties in a natural disaster rather than the predictable results of human-made systems.

Every one of these little lessons are like arrows with barbs around the edges. Unquestioning obedience is virtuous, the individual suffering for the ' greater good' is noble and leaders who enforce harsh rules are moral (not cruel). When Ram exiles Sita based on public gossip, he's not shown as a weak leader caving to pressure—he's shown as a noble king putting duty above personal feelings.

Ancient history? Sure. But people are still acting out the same worn-out roles from the script while refusing to acknowledge that the set has changed. You see this same pattern everywhere: 'respect your elders' being used to shut down criticism of harmful traditions, 'greater good' arguments that always require sacrifices from the marginalised, political rhetoric that frames dissent as unpatriotic. People are still asking #WWRD and then going out and vandalising mosques in his name—something he would never have countenanced.

Texts like the Ramayana were once part of oral traditions and public storytelling (like in Ramlila performances), where questioning, interpreting and emotionally reacting were part of the experience. Problematic episodes provoked discussion, introspection and reinterpretation. These weren't meant to be regarded as timeless truths; they're cultural snapshots. Including these elements allowed later generations to critique and question them—like many modern retellings do. Somewhere along the way, people lost their appetite for questioning and began to demand blind allegiance.

We've turned a complex story about flawed people making difficult choices into a simple morality play about good versus evil. And we wonder why authoritarianism keeps finding fertile ground.

But hey, that's just my take. I'm sure the traditional version makes for better bedtime stories. After all, who wants to tell children that their heroes are complicated, that good people sometimes do terrible things and that happy endings often come at someone else's expense? Much easier to stick with the sanitised version where everything works out and everyone gets what they deserve.

Except for Sita, of course. But she is a woman, so who really cares about her opinion?

CHAPTER TEN

K's friend Jane had a pretty caustic observation to make:

'It is a truth universally acknowledged, that a single man in possession of a good fortune, must be in want of a wife.'

What they don't tell you is that the unspoken corollary is just as absurd:

A single woman—regardless of age or common sense— may still choose a dishevelled, possibly undead-looking ascetic as the husband of her dreams.

Enter Sati, an eight-year-old with the unshakeable convictions of a teen environmentalist. Despite Shiva being older than time and his dreadlocks and live snake accessories, she decided age is only a number and declared only he would be her husband. Her father Daksha dismisses Shiva as a homeless vagabond, which was harsh but accurate. However, parenting in epics follows one rule: if your kid is stubborn enough, you cave. So, he did.

Fast-forward to a lovely family gathering where Daksha decided to insult Shiva.

Sati, rather than rolling her eyes and leaving, decides a massive overreaction is needed. She immolates herself.

When your wife folds herself out of existence, you don't just call, you raise with divine vengeance. Shiva went all in—by slaughtering his father-in law.

Patricide didn't make him feel better and so he placed her on his shoulder and wandered the world. Carrying your dead wife's body like a backpack might seem excessive, but in the pre-digital age, grief processing options were limited.

Vishnu decides to intervene. Ever practical, he studies the scene and surmises that traditional options like a kindly word or a shoulder to grieve on might not be as effective. Instead, he hits upon a brilliant solution. The template for dealing with problems by men for the next several thousand years. It was called out of sight, out of mind.

Vishnu severs Sati's body into fifty-one pieces which land all across the sub-continent. Shockingly that worked. Shiva went back to the Himalayas to meditate, feeling like a weight had been lifted off his shoulders. Meanwhile, humans gained fifty-one new sacred places to worship, because what the subcontinent perpetually had a shortage of was ... more temples.

Soon after, the Devas were being persecuted by a demon named Tarakasura. Tarakasura had received a boon from Brahma that only a son of Shiva could slay him. It was oddly specific and for good reason; Shiva was very much a loner—the OG social distancer. That alone was enough to make me respect him greatly. The secret to longevity, among introverts, is to not be around other people and Shiva had no qualms whatsoever staying away from the world.

But the Devas, ever resourceful, hatched a plan that could be summed up in four words ...

Let's get Shiva laid!

They chose to pin their hopes on Parvati, a beautiful young girl who, coincidentally, was Sati reborn. Parvati and a bunch of other pretty Apsaras frolicked in front of him. Unfortunately, our Lord of Earth and the heavens didn't twitch so much as a single muscle—he used to meditate with his eyes shut.

Kama, the God of Love, was requested to assist.

Matchmaking in the divine realm required surprisingly literal arrow-shooting. Obligingly, he shot a flowery arrow into Shiva's heart.

Shiva reacted like any sane person would react when someone shoots arrows at you—he killed Kama. To be more precise, an eye on his forehead opened up and flames immolated him.

With all eyes open, Shiva finally saw Parvati and succumbed to her advances. Soon they had a son, the son killed the demon and everyone on heaven and earth were happy again. Well, except the charbroiled piece of meat that he had burnt to a crisp.

The love God's physical body was gone. The essence of Kama diffused all over the earth and humans thus experienced love for the first time.

Now, before this, people were still going at it like rabbits—but it was more ... wham, bam, thank you ma'am. No romance. No sonnets, no coy little requests of 'send bobs and vagene'. Just... business.

But thanks to Kama's explosive career change, poets finally had something to write about besides the weather. And thus, humanity upgraded from 'ugh, fine' to 'sigh, my soul aches for thee.'

(RIP Kama. Your sacrifice was ... oddly convenient for literature.)

—The Private Journals of Akran

'Are we there yet?' I asked for the sixth time.

Sars gave a low growl. 'The answer hasn't changed in the last one minute, Akran!'

Seated next to Sars, Tamara gazed up wistfully at the moon.

'It's so beautiful,' she sighed. 'The way the light blends with the shadows. The smell of street food. The feel of the breeze!' She gave me a sideways glance. 'Honestly, I don't understand why you couldn't be happier when you have so much to be grateful for.'

I grunted. Wide-eyed wonder was tolerable for the first hour or so. After that, it got annoying.

Besides, I didn't really see what Tamara was so excited about. I remembered a time when civilisation meant something else entirely. Cleaner air, for one. Less noise. Most of all, significantly fewer people. No TikTok dances, no Instagram filters, and nobody asking if you wanted to hear about their podcast. Paradise lost, indeed.

We were in a car driving down the Eastern express highway towards a farmhouse in Mira Road. I couldn't stand it. Trapped in a steel coffin hurtling down the road at a hundred miles an hour—how could anyone put up with it? It felt claustrophobic, not to mention insane. I would have rather walked. Or swum. Or been shot from a cannon.

Sars was somehow unaffected. As a new-age Goddess, none of this bothered her. And clearly, Tamara didn't care either. Which left me as the grumpy old fart driven up and down by the Celestial equivalent of teenagers.

Our reaction to Tamara's announcement ranged from disbelief to elation—an emotional spectrum that somehow managed to skip right over 'reasonable concern,' which would have been the sensible middle ground.

K wanted to head out at once and celebrate the 'first solid lead' in the case. His idea of a celebration was usually an orgy that lasted for at least a few days, which, understandably, did not receive an enthusiastic reception from the rest.

I was halfway through the door; if I could murder whoever had put this hex on me and be home for breakfast, I was more than willing to do so. Lyla and Tamara appeared carefully neutral. Sars was the only oddball who suggested that rushing headlong into obvious traps might warrant a brief discussion first. Who even does that anymore?

'Akran, think about it for a minute. This could be a trap designed to get you there.'

I have always valued her counsel, except when it conflicted with my burning desire to hit something.

'Sars, this is it. They don't know we are on to them.' I felt a fierce exultation in my chest. 'We strike them hard, now, before they can react. Before they slither back into the shadows! No waiting for them to make the first move.'

'Nothing about what you are saying addresses my point about it being a trap,' Sars said calmly. 'And this isn't you! It's too hasty. You are the one always telling us to be careful. To work out all the angles before we commit to an action. Even you must admit, heading there now is foolhardy. Especially when you know you have assassins on your trail.'

She had me there. It was easy to dismiss me as reckless and short-tempered, particularly since I didn't back down from a fight. But I hadn't survived millennia on the run by being stupid. Give me some credit!

'You are right,' I said heavily as I forced myself to sit on the couch. My whole body thrummed with this nervous, excitable energy. I was experiencing something I hadn't felt in a long time: battle lust. Right now, I needed a rage room, a place that could soak up this desire to fight.

This wasn't me. Or rather, this was not me anymore. From being a battle leader of the Yakshas, I had undergone a massive transformation to the relatively sedate lifestyle I had here. Clenching my fists, I tamped down on the fervour, willing it back into a tiny place in my soul that I had left forgotten. A place where all the dark emotions were stored. The time would come when I would need to bring them to the forefront again, but this wasn't it. 'Not today,' I whispered.

Unaware of my inner turmoil, Sars addressed the rest of the group. 'Let's wait till sunset. That gives us a few hours to study the place and see what we can learn about it. After that, we could take a quick peek in the dark, just a few of us.' She looked around, seeing if anyone had any objections.

Lyla raised her hand. 'Let me inform my father. He will bring a group of Nagas to assist us.'

Sars shook her head. 'Your father told us there may be moles in his organisation. We can't risk tipping them off. Let's keep this on a need-to-know basis for now.'

'Then I'm coming along. You'll need every hand you can get.'

I spoke up. 'I don't think that's a good idea, Lyla. We promised to keep you safe, so we will do that. I can't think of a single place in the city safer than this. With the number of protective spells I've cast on this place, the penthouse is a fortress. Single entrance through the lift, reinforced glass and concrete. Even if someone fires a bazooka at us, we will be okay.'

'That's not what I meant,' began Lyla. She turned to Sars. 'No offence, but why is it okay for you to head out and not me? Do you have some special abilities of any kind?'

'Not offensive ones, no,' I said. 'But Sars can put together clues and figure stuff out much faster than anybody else on the planet, thanks to her intuition. She's definitely going with us!' I chose not to mention that I had promised Sars I would take her on our next field mission, and this was it.

'And what about you, Tamara?' she asked. 'What can you do? Or K, for that matter.'

Tamara gave her a bemused look. 'I think I can keep Akran safe. I'm not sure how exactly, but I'll know more when it happens.' She raised a hand, palm facing upwards, and a ball of white flame about the size of my fist appeared. It floated lazily in the air, a foot or so above her palm, and she gazed at it in delight. I could feel the heat radiating from it, even at a distance.

'I couldn't do this last night. And now I can. Isn't this exciting?' She squeezed her eyes shut, and the flame turned into a ball of ice.

K and I exchanged a look. I could do this earlier when I had access to my mana pool.

Lyla gave a tight-lipped frown. Nagas didn't have powers of their own. They were long-lived like most Celestials, could see on multiple planes and shape-shift into snakes when they chose—but that was about it. A few of the really powerful ones had other abilities, but most of them lived ordinary lives.

Tamara closed her palm, and the temperature of the room went back to normal.

'That's great, Tamara. We also need to deal with the RBs,' I said.

'I could set fire to their chapter house,' offered K. 'You know, as payback for what they did to your other apartments.'

'Let's indulge in arson another time. For now, finding out who hired them would be helpful. K, maybe you could snoop around their headquarters? See if anything turns up?'

'Gotcha,' K dead-panned. 'First, find their client's name, then we can smoke them out.'

'To summarise,' I said. 'We move in a few hours. Sars and I will visit the farmhouse. Tamara and K can check on the RBs. Lyla, don't leave the apartment, even to wander about in the building. There's food in the fridge, and we'll order more before we head out. Stay holed up in here till we are back.'

Lyla didn't look pleased. I couldn't blame her. Despite her bubbly charm, I could see why anyone would be intimidated by someone like Tamara.

Our plans changed somewhere between the lift and the parking garage, and Tamara joined Sars and me. Which was good since Sars tends to be chatty on road trips, and I'm not. The farmhouse was at least a couple of hours away, if not more, by road, and I could wallow in my misery at being trapped in a car while the two of them chatted.

Sars took me aside in the garage to explain why she thought Tamara should join us. Less than two minutes into her explanation, I knew where she was going. I've always acknowledged her as the smartest among us because her innate abilities allow her to make leaps of intuition that bridge the gaps in our knowledge. She then weaves those disparate threads of understanding into a single coherent narrative—which is what she did now.

'This makes sense to me. Does K know?'

'He's been briefed.' She made a face. 'He seemed way too excited about this assignment.'

I could see that. Still, if he was off doing his part, we needed to be heading out to do ours.

Which was why I was now in this metal coffin, heading to our destination.

Tamara gave a deep, dreamy sigh. 'You lead such a wonderful life. I wish I could spend more time here with you all.'

'Why don't you?' I asked. 'After we get done with these assassins and other nonsense, take some time and visit us. Spend a week or a month if you'd like. There's plenty to see here.'

'I've got people and animals depending on me. Goats to be milked, eggs to be collected, pigs to be fed. Not to mention my responsibilities in the village. This life of luxury is one I can only dream of.' A thought occurred to her. 'Tell me, since you have lived for so long, are all Celestials rich? Have you all been accumulating wealth since ancient times?'

I laughed. If she had seen how I had survived those first few years … Living on the banks of the Ganga, stealing the gold, silver and copper coins they would throw into the river on festival days. Working as a mercenary, a caravan guard, a soldier, a sailor, a bouncer in an ancient bar, even a pit fighter for a brief time. Fighting was the only thing I could do well and I spent a lot of time travelling the ancient world, taking up odd jobs and being a part of history.

'I wish. Before I met Sars, I wasn't really living this hedonistic lifestyle. She transformed my finances within a few months.'

'How did you all meet?' Tamara leaned forward, eyes bright with curiosity.

A mischievous grin spread across Sars's face. 'K tried to pick me up at a bar.'

'No way!' Tamara's jaw dropped.

'Oh yes. I friend-zoned him,' Sars jerked her thumb towards the back seat, 'and his wingman too.'

I sank deeper into my seat. 'I was dumber back then,' I muttered. And it was true, K was always dragging me into his half-baked schemes, chasing everything in a skirt, from wealthy widows to tavern maids, with me stumbling along like a lost puppy.

Tamara slapped a hand to her forehead. 'That reminds me! I had a thought a while ago, and then I filed it away as "it's too stupid", and then forgot about it until now when you spoke about being young and stupid.'

I waited for Tamara to continue, but it seemed like she thought she had explained enough.

'Tamara?'

'Hmm?'

'What was the thought?'

'Oh, I don't think your powers are really gone!'

'What do you mean?'

'Based on everything you told me, during your last encounter with Ashwatthama the gem destroyed the block on your powers and cleared your mind. You shouldn't be facing any limitations anymore.'

'Except I am.'

'Except you are,' she agreed.

There was another long pause as I counted to ten in my head.

'So, why did you think my powers aren't really gone?'

Her face brightened. 'Oh, I thought you understood what I meant. Your powers aren't gone. You are just unable to tap into them fully.'

I bit back the sarcastic retort at the tip of my tongue. 'How do I tap into them fully?'

'When did you last use your powers to the most of your ability? Not constrained by whatever limitations that are holding you back, tapping straight into your mana reservoir and letting loose?'

I frowned. The last time I did so was fighting the demon prince Shambha-La, which seemed a lifetime ago. Or was it?

A memory bubbled up from the murky depths of my mind, reluctant and blurry at first, then snapping into focus like a developing photograph. I was sprawled on the floor, arm outstretched, raw lightning crackling from my fingertips as it turned one of Narada's cards to ash. But what was on that card? The memory felt like an itch just out of reach, and something about it made my skin crawl.

'I used it a few days ago. Narada was showing me a card of some kind and I set it on fire.' Just thinking about it made the back of my brain itch. Something I had seen there had really upset me.

'How were you feeling at the time?'

'Angry,' I said, though that barely scratched the surface. Afraid. Self-righteous. That cocktail of helplessness and rage was burned into my bones, I doubted I'd ever forget it.

'So maybe that's it then.' Tamara's eyes sparkled with excitement. 'Your powers aren't locked away, you're locking them up yourself. There is nothing, as far as I can tell, that is holding you back unless it's in your head. Maybe you fear what you might become if you use your powers excessively. Maybe you are afraid of killing someone. I don't know what the issue is. When you stop thinking, when you just feel and flow with the moment, your heightened emotional state lets you blast right through whatever mental wall you've built.'

'There may be something to this theory,' Sars said thoughtfully. 'It's not the first time it has happened. People with anger issues often find they can't function very well.'

'Except those people usually need to find a way to let go of their anger. This sounds like I should get in touch with my inner anger. Maybe muster up enough rage, break a few things, go start a fight.'

She gave me a grave look. 'If what Tamara is saying is right, then this seems to be self-inflicted. You've done this to yourself. Not intentionally,' she hastened to add as I opened my mouth to argue. 'But maybe … 'she hesitated. 'Perhaps you feel guilty about leaving Ashwatthama the way you did. Or maybe this is just some pent up thing from all the years of conflict with the Celestial council. Either way, we should give it a shot. It might break this mental block on your powers.'

This sounded exactly like what I would expect to hear on a psychiatrist's couch. Feel anger? I was annoyed most of the time. How would that help?

Still, If I combined all the possible explanations of why my powers were fritzing, including this one, then I had with me a grand total of one explanation. I filed it away as something else to look into when we had the time. Maybe visit one of those rooms with breakable items and really let go. See if that would make me whole again.

'So, what's it like over here?' Tamara asked. She seemed to be given to flitting from one topic to the next. 'Are you all worshipped like Gods?'

Sars gave her a bemused look.

'I don't go around telling people I'm a God. None of us do.'

Tamara looked gobsmacked. 'None of you do? Not even K? I thought that would be the first thing he would do when he ...' she gestured vaguely, 'went out doing whatever he does.'

Sars burst out laughing. I realised that she probably enjoyed finally having some female company around. Let's face it, K and I are both delightful, but we are a bit of an acquired taste.

'I don't think K claiming he is a God will have any discernible impact on his sex life,' I said. Which was true. Part of being a fertility God meant that he could never keep it in his pants and there was no shortage of action he was getting in the nightclubs of Mumbai.

'Besides,' Sars added, 'plenty of Indian men already think they're God's gift to women. His claim wouldn't be as exceptional as you'd think.'

'I don't think that's restricted to only Indian men,' I muttered but nobody was really paying attention to me.

Tamara was still trying to solve the puzzle of why we were being modest. 'Seriously, why would you not tell people?'

'We don't break the First Law,' Sars said, then caught Tamara's blank look. 'It's not really the "First" law—more like the only rule. When we live among humans, we swear to keep our existence secret. It's not just a rule, it's ...' she searched for the right words, 'it's the foundation everything else is built on.'

Tamara turned to look at me. 'Didn't you tell me a few minutes back how you threatened a bunch of goons the last time you were on a case?'

I shifted uncomfortably. 'Those goons I mentioned? I could get in serious trouble for that. But after living among humans for so long, you learn to bend the rules when no one's watching. Just don't get caught on camera throwing magic cards around or floating in mid-air, and you're usually okay.'

'What happens if you do?'

The memory made me wince. During the Ashwatthama incident, some young, hot-headed Celestials had decided to throw the rulebook out the window, launching a brazen attack on the Tea Room, a café in Bandra where my friends and I hung out. The Celestial council had been slow to respond, but when they did, they stamped down hard, executing those involved.

Excluding the three I had personally killed, at least half a dozen others were hunted down or forced into hiding. The tracker they appointed, a dour-faced sage named Parashuram, was well known to me—a stone-cold killer who personally executed twenty-one generations of warriors in his lifetime.

'There are kill squads that will be sent after us if we expose the existence of Celestials to the world. Seriously, Tamara, I cannot emphasise how much the Celestial court values its secrecy.'

Nothing humbles you quite like realizing you're not as mighty as you thought. I strutted around like a peacock for about two weeks, cocky and invincible, right until my powers started going haywire. Parashuram, after picking through the evidence like a vulture and grilling every Celestial involved, eventually declared me innocent. I'd done my best to prevent disaster, he said. The accusations stopped after that, though plenty of people still blamed me—they just learned to mutter under their breath instead of pointing their fingers in the open.

'They take the Yugas seriously,' Sars was saying. 'The Kali Yuga is the one we are in now. It is called "the age of darkness" because it is the period where man wilfully turns away from God, and the Gods no longer walk openly among mankind. We don't openly display magic, and in turn, they are forced to rely on their own creativity. They find their own path. It is why we also call this era the age of science. They replicate the achievements of the past but this time on the strength of their own merit. The fruits of their labour are what pushes them forward. They've built technology to reach the stars without our help. If they learn that a select few of us can do magic …'

'Or that some of us have walked the earth for millennia,' I continued, 'there would be riots. Many don't even have the temperament or maturity to co-exist with other religions. Half of them are still frothing at the mouth because of one dead Mughal emperor from four hundred years ago. The last thing we need are modern-day holy wars and blood spilling on the streets.'

Tamara slumped back in her seat. 'So, you all can never let the world know that Gods walk the earth?'

'There have always been Gods walking the earth. Most of them didn't choose the life they were born into. They don't want to be dragged into wars in their name. They just want to be left alone without all the adulation and expectations constantly being piled on them. Someday, when that happens, we can announce ourselves to the world.'

'On that cheery note,' said Sars, as she shut off the engine. 'Here we are!'

'Here' turned out to be five minutes away from the main road, where a large red-and-yellow farmhouse stood. It was at least a kilometre away from the next farm, so it was quite secluded and allowed for plenty of privacy. Exactly the kind of place I would want to look for if I was indulging in nefarious activities.

We were crouched in the bushes, studying the place, when Sars grabbed my arm. 'RBs!' she whispered.

I counted six of them guarding the place. They were all heavily armed and made no real effort to conceal themselves. It was a full moon, and we could see them clearly as they patrolled the area.

'We need to get past them.' Sars whispered.

'Let me try,' I said. I focused on the one furthest away from the others and tried to muster anger.

I didn't personally have anything against the RBs. They were nothing more than worker drones carrying out their leader's instructions. It was hard to think of them as separate entities with feelings and lives. But we were on two sides of a conflict, and I had no qualms about taking one down.

I raised my hand and pointed straight at him. Every little bit of frustration that I could drum up, I channelled into my fingers. Fucking Narada and his cryptic clues; this pain-in-the-arse rift that wasn't healing; the little scratch on the back of my neck that now had yellow pus seeping out. I channelled all my frustration through my arm and, by extension, at the RB smoking a cigarette.

About a minute later, I felt a pain in my arm. I had been holding it up for too long.

'You are turning blue in the face,' Tamara whispered.

I lowered my arm and massaged my aching elbow. 'It's no use. I can't seem to channel my anger in any way.'

'A shame, since you usually are so full of it,' Sars commented drily.

'You know, there is a graveyard nearby,' Tamara said thoughtfully. 'I can sense it.'

Sars and I exchanged a glance. 'Now may not be the best time to go sightseeing.'

'If I had my staff, I would have been able to raise some of those bodies, made an army of our own.' She caught the look Sars and I gave her. 'What? You've never imagined how you would handle things in one of those zombie survival movies? Its kind of cool.'

'I've never imagined a zombie apocalypse where I'm leading the zombies, Tamara, seriously, wtf?'

'It's not that big a deal, honestly. If you've ever seen kids playing with dolls or action figures—it's kinda like that … Only on a slightly larger scale.'

I had a mental image of hundreds of shambling corpses stumbling across the field. 'I think we are good, Tamara. Thanks for your suggestion but let's call that Plan B for now.'

She looked interested. 'Oh? What's Plan A?'

'Right now, I would say literally anything but that.' I had to stop myself from shuddering. Zombies! What on earth would she think of next!

'Look, one is coming towards us right now,' Tamara said as she pointed to the left. One of the RBs was walking in our direction.

We crouched lower as he came straight towards us. I kept my eyes lowered to the ground—if we looked directly at him, I was afraid our eyes might reflect the moonlight and he would see us staring at him, like three cats sitting in a row.

Barely ten feet from us, he stopped and unzipped his pants. Tamara wrinkled her nose as he urinated, a thick yellow stream splattering in our eyeline.

'For fuck's sake,' said Sars. 'I'm done with this.'

She rose from the bush, menace in her eyes. Her invisibility wasn't perfect—if you stared in her direction for long, you could make her shape out, but it sufficed at night. She moved with lithe grace as she stepped to his side and jammed something that looked like a hypodermic needle into his neck. His eyes rolled to the back of his head, and he fell face first onto the ground.

'I'm not waiting for the next chap to piss on us. I'll be right back,' she said.

We watched in awe as Sars moved deftly, like a ballerina weaving through the shadows, quietly striking each guard so that none of the others knew until it was their turn. I used to think of Sars as ... well, a bookworm. Not in an unkind way but as someone unsuited to these cloak-and-dagger escapades. Shows how little I knew.

'Akran,' Tamara murmured.

'Hmm?'

'I was thinking about what is so special about you.'

'Umm ... okay?'

'You are special because you are surrounded by incredible people. You need to take better care of your friendships.'

That brought back a memory. The dreamwalker Jill and I had parted on not-so-friendly terms … She had accused me of withholding information and manipulating people. She wasn't wrong. I didn't trust easily.

I resolved to call Jill to apologise when this was over.

'I'm trying, Tamara. I'll do better.'

She nodded once before turning away.

Sars returned when all six RBs lay unconscious. 'Let's check who's inside.'

***

'Do you want to do the honours?' Sars asked.

'Allow me,' Tamara said as she stepped forward and raised her hand.

The door blew apart like a commercial airliner had rammed into it. It exploded inwards, sending shrapnel flying everywhere. The beams holding the doorway cracked as she stepped in. Dazed, Sars and I followed.

Inside the room sat a half-naked, pot-bellied man with a biker-gang beard. He looked at us with bleary eyes that struggled to focus. 'Wh … W … Who?' he mumbled, clutching his head. Some plaster from the roof appeared to have fallen on him from the massive overkill Tamara had employed on the door.

'I'll check if there are others inside,' said Sars as she headed towards the rooms at the back.

I studied the room we were in. It had very little furniture, almost nothing except the couch and two small tables.

There were no paintings on the wall, no personal touches of any kind.

Still clutching his head, the man stared at me. He looked vaguely familiar. There was something about his short, squat appearance and frown.

Abruptly, his eyes widened in recognition.

'Defiler!' he screamed.

So he was one of those. The people who continued to believe that Kali Yuga was my fault.

I'm willing to admit one tiny flaw in my personality—I'm a bit of a grammar Nazi. There may be a variety of adjectives you could use to describe what I was, but I had never defiled anything. All I could be accused of was destroying the Yadava race, losing the sacred weapons and kickstarting the age of darkness.

An orange flame shot out of the man's palm. I was less than eight feet away from him and had no powers to call upon; I guess he liked his Yakshas medium-rare.

Thankfully, Tamara planted herself between us, hands on her hips, and the flame dissipated into a mist of perfume. Something fruity and floral.

The man blinked. He wasn't expecting that.

I tried to reason with him, 'Calm down. We just want to talk.'

The man spat and muttered a string of obscenities. He seized an ashtray, whispered something into it and flung it at Tamara. The ashtray turned into a hissing snake as it flew through the air.

Except ... less than three feet from Tamara, it changed back into an ashtray. Even worse, it lost all its forward momentum and fell to the ground.

This was fun. I had seen this happen to me once. My first encounter with Ashwatthama was me throwing everything I had at him and him shrugging it off. In desperation, the man shut his eyes and muttered another spell. The two ornate tables on either side turned into giant dogs, each half as large as a horse, sniffed the air around us, and turned towards Tamara, growling. Clearly, she was the biggest threat in the room.

Tamara seemed unperturbed as she clenched her palm into a fist. The dogs leapt at her, jaws wide open, malice in their eyes.

The next moment they were gone. Two purple monarch butterflies hovered in the air. They flitted around her face before falling to the floor next to her feet.

Much as I was enjoying the man getting his ass kicked at the hands of a fourteen-year-old, I was done with this. Sidestepping her, I grabbed him by his neck and slammed him into the wall. 'Enough of this! We just want to talk!'

The man began to speak but I covered his mouth with my hand. 'If you are thinking of attempting another curse, you should know that my friend here has been looking for a pair of shoes to go with her outfit.' I looked closely into his eyes, so there was no ambiguity in my threat. 'Do you really want to offer yourself up on a platter like this?'

The man gave me a sullen look. 'What do you want?' he muttered as I loosened my grip on him.

'First, who the fuck are you? And second, why the fuck have you been doing whatever this is you are doing?'

The man glowered. He seemed to be hawking up saliva to spit on my face; my grip on his neck tightened. Then his eyes slid over to Tamara, and whatever fighting spirit he had in him drained away.

'I am Rishi Durvasa,' he muttered.

Ah, crap! I knew him.

Durvasa was a really ancient, grouchy sage. I don't know how to say this politely, so I'm just going to say it: he was a massive dick.

The main problem with Durvasa was that he was exceedingly short-tempered. His second problem was that he was a bit liberal with his curses. Anyone who annoyed him—and in those days it would take very little to annoy him—would be cursed.

Sages, being human, did not have an infinite supply of cosmic power. Everything they gained, they did through the penance and hard work they put in. So it was natural for them to hoard this power and use it judiciously, i.e., when they felt they could do the most good or when someone really deserved it.

Durvasa, on the other hand, cursed someone every few days. It may have been coincidental, but way too many of them just happened to fall on women, including but not limited to his wife Kandali (cursed into a heap of dust for quarrelling with him), Rukmini (wife of Krishna, cursed to be separated from her husband because she drank water without his permission), Saraswati (the original Goddess of whom Sars was an Aspect, cursed to be born as a human because she laughed at him when he recited the Vedas incorrectly), Shakuntala (cursed to have her husband forget her), Banumati (cursed to be abducted) ... you get the drift. Durvasa also cursed my friend Shukracharya to forget the Sanjivani mantra (the curse was lifted eventually), and was responsible for the curse that destroyed the Yadava civilisation.

Even when he offered a boon, it had its own ramifications. Durvasa was the sage who gave Kunti the boon that enabled her to call any God to her bed using a magical hymn (seriously, who gives a teenage girl access to sex with Gods?). Kunti, eager to test this out, begot Karna from Surya, the sun God, before marriage, and a whole series of unfortunate events unfolded from there.

With such a reputation, one might expect me to have eagerly dispatched him, but instead, the realisation of who he was filled me with deep dismay. This was no ordinary sage. He was said to be the living embodiment of Shiva's anger, born when the God of destruction bundled up his fury and cast it aside. Durvasa, they called him, a name that meant 'difficult to live with'. And difficult he was, for his power was said to rival even that of the Celestials themselves, and it was rumoured that every time he lost his temper, another century was added to his lifespan.

Despite his immense dickishness, I could not bring myself to harm him. Part of me—the part still clinging to the ancient codes I'd lived by for centuries—held me back. Another part—the one that had evolved with the modern world—wondered if maybe some traditions weren't worth preserving, especially when they involved not punching insufferable sages.

For all my bluster about attacking sage Narada and wondering if I could take him down in a fair fight when it came down to it, I would only attack Narada in self-defence. Yes, he was a pain, but he was a pain on the side of good. He never acted selfishly or to aid evil in any way. And for that, despite me thinking of him as a prick, he had my respect.

Durvasa on the other hand? I felt sorry for him. His inability to control his temper meant he kept using up the yogic powers he accumulated through penance. Which prevented him from ever living up to his full potential. He needed a course in anger management.

I let go of him and took a step back.

'Rishi Durvasa,' I said respectfully, bowing to him. 'I'm sorry for attacking you. Could we please talk?'

Durvasa had still not fully regained the colour on his face. He shrank away from Tamara in fear. 'Where did you get her from?' he whispered. 'Are you cavorting with demons now?'

I shook my head. 'This is Tamara, a friend of mine. She's not from around here, but she is not a demon.'

He snorted. 'You take me for a fool? I can see the demonic energy in her aura.'

I nodded to Tamara who unclasped the locket and handed it to me.

'Look at her again.'

Durvasa's eyes widened.

'How is this possible?' he demanded.

'It's a long story and I'll be happy to tell you if it will ease your mind.'

I raised my hands, palms outstretched, trying to show him we meant no harm. 'We didn't realise a revered sage such as yourself would be here today. I came seeking answers. It is my hope that you will be able to help.'

'I could compel him,' Tamara whispered. 'I can remove his spirit from his body, and then it will sing like a canary.'

I couldn't decide if she was trying to intimidate him or if she was serious. I wasn't sure I wanted to find out.

'No removing of spirits. For now,' I amended under my breath. Turning to him, I spoke politely again, 'Will you help us?'

He stared at us for a long minute. Sars had wandered off to explore the other rooms. Finally, Durvasa nodded.

'What do you want to know?'

'All of it. Who are you working with and why?'

'I was contacted and asked if I could help fix the tear in the fabric of the cosmos.' He gave me an accusatory glare. 'I heard you were involved in that as well.'

'You put a hex on me. Why?'

'I was told that you would try and interfere with the ritual, like you did with the last one. This was only to know your whereabouts so you wouldn't interfere.'

'What about the dizziness and the fainting spells? Why was that a part of the hex?'

He looked bewildered. 'What do you mean?'

'Your hex is doing something to me. Weakening me in some way.'

'That's got nothing to do with me. This is a simple tracking spell.'

'Can you get it off me? Right now!'

Durvasa muttered under his breath but shut his eyes and mumbled a few words.

'It's gone,' Tamara confirmed as she stared at a spot a little above my head.

I could feel no discernible difference, so maybe the hex wasn't causing the other discomforts I was experiencing.

Sars chose that moment to pop in. Durvasa flinched. He didn't recognise Sars, and she didn't introduce herself.

'There's another summoning circle in the next room.'

I turned to Durvasa, the warmth having left my voice. 'Did you kill Nahusha?'

His frown became more pronounced. 'Who?'

'Nahusha, Ex-Indra—we found him dead in his apartment with a summoning circle drawn in his room. This was four, maybe five nights ago.'

He paled. 'I had nothing to do with that.'

'What's the summoning circle for?'

'I just told you. To fix the damn hole. It's leaking away the essence of magic.'

'Why do you need a summoning circle to fix the problem?'

'The yagna that Ashwatthama was undertaking required the use of all three primal races that make up the world: demon, human, and Celestial. Leaving the yagna incomplete has created a tear in reality. We need to heal the tear. We need to get the three primal races together, and then sacrifice them. The spell should be enough to fix the tear in the fabric of realms.'

Sars spoke up. 'I thought sages were not supposed to murder people in cold blood.'

Durvasa bristled, 'We aren't killing the human and the Celestial. They both need to be there; the only sacrifice will be the demon.'

'That doesn't make sense. How can you kill the demon and leave the human and Celestial untouched?'

'I didn't say untouched. There will be some injury to the others as well. As far as I know, it won't be fatal.'

'As far as you know?'

'Nobody has ever done this ritual before. It's impossible to say if it's completely safe for the human and the Celestial.

The sacrifice may result in a huge outpouring of energy that might harm them. I'm going to do my best to protect them but I can't guarantee their safety.'

I stared at him. This blasé attitude to human life was not something I would expect from a sage of such renown.

Durvasa looked defensive. 'I'm not forcing anyone to participate in this ritual. The choice is between the lives of hundreds of Celestials and a volunteer. It's for the greater good.'

Oh, yes, the greater good. The justification that ties mass murders and evil men everywhere.

'Besides,' Durvasa continued doggedly. 'I already have a volunteer human and a God. Now I just need a demon.'

Sars and I looked at each other. 'Who would volunteer for this?'

He gave me a smug glance. 'An Indra. It kills two birds with one stone.'

Wait, what?

'How does an Indra kill two birds? Don't you still need a human?'

Durvasa frowned. 'Weren't you an Indra yourself? Why do you ques …' A change came over his face as a realisation struck him. 'Aah, yes, I see now. That makes sense.'

Did it? Really?

'What do you mean? What does my having been an Indra have to do with anything?'

Durvasa's belligerent tone softened. 'I apologise, Yaksha. I thought you were being arrogant. Now I see you were only ignorant.'

As apologies go, that was far better than others I have received. Durvasa was smiling again. He was in the role that he enjoyed the most—teaching someone by being condescending.

'Answer me this: where do the Gods come from?'

The question was so left-field that it took me by surprise. I had always assumed the Gods, being Gods, were just there.

Durvasa answered his own question when he saw the confusion in my eyes. 'The Gods didn't create humans. It was the humans who created Gods. When the first apes climbed down from the trees and began to walk on two legs, they struggled to understand everything they had no control over—the big ball of fire in the sky, the fire that could burn them and make their food taste better, the wind, the water, the earth. They anthropomorphised them and gave them names. Surya. Agni. Vayu. Varuna. They worshipped these beings and made sacrifices to them. In doing so, they tapped into the power of the primal cosmos, the eternal void, the energy of the universe, and shaped primal beings that reflected these beliefs.'

'Boltzmanns brain,' Sars whispered. I nodded. I was familiar with the thought experiment—random fluctuations in the universe creating ordered consciousness—but I'd never considered its application to divine beings. Had we Gods simply popped into existence because enough humans believed in the same idea at once?

'These beings were not made of flesh and blood but pure energy. They took on the roles envisioned by the people who worshipped them. These were the first Gods. And as storytellers across hundreds of fireplaces around the world spun their own stories, they turned these beings of energy into what we see today. It gave them personalities, purpose and emotions. These "Gods" then took on lives of their own. They created a whole sublayer of minor deities and divine beings to help them. Gandharvas. Apsaras. Yakshas.

'The farmers naturally expected Indra to be the king of the Gods since monsoon was so important to their survival. And kings, in their experience, were rich, powerful and promiscuous.'

I frowned. I had been one myself.

'That's not true, all Indras were not cut from the same cloth.'

'Their individual personalities might have differed, but they shared common traits. The common people also had one more belief about their rulers. Kings, good or bad, would not last forever. They would change over time. And so while the rest of the Gods remained, Indras kept changing.'

'How is this relevant to ...'

Durvasa waved his finger at me ... 'Patience, Yaksha. I am getting to the point of the story. The problem was, who would inherit the throne? It could not be another Deva since they already had their own responsibilities. It could not be a demon since they were the opposite of everything that the people believed in. The demons themselves, like the Devas, were formed of the fears of humans—nameless, shapeless dreads of the things that go bump in the night. Is it any wonder that the demons were always so numerous? So powerful? So much stronger in the dark?

'You could not have one of them occupy the throne of heaven. So naturally, it fell to ...

'A human,' I realised.

'Exactly. So all Indras, barring the very first one, were originally human. Virtuous, noble kings loved by their people and deemed worthy warriors were successively, over and over, appointed Indra.' He gave me a compassionate look. 'Even you, once upon a time, were very much human.'

His words were making my head spin. I knew about Nahusha being human and his ascension and fall from grace. But all the Indras being human? That was new information.

'I don't remember anything of my old life as a human.'

'Nor should you. The first thing when an Indra ascends is for his memories of life as a human to be wiped out. Or you would never be a good king to heaven.'

'So that means an Indra who volunteers to be sacrificed ...'

'... is already human as well as a Celestial. So all that is needed is a demon. Summon one, make him take possession of the human/Celestial body and sacrifice it. The ritual is complete, and the rift will heal.'

'Fascinating,' murmured Tamara in my ear. 'But we should wrap this up. I cannot do much more in this body, I must recharge before the next fight. If his friends return ...' She left the rest unspoken but I knew what she meant. We couldn't afford to be caught off guard.

'Understood,' I replied, turning back to Durvasa. 'Just a few more questions before we go.'

Durvasa gave me a benevolent smile. His distaste for me seemed to have abated.

'Which Indra was it? Who was this volunteer?' I asked.

Durvasa's smile turned wistful. 'I have seen dozens of Indras, if not more, across three Yugas. I cannot say which one he was. He still had his powers of lightning, though, which is how I knew he was who he claimed to be. After all, when you lose the position, there is a ceremony where the power is transferred.'

I frowned. 'Unless one of them found a way to hoard a portion of the power and not transfer it all to the next Indra,' I mused aloud.

My unease grew as I thought of the one Indra I had disliked, even hated. He had hazel green eyes, a distinctive feature in this part of the world. If it was him, we were in serious trouble. 'Thank you, Durvasa. You have been most helpful,' I said, turning to leave.

Durvasa was still speaking. 'He had wonderful green eyes, though. He looked completely trustworthy.'

@#$%^!!

Durvasa saw the sudden change in my demeanour and frowned. 'What's wrong?'

'You have been deceived.'

His frown grew more pronounced. If it wasn't for Tamara standing there, he would probably have started cursing.

The irony of a sage renowned for his wisdom being so easily fooled wasn't lost on me. Perhaps age doesn't improve one's critical thinking skills after all. Who would have thought?

'There is no so-called "volunteer" who intends to partake in this rite. I suspect that the Indra you encountered sought to sacrifice another Celestial–human hybrid, namely, myself.'

Apparently 'volunteer' now means 'completely unwitting sacrifice'. Semantics are so flexible these days.

I proceeded to tell him about the assassination contract.

Durvasa appeared perplexed. 'But why would he lie?'

'Because he lacked the ability to carry out the deed himself,' I elaborated, recounting our discovery of Nahusha's murder. 'Perhaps he attempted it and failed. So, he decided to try again, this time with the aid of a sage—someone with greater expertise and, regrettably, someone he believed to be easily duped.'

Durvasa shook his head. 'An Indra would not do this. No, I refuse to believe it!'

'That's what sucks about people. They don't need you to believe in them to be world-class assholes.'

Durvasa stiffened. 'I will not tolerate this disrespect.'

'Ask yourself, Rishi, among the many Indras that you encountered, wasn't there at least one that you thought might have been a bad choice? You may not remember their faces, but just by their deeds, is there one that you thought was a bad apple?'

'N-No. I … Wait …' his eyes widened. 'Are you talking about …?'

I gave a grim nod. 'That's exactly who I'm talking about.'

'It can't be! He was stripped of his power!'

'And as we have just discovered, he's obviously found a way to hide a portion of those powers.'

Durvasa slumped. 'I was a fool.'

'We will get to the bottom of this. You have our word.'

We left the farm, leaving behind a very sad old man in his house with a ruined door, looking dejectedly at the floor. I pitied him a little. Not too much. I had plenty of my own problems.

***

Sars grabbed my arm as we stepped outside. 'We should talk.'

I gave her a quizzical look. 'What about?'

'You've got that idiotic look on your face, that look you get when you plan on doing something noble and heroic, which is also inevitably stupid.'

I glared at her. 'I have no idea what you are talking about!'

'Oh, really?' Sars stuck one hand onto her chest, raised the other to the sky and stuck her nose in the air. She began speaking in what I can only assume was a terrible impersonation of me. 'Sars, I have got to sacrifice myself. All of this is my fault, every single thing that's ever happened since the day I was born is my fault, and only a heroic death will redeem me.'

'Okay, first, I sound nothing like that. Second, I'm not thinking of being a hero.'

'My point,' Sars interrupted, 'is that you don't intend to do anything noble and heroic because it's the right thing to do. You want to do it because you are carrying a mountain of guilt over everything, and you'll just find a way to make this situation all your fault.'

'It *is* mine,' I pointed out. 'If I had known the right way to stop the yagna, we wouldn't be in this clusterfuck we are in today.'

'You didn't know the right way to stop the yagna, so you did the best you could.'

They wouldn't get it. I wasn't sure I got it myself. But I did know that if magic leaked out of our realm, all Celestials would die. Including me. So someone would have to step up anyway. I didn't mind it being me.

Sars stepped away to answer her phone while Tamara and I spoke.

'What did he mean when he talked about ascending?' Tamara asked.

Ascension was an incredibly rare event among Celestials. It was when a celestial, moulded into shape by the weight of people's beliefs, broke free into something else entirely. Like a butterfly from a cocoon.

In human terms, it was the equivalent of when fish first walked on land or when primates came down from the trees. Or, as Durvasa explained it, the point when dreams and stories became the first Celestial beings. It was still intrinsic to our nature A God of fire didn't magically turn into a water elemental but it was a dramatic transformation. Like levelling up in a video game except going from level 1 to 10 instead of a slow natural progression.

'He was talking about it in the context of a human being elevated to an Indra. But ascension can occur to any Celestial. We don't really know how or why it happens. Of course, now that there is a rift, I doubt it will come about.'

'Well, I think you should stop calling it a rift,' Tamara declared. 'Or a tear. It's more like a sponge. It sits there absorbing the magic, but if we could prick it like a bubble, the magic should just flow back in.'

'You can see the rift?'

'Yeah, can't you?'

'How many planes of existence can you see, Tamara?'

'I've never counted. Let me check. She shut her eyes tight as she counted. 'Eleven, I think.'

She frowned. 'Also, I think I can shut it down!'

'You can close the rift?' I wasn't quite sure what to make of that. She had been with us for barely twenty-four hours, and she was already talking about something Sars, Durvasa, and I'm guessing a whole lot of other people had been struggling with for months.

She shrugged. 'I had a little help. You know that thing I can do where if someone is thinking about something a lot, I can sense it? It was something I picked up the last time we met.'

On our first meeting in London, Tamara had met K and picked up what Sars and I call his 'low-grade telepathy'. Turns out it wasn't so low-grade after all; she was just able to use it more effectively than K could.

'I peeked into Durvasa's mind while you were interrogating him. Well, not really peeked because it was right there on the surface. He's been thinking about it a lot. The biggest thing holding him back is the way you all—sages and Celestials—interact with magic.'

'You really need to explain that a bit better, Tamara.' I looked for Sars. She was still talking on the phone. 'We should wait for Sars. She can understand this much better than I could.'

Tamara shook her head. 'It's not that complicated, really. It all comes down to mana—what you use as fuel for magic. Think of it like this: there are two types of gas for your magical car.' She gestured at the air around us. 'First, there's what you use—ambient mana. It's like solar power—all around us, free to use, especially abundant in this city for some reason. Different cultures tap different sources. Maori practitioners draw from the sea, Druids from sacred groves and ley lines, shamans from ancestral spirits. Each place has evolved its own filling station.'

'I'm following so far.'

'Now, for the second type,' she continued, her expression growing more serious. 'Imagine every living thing has a battery inside. Birds, animals, trees, even the worms in the soil. Take that away, and the creature dies. It's tied to your life force. Let's call this life-battery "red mana". It's concentrated, compact and way more powerful than the ambient stuff.'

My stomach tightened as I caught her meaning. 'You're talking about death magic,' I said, the words bitter on my tongue. Every ancient civilisation, from the Carthaginians to the Mayans, have used blood sacrifice to harvest power.

'Exactly,' Tamara said. 'Voodoo is the same. Animal sacrifices for the most part. When something dies violently, that red mana bursts free. A priest who knows what they're doing can capture that energy, like catching lightning in a bottle.'

She leaned forward. 'Everyone working on this rift problem is trying to use ambient mana—the solar power. But voodoo is the exact opposite. Using one's life-force to sustain another is one of the first and most basic spells we learn to do. Everything follows from there. Because there's so much more power in a life-battery, Vaudun shamans can work with far more juice than your average nature witch.'

'So you're saying this red mana could close the rift?' I asked, wanting to be crystal clear.

'Like lancing a boil,' she said simply. 'A red-hot spear of energy can pierce the boil and let the magic flood out.'

'So why use a demon and a human?'

'As far as I can tell, bringing all of these together creates a more volatile mix.'

'But you have another solution?' I asked hopefully.

'Unfortunately, not. I can pop the blister that's sucking away your realm's magic. To do that, someone needs to die. There's no way around that. Preferably a Celestial. Or a half-

Celestial, half-human. Or a Celestial and a human. You get the idea.'

I did. It wasn't a solution I was pleased with. Then again, it was better than us scratching our heads for the next few weeks while we all got weaker and eventually died.

She hesitated. 'There's also the very real risk that doing so might leave me vulnerable. The psychic backlash from channelling this energy might displace me out of this body and leave me disoriented and unable to defend myself.'

'I will make sure nothing happens to you,' I promised. 'Tamara, this is amazing!' A thought struck me. 'Can you also heal people? As in, if someone is on the verge of death after we use the red mana to pierce the boil, could you maybe shove it back into their body?'

Something flickered on her face, too quick for me to determine what it was. 'Akran, that's the one thing I can definitely not do. I can't heal people. It's outside my abilities.'

'Unless you met a healer and could ...'

'No,' she said emphatically. 'Yin and Yang. Life and Death magic are entirely different. The only way I might be able to heal someone is if I'm forced to kill someone else. Even that may not work.'

'Noted.' This seemed like a sore point for her, so I cast around, looking for something to change the subject.

'I made a mistake,' Tamara said finally.

'What do you mean?'

'I hadn't tried this body swapping before. I was eager to get here quickly, but this was a bad idea. I have very little access to my powers.'

'You were doing alright in there!'

She laughed. 'You didn't notice then?'

'Notice what?'

'I didn't do anything. I can't access most of my powers in this body.'

'You defended yourself pretty damn well in there.'

She tapped the amulet around her neck. 'That was because of this. I stole it from a demon a while back. It absorbs magical attacks and allows me to redirect that energy.' She laughed. 'If he had just thrown that ashtray at me, it would have probably knocked me out.'

'Wait, I saw you blow the door open!'

'I suspect that is what Sars wants to talk to you about. She used her powers on the amulet and stored that energy within. I used that on the door and it worked!'

'Tamara, why on earth would you do this? You're telling me you are at your most vulnerable right now. You have no powers; you could easily be killed. Why did you not just wait? I could have handled this till you got back.'

'Do you remember what I told you'll when we last met?'

'That you will come whenever I call? I …'

'Not that,' she interrupted impatiently. 'I told the dreamwalker all about it. I can't imagine she didn't mention it to you.'

I gave her a blank look.

'The world teeters on the edge of a broken blade. If I am not here now, in this moment, then you will die. This much I am certain of.'

I stared at her. 'Without your powers, you being here will keep me alive?'

'I didn't say I have lost them completely. It's like your well of mana. I have a finite supply of it that I am saving up for the right moment.'

'The right moment,' I repeated. 'When will that be exactly?'

'I'll know it when I see it.'

'What will you being here accomplish?'

'Maybe nothing. Maybe everything.'

'That isn't vague at all, Tamara.' I've heard fortune cookies with more specific predictions.

'I don't know if anything I am doing will make a difference. I know where I'm supposed to be but not why. Or sometimes I know the why but not the who. Or sometimes the who but not the how.' She shook her head. 'I'm a butterfly flapping its wings. A boy with a stick beating the bush. A child with a boat wishing for a storm!'

My unease increased as she spoke. 'Tamara …'

'All I know,' she said quietly, 'is that sometimes, just sometimes, a tiny nudge can change a boulder's path. It can end one's life or create another, it can make or break your fortune, it can unmake galaxies or Gods. The kingdom is lost for want of a horseshoe nail.'

She gave me a wry glance. 'Life for everyone else I know happens in the moments they live in. For me, it lies between those moments. In the realm of possibilities. Where uncertainties abound.'

I kept forgetting she was still a teenager.

She sighed wearily. 'I'm tired, Akran. Sometimes, it feels like I spend my whole life in the in-between place. Nudging moments to make the best outcomes. I don't even know if this is the best one. Maybe my saving you will end up killing someone else. But I know this moment is important, that you are in great danger, and that I owe you my life.'

I opened my mouth to protest but she shook her head to indicate she was not yet done. 'So I will save you and let the consequences be damned. I know that in the future, when I need help, you will have my back. And that's what counts in the end.'

I had no words. Her problems were different from mine by several orders of magnitude.

We spoke for a few minutes more before Sars joined us, fit to burst.

'Sars, you had something to tell us?'

'K called.' Briefly, she told me what she had found out. Tamara and I listened in silence. Many pieces of the puzzle were starting to fall into place.

'I have an idea,' I said, and turned to Tamara. 'And I'll definitely need your help.'

'For sure. What do you need?'

'An honourable demon. One with whom I can make a deal.'

CHAPTER ELEVEN

Meghnad ('thunderous' in Sanskrit, because subtlety was never a demon's strong suit) was one of Ramayana's most illustrious antagonists. Born the crown prince of Lanka, and son to Ravana—who had modest parenting goals like conquering the universe—Meghnad was deemed more powerful than his father by some scholars. (These accounts were, of course, whispered in dark corners, because Ravana's ego was the one thing in Lanka more flammable than its capital.)

Meghnad earned himself a boon from Brahma for sparing Indra's life in battle. The prince, displaying characteristic demon optimism, asked for immortality. Brahma, displaying characteristic divine determination to screw him over, declined. Instead, Brahma demonstrated his skill in the art of the deal and countered by offering a fantastical, too-good-to-be-true, once-in-a-lifetime offer that Meghnad, clad in the military fatigues of the bronze age, was forced to accept because he didn't hold any cards.

The prize was: knowledge of a ritual that would summon an invincibility-granting chariot, and a promise that Meghnad could only be killed by someone who had defeated sleep—a human who could stay awake for years without rest.

As the war neared its end and all other means to halt the invasion had failed, Meghnad decided to conduct the yagna. Unfortunately for him, Vibhishana—Ravana's brother and the family's sole brain cell—had defected to Ram's side, and he just happened to know all about the yagna and how to disrupt it.

Meghnad put two and two together and arrived at a startling conclusion. These two random fellows slaughtering the demon army by droves weren't your garden-variety humans. There was definitely a divine plot involved. Even worse, one of the dynamic duo, Lakshman, had received a boon from the Goddess of sleep (one we have never heard of before except in this epic) that allowed him to remain awake through the fourteen years spanning Ram's exile—a feat matched only by modern-day parents of newborns. Thus, he had 'defeated' sleep.

Yes, it was sneaky wordplay—kind of like 'none of woman born shall harm Macbeth', but that's always what the Gods excelled at and Meghnad recognised it. He pleaded with his father to make peace. Ravana, maintaining his flawless record of poor decisions, refused and called his son a coward. Meghnad apologised and promised to go out and fight, even though he knew it would mean his death, because it was a son's duty to obey the father. For this and other stupid things people believed back then, I should also talk about Parashuram at a later time.

As expected, Meghnad died. It is claimed that he killed over six hundred and seventy million vanaras in a single day. (Ever since the concept of zero was discovered by early

Indians (second century BCE), numbers in epics got randomly multiplied by 100 million. This figure surpasses even the human population of that era, for humans hit their first billion only in 1804. Trust me, I was there.)

What makes Meghnad remarkable was his obedience to traditional Vedic values—the ones where your parents are always right even if obeying them meant certain death. That is what dharma is all about: doing your duty, even when your duty involves getting killed because your father made a series of spectacularly poor life choices.

—The Private Journals of Akran

It was nearly 4 a.m. when we returned to the penthouse. Sars was in a foul mood. She stormed in and headed for the bar to pour herself a drink.

Lyla was awake and pacing about the house like a caged tiger. She stopped short when she saw us.

'What took you so long?' she demanded. 'Where is Tamara?' she stopped to look at me more closely. 'What on earth have you done to yourself?'

I swaggered to the full-length mirror in the corridor and took a long look at myself. I looked different. The Akran she had last seen was weary and weak, without access to his mana pool. Now I flexed my hand experimentally, and tiny sparks of lightning crackled across my fingers. I was feeling better. Better than I had felt in the past couple of days. Eager to fight. It showed in my face, eyes, and in the way I was holding myself. This was not a Yaksha you could trifle with.

'What's happened to you?' Lyla asked.

'Take a look,' I invited, flexing my arms. Lyla's eyes narrowed as she studied me. I watched as her eyes took in my appearance on this plane, then the next and then widened as she spotted it—the dark demonic energies shrouding me on the other planes.

'You have a demon riding within you?'

I laughed. It came out more booming than I intended. 'He's not riding me. I am in control. We came to an agreement. He gets to experience walking around in my body for three days, and in exchange he shares a portion of his power with me. This is the only way to close the rift.'

She gasped. 'You are going to sacrifice yourself?'

'Not at all. We went to the farmhouse and met Rishi Durvasa. Closing the rift will require the presence of a human, a demon and a Celestial. But ...' I wagged my finger like I had seen Sars do once. Somehow it looked better when she did it. 'There's no need for all three of them to die. Any one of them can be sacrificed. Ordinarily, we would expect to sacrifice the demon. Perfectly understandable because, well, demons are bad and all that. Except, since I was an Indra, I have another option.'

'You are going to sacrifice the human part of you,' said Lyla slowly.

Sars gave me a sharp look but said nothing. I nodded.

'That's right. Tamara thinks she knows a way to heal the rift. All I need to do is "sacrifice" the human part of me.' I shrugged. 'It might be painful, but it will close the rift. There is a chance I will emerge even more powerful than I am now when I shed the human side of me.'

'You are assuming he can be trusted,' Sars said. Her voice was flat and weary, like she was tired of arguing.

'I chose a demon known to be honourable. Meghnad. A prince among demons. He and I knew each other. We were on opposite sides in prior conflicts, but he was as honourable as they come.

'The power he has shared will be useful in dealing with these assassins. In return, I will give him a few artefacts that were in my possession, which he can use to further his influence in the underworld. Once the rift is healed, we undertake a decoupling ritual, and he goes back to the underworld.'

'Assuming he doesn't break his word,' said Sars.

'Then Tamara has a way to forcibly evict him from my body. Sars, relax. I've planned this well. Nothing can go wrong.'

'Where is Tamara anyway?' asked Lyla, looking around.

'Tamara's gone,' said Sars as she poured herself a drink. 'Now that the crisis has passed and Akran is strong again, she will swap bodies, return the girl she hijacked back to her mind, and then use more conventional channels to visit us. Possibly in three days or so.'

Sars checked her phone. 'K messaged. The RBs' chapter house didn't reveal much but they have a data warehouse in the city. They may have a paper trail there. He plans to check on it tomorrow.'

Lyla nodded, coming to a decision. 'I spoke to my father. He asked that you bring me along tomorrow evening to a place he has by the docks. He will meet us there with his men. He will tell you about the gem and who currently possesses it.'

'That's excellent news, Lyla'. I beamed at her. 'K and I will get you there safe and sound tomorrow.' I turned to Sars. 'Would you like to come along?'

Her silence said enough.

***

The warehouse wasn't hard to find. It was a secluded little spot close to the docks where we had fought Vritra, a forlorn neglected building with rust and moss climbing up its sides. Inside, we found piles and piles of boxes which I assumed were filled with food, machinery, or whatever else people normally store in warehouses.

Lyla, K and I crept in together, our footsteps echoing in the darkness. It was past 7 p.m., and the sun had already set. There were no dock workers in sight, and nobody was inside the warehouse. Bare bulbs hanging from the ceiling created pools of sickly yellow light, bright enough to read by in some spots, while some corners stayed hidden in deep shadows.

'He'll be upstairs. There's a little room on top,' said Lyla, her voice bouncing off the metal walls as she marched ahead. K and I followed not too far behind, scanning the place, wondering where an attack might come from.

'This is a stupid idea,' muttered K.

'Trust me on this, I know what I'm doing,' I muttered back.

'Oh, do you? Coz I thought us once again marching into a lion's den, where there will no doubt be many hostile … lions, is definitely a sign that you don't know what you are doing.'

'K, you know what the best part of being human is?'

He nodded. 'Yes. The small intestine!'

'What? No!' I mean, what?

K began to explain, but by then I noticed Lyla was already a bit too far ahead of us.

'Wait,' I called out as I picked up my pace.

'We'll pick this up later,' K whispered. I forced him out of my mind as I ran ahead.

'Lyla, don't rush ...' I called out as I came closer. 'Let me and K scout—'

That's when the shit hit the fan.

Invisible walls slammed shut around me. The air within felt dense and cloying. I could still move within the confinement, but it felt like I was wading through water, my movements sluggish.

A panicked warning flashed through my mind, complete with bulging eyes and a bulbuous fish-head, but it was too late.

I was stuck, like a rat in a cage.

'Akran, what's wrong? Are you okay?' K's words were coming from far away. Lyla froze mid-step and turned back, her face a perfect mask of concern.

I studied the confines of the trap. I could feel the force field extending four feet around me in every direction. The floor was tiled stone with a thin layer of dust. There was no carpet covering mystical symbols, no visible markings on the floor or walls. What was I missing?

There! Above my head was a pentagram etched across the ceiling, its lines glowing faintly like dying embers. The same symbol we'd seen at Nahusha's place and the farmhouse—a demon trap. Some genius had gambled on the fact that nobody ever looks up, and I'd walked right into it like an amateur. My throat felt dry. All this planning and I hadn't expected this. What other surprises were we missing?

'K, Lyla,' I called out, my voice hoarse. 'I'm trapped. Help me destroy that pentagram so I can free myself.'

K glanced helplessly at the pentagram above me. He continued to stare at it as Lyla extracted a glove from one of her pockets, slipped it on and picked up an iron bar that had been leaning against a crate.

'Lyla, wait, don't!' The words died in my throat as she brought the bar down on K's head with a sickening crack that seemed to echo forever.

Ah, Crap!

Any ordinary human would have died with the force of that blow. Granted, K was not human, but it would still take him some time to recover. I felt a leaden weight in my stomach as he crumpled to the floor, his body making a dull thud against the concrete.

'What did you do, Lyla?' I whispered. This had been my hare-brained idea. And K was paying the price.

She chuckled. 'What do you fucking think?' she purred in a voice like honey-coated poison.

Out of the shadows stepped a familiar face—Takshaka. He looked ill at ease, like the last time we had met. I felt a stirring of hope. Maybe she planned this without him. He would express horror and outrage and demand for me to be freed.

No such luck. Takshaka ignored me and made a beeline for Lyla.

'My part in the bargain is done!' he hissed. 'Now it's your turn!'

Some part of me knew that Takshaka had to be involved.

'Takshaka, why would you do this?'

He pretended to not have heard. No matter. Hanging out with K for several human lifetimes had taught me a thing or two about getting under people's skins.

'If this is about that joke I made about snakes having two willies, it was from a show on NatGeo.'

He gave me an angry look. 'Virach was my brother!' he grated.

'Virach? Who the fuck was Virach?' And then it came to me. I had met the nervous little Naga collector a few months ago; the humble, unassuming chap who was also greedy and foolish. The one who invited Ashwatthama and me for a sit-down. I winced at the memory. Ashwatthama had snapped his neck with a flick of his fingers.

Once he mentioned it, I could see the resemblance—they were practically twins. Had they stood in front of me in their birthday suits I wouldn't have been able to tell them apart. It's just that when they were fully dressed, Takshaka dressed with understated elegance, while Virach used to dress like a peacock that had mated with a rainbow.

'It sounds like you are blaming me for his death.' I ventured. 'If so, may I point out it was entirely your brother's fault? And also Ashwatthama's. I was merely a witness to that shit show. Heck, I almost got killed myself.'

Takshaka clenched his fists. 'It doesn't matter anymore. They told me you were responsible for his death. I only found out much later that you had nothing to do with it.' He gave me a beseeching look. 'I had no plans to kill you, just teach you a lesson.'

I was hooked. I rarely hear such stimulating confessions.

'I'm on the edge of my seats, Taks, don't leave me hanging! What happened next?'

Takshaka gave a defeated sigh.

'You have powerful enemies, Akran. You won't believe how many people you have pissed off!'

'I know some of them. We recently encountered Durvasa at a farmhouse. He laid out the plan's details.'

'Durvasa?' Takshaka's laugh sounded forced even to my ears. 'Try …'

'Ah, ah, ah,' Lyla wagged a finger at him. 'No names! He doesn't get to know who is behind this!'

Damn! Why is it always so much easier in books and TV, with villains eager to crow about their master plan? Reveal every detail of what they were plotting so that when the hero makes a last-minute escape, he knows everything!

'I found someone who was most eager to help,' Takshaka amended. 'But then …'

'Then our little snake got himself entangled in his own coils,' a booming voice said as a third person stepped in from the shadows.

And with that, I sensed the puzzle was nearly complete.

Indra Meghavahana, the most narcissistic of the pantheon of Indian Gods and quite possibly the biggest asshole I have ever encountered, stepped up to the edge of the circle. He twirled his oily moustache as he smirked at my predicament.

Okay, look, I know I use the word 'dick' to describe way too many people. Uriah, Durvasa, Narada, Indras in general. Maybe it is because I lack the breadth of vocabulary to really articulate how I feel about most of them. And maybe I'm also emotionally stunted like K says I am. But I've never called Meg a dick! For a very special reason. Douchebag, twat, quim, minge and beaver, yes. Dick, no.

'Meg! What brings you here after all this time?' I called out in a cheerful voice.

'If it isn't Akran the Yaksha,' he said. 'What an absolute joy it is to have you here with us!'

'In the flesh, Meg. I would shake your hand, but …' I gestured at my invisible prison. 'You can see I'm a little occupied.'

'You have no idea how long I have been looking forward to this!'

'I might. Since, unlike you, I can actually count.' Damn, I was on fire today!

He didn't seem too bothered by my wisecrack. I didn't expect him to be fazed either. Meghavahana was a stone-cold sociopath who never took his eyes off the prize. These little zingers probably only made the final outcome sweeter, as far as he was concerned.

'Enough about me, though. What do you mean he got caught in his own coils?'

'Takshaka wanted you dead, because he thought you killed his brother. But there are lines he won't cross.' He walked over to Takshaka, who stood there mute, glaring at everyone else.

'So we kidnapped his daughter,' Lyla chimed in. 'And I took her place.' She made a show of patting Takshaka's arm as she spoke. 'She is safe, by the way. We set her free before Takshaka made his way here.' She cast a sly look at Indra … 'Didn't you?'

Meg chuckled. 'I set her free,' he said in an amused voice.

Something about the way he said it made my heart sink. If I knew Meg, the girl was dead. But Takshaka believed him.

'I felt like I owed you an apology,' Takshaka said to me stiffly. 'I had a blood debt. This … This is not what I was …'

'Hush, now,' Lyla whispered as she moved to stand behind him. 'Don't spoil the surprise just yet.' She caressed his shoulder, and a look of revulsion passed over Takshaka's face. He was using every bit of self-control to avoid recoiling from her.

Abruptly, Takshaka stiffened. He gave a low moan and collapsed to the floor, clutching his chest.

I realised at that moment what she had done. That strangely intimate gesture where she clutched his shoulder—I had felt it before.

Takshaka was curled into a ball, frothing at the mouth, whimpering. I tore my eyes away from him.

'You poisoned him! And me.'

'Clever of you to finally figure it out. Didn't you wonder why the little scratches I gave you didn't heal?' She held up her hand, her green nail polish glistening. This little neurotoxin is my own invention. 'My feelings for you in distilled form.'

I had thought the little puncture wounds not healing were a symptom of my weakness, my inability to deal with magic leaking from the world. Lyla had poisoned me and that was what was responsible for my headaches and sickness.

Meg slipped his arms around her waist, his eyes on me. She arched her back and wiggled her hips as she gave me a sly look from the corner of her eye. 'Are you scared yet, Akran?'

'Scared? Not really. Grossed out? Yes. Both of you are older than the pyramids and are still as handsy as horny mice. You ever heard the expression, Get a room?'

You didn't even receive a lethal dose,' she continued, ignoring me. 'Just a tiny little taste to keep you off balance. A neurotoxin that neutralises your powers. Gave you a little less sleep and a little more paranoia. Made you a bit more susceptible to rash decisions.' She smiled, a cruel look full of sharp teeth and malice. 'Like putting demons inside you! How noble and self-sacrificing. How utterly stupid!'

I shook my head. 'You do know you are insane, right? I put a demon inside me to help close the rift. The one that's letting magic leak out. The one that, if we don't find a way to close, will mean the end of all of us—Yakshas, Nagas, Devas … Of all the screwed up things you could be doing, why interfere with the one thing that will actually save your life?'

'We aren't trying to close the rift, you fool! We are planning to widen it!'

WTF?!

'The Dead Queen rises. Her disciples will clear the weeds and prepare the path.'

For fuck's sake. I thought Ashwatthama was the loon. This chick had taken crazy to a whole new level.

'Lyla, what the fuck are you on right now?'

Her eyes gleamed like shiny sparkly glass. Crime master Gogo would have loved to have made her acquaintance.

'The Elder Gods will once more walk this world. No longer will they remain steeped in shadows. And you, Akran, will be responsible. Your blood is what will make it happen.'

I could feel another headache coming on, just listening to this garbage. Turns out poison isn't the only thing that can trigger that reaction. I'm also allergic to sheer fucking stupidity.

'This Dead Queen. You can see her right now? Is she telling you what to do?' I gave her a pitying look. 'Lyla, if no one else can hear her, have you considered that she may be a voice in your head and nothing else?'

She laughed. Hysterically and for a touch longer than your standard level of crazy, if you ask me.

'I don't blame you for your ignorance, Akran. You only know what the Trinity has taught you. A lamb trusting the butcher.'

I shot a quick look at Meg. He had this carefully neutral look on his face. The face of a man who knows his girlfriend is crazy but also hot, and who's willing to pretend she's sane so he can continue to get laid.

'The world is older than you think. When she ascends, all who were banished will flock to her throne. That which is hidden will soon come to light.'

This reverse interrogation thing was going quite well. She was spilling everything she knew. It's too bad she was an insane broad with grass in her head.

'You know, I did wonder, how were you able to kill all of the demons in that club?' She narrowed her eyes. 'I'm going to wring the truth out of you anyway in the next few hours, so you might as well tell me now.'

I shrugged. 'Clean living, eating healthy, that sort of thing. The demons should have included more veggies in their diet.' Another thought struck me, the confirmation of a suspicion at the back of my mind.

'You sent the RBs after us. You knew we were coming, so you told them to attack me. You wanted to test my abilities.'

She laughed again, a shrill, mocking sound. Has anyone else ever noticed how often the insane really laugh?

'We heard about how you defeated Ashwatthama. That was a shock to everybody. Everyone thought that maybe you are dangerous. "We should study him for a while, see what powers he has".' She spat on the floor. 'If I had known what a pathetic loser you were, I would have killed you that night instead of going through that charade of being Takshaka's daughter.'

Meg draped his arm over her shoulders, an oddly intimate gesture. 'You know what's ironic? We would have paid for the opportunity to have you killed. Instead, someone is paying us!'

I wasn't surprised—Meg and I had history. Lyla, on the other hand … I recalled the night at the club when Lyla was giving me those 'come hither' eyes one minute and looking to incinerate me with heat vision the next. I would've liked to believe she was a pretty inept assassin who couldn't decide whether to seduce or kill me, but that was delusional. She clearly had a hard-on for me, and not in a good way.

'Did I sleep with you and never call you back? Is that what this is?'

'In your dreams, Yaksha.' She circled closer to my invisible prison, her movements predatory. 'You don't recognise me, do you?'

'Umm … No. In fact, you may be confusing me with someone else. I'm pretty sure I've never known a Lyla in my life.'

She reached into the waistband of her slacks and pulled out a glowing red knife. It looked like a jagged piece of ruby, filed into a shiv. The light shone across the blade as it gleamed.

She cut herself with the ruby blade and closely watched my reaction. I stared with a sick fascination as the knife appeared to drink the blood greedily, absorbing it as soon as it touched the blade. The blood seemed to give it an extra glow.

'I'm going to use this on your eyeballs, Akran,' she whispered. 'Then your tongue. Then your fingers and toes. And after that, I may write the story of how we met on your body.' She gave me a chilly smile. 'In very tiny letters.'

'Could we get back to the fact that we don't know each other, you little freak?'

She reached behind her neck to release the clasp of the choker, and her power flared to life. She wasn't a Celestial after all. She was a yogini, a female ascetic, also known in some circles as a Tantrika. Plenty of power, all tamped down and tightly hidden by that necklace.

'We've never met, Yaksha. But you ruined my life all the same. Lyla is an alias. You know me by my actual name, Ahalya.'

Fuck me with a sword! I did know Ahalya!

Her story is one of those cautionary tales against infidelity that has become the stuff of legend. For centuries afterwards, the mere mention of her name was enough to shrivel the dicks of any wannabe Casanova who thought seducing someone's wife was a risk worth taking.

Early Vedic texts describe Ahalya as a 'shapely and slim-waisted woman', proving, if nothing else, that these texts were written by a man. The first of the Trinity, Brahma, created her as the 'perfect woman', because, again, as a man, he was considered an expert in what that entails. She was said to be more beautiful than the apsaras (dancing girls that adorned heaven). There were no good female role models around at the time—and so Brahma handed her over to a Sage named Gautama to raise as his daughter.

Rishi Gautama looked after her until puberty and then returned her to Brahma. Brahma decided it was time to find her a suitable husband and naturally, given the prevailing wisdom of the time, decided to have a contest among the suitors instead of asking her whom she would like to marry.

This attracted the randiest celestial of them all, Indra Meghavahana. I had nicknamed him Meg for short, a nickname that became wildly popular and which he despised. It was hard to look all macho and godlike when people gave him irreverent nicknames.

Even among the many Indras, Meg was regarded as one of the worst. Which is saying a lot. He looked at humans with contempt, often referring to them as apes. He tormented one of my closest friends, Mayasura, incessantly because of his dark skin. He used to play pranks on the sages and find ways to disrupt their yagnas because he was worried that any sage who acquired too much yogic power through their penance would one day challenge him or seize his throne.

In plain terms, Meg was a bully used to getting what he wanted.

In the interest of fairness (no pun intended), I must also state that he had a few redeeming qualities, most of them physical. He was fair, handsome and broad-shouldered, a skilled warrior, and he had led the Devas to victory against their mortal enemies, the Asuras, in multiple skirmishes. Everyone was willing to turn a blind eye to his excesses as long as he gave them victories. Still, his behaviour in general was despicable, and I was always looking forward to an opportunity to teach him a lesson.

His contempt towards humans did not stop him from chasing the women of Earth.

Meg announced his eagerness to participate in the contest. He wanted to take a break from diddling the nobility's nubility and decided to tap a Tantrika's tushy instead.

What was incredibly creepy, by today's standards, was that his opponent, who also decided to try win her hand, was none other than Rishi Gautama himself, the man who had raised her like his daughter. Did it make people wonder if he had been the right choice to raise her as a dad? Doubtful. He was a man and, hence, above reproach or suspicion. Also, irony hadn't been discovered yet.

The challenge was to circle the three worlds (Heaven, Earth and the underworld), and the winner took all. Indra set off immediately and was quite confident he would win. Unfortunately, he didn't. Our good friend Narada made an unexpected appearance at the end of the contest and announced that Rishi Gautama was the winner because, as part of his daily rituals, he went around the wish-bearing cow Kamadhenu (described in Hinduism as the mother of all cows) while she gave birth. Through some weird-assed Vedic logic, encircling a mother was the equivalent of encircling the world—something about how, to a child, their parents are their whole world or some such word play. Rishi Gautama was declared the winner.

It occurred to me as I ran the story through my head that, once again, that goddamned troublemaker Narada was responsible.

Ahalya possessed what women weren't supposed to have in those days: a sex drive. Desires, feelings, actual human emotions—absolutely shocking stuff that was perfectly admirable when found in men but apparently a moral catastrophe when discovered in women. Because it wasn't really part of Indian culture at all -we became the most populous country in the world purely through meditation and yoga. With possibly some Ayurveda thrown in.

Turns out that being married to your dad doesn't lead to a happy marriage. Shocking, I know!

The scriptures are a little vague about what happened next. In one version (Uttara Kanda 4th–16th Century CE), Meg forced himself on her. According to this version of the scriptures, she was an archetype of female chastity who would never have consented to sleep with someone other than her husband. In another version, the Bala Kanda (4th–5th century BCE), Indra seduced her. Rishi Gautama was one of those sages who spent all his time praying. And while that may sound like a euphemism for 'celebrating palm sunday' or 'getting to know himself better' as it was called in those days, sages back then were really strict about denying themselves all worldly pleasures. They only took on wives to have kids, and even then, they probably promised themselves not to enjoy the act of making the kids.

Fed up of dealing with a husband with no sex drive, Ahalya decided to give in to Indra's advances. In yet another version, Indra tricked her by taking on the form of her husband, Rishi Gautama. What everyone agrees on is that the two slept together. And somehow the Rishi found out. Nobody really knows how that happened; it's one of those details that is unimportant to the story. Certainly not something for anyone to make a big deal about. In fact, it is so unworthy of consideration, I should not even be giving it the attention I am giving it right now.

The Rishi was livid. It was one thing for him to not sleep with his wife, how dare she go about making her own choices? If he allowed that, there might be no end to her list of unreasonable demands. Education! The right to work! Equality! Who knows where it would end?

Rishi Gautama decided they must both be punished for their transgressions. He turned Ahalya into a rock. A few different variations of her punishment exist (pebble, boulder, Dwayne Johnson, etc., but they were all fundamentally rocks). She remained in that state for several thousands of years until the time of the Ramayana. Prince Ram, exiled from Ayodhya and destined to spend fourteen years of banishment in the forest along with his wife Sita and brother Lakshman, is met by sage Vishwamitra, who tells them the tragic tale. Ram happened to be the seventh avatar of Vishnu's. Moved by her plight, he touched the rock with his foot, for that is exactly what you are supposed to do when you find out the stone is a human being—give it a foot rub.

The meeting of divine foot and human head releases Ahalya from the curse. Also, in the grand tradition of women in epics being mainly around to father kids, instigate war or be damsels in distress, she is dropped from the story like a hot potato after making Ram look good. Presumably, she picked up and went on with her life. It's a heartwarming tale of divine mercy—rescuing a woman from a fate worse than death, then immediately forgetting she exists because her narrative usefulness has expired.

But Meg? Oh, he received a far more epic punishment.

I am paraphrasing here since Rishi Gautama's exact words have been lost to the world, but the essence of his curse was this: You can't seem to stay away from vaginas, huh? Well then, let me give you a thousand of your own and then maybe you'll leave everyone else's alone'

All over Indra's body, a thousand vaginas popped up. To add insult to injury, and to make sure he never actually got any pleasure from that curse, he also lost his testicles.

This was one of the dangers of messing with a sage. Not only did they have fearful powers, but they could also craft really fucked up curses. This one sounded like an emotionally stunted adolescent male's idea of a curse—or fantasy, depending on how you look at it. As K put it, 'Why would he give him a thousand vaginas? That's just bad thinking. You want to torture somebody, give them a thousand itchy ball sacks, see how that would feel!'

So ... Meg was no longer deemed fit to rule. I'm guessing this was primarily because a thousand vaginas got in the way of EVERYTHING. He was also stripped of his title as war leader. He would have been laughed off the battlefield if he made an appearance. It also put a cramp on his hedonistic lifestyle—no woman wanted to be anywhere near him. He did receive a fair bit of unwanted male attention, but by and large, he was well and truly screwed (again, no pun intended).

A completely unexpected consequence of this was my being promoted to the role of Indra for a short while (a few thousand years). I didn't begrudge the next Indra when they found a worthy successor. I relinquished my position gladly and, with my newfound abilities, became the First of the Yakshas, a martial role I felt well suited for.

More action, fewer responsibilities.

What about our friend Meg? Eventually, the curse was lifted—there was a lot of grovelling involved, and there was a multi-step process where the vaginas were first converted into eyes. Because eyes are the windows to one's soul and a vagina is the ... you know what ... I'm just going to admit I have no clue why they had to be converted into eyes in the first place. It's not like they are interchangeable; they don't even look alike—It's just one of those things people back in the day seemed to accept without asking for any explanations.

Those eyes were also eventually removed but it was a long and humiliating period in Meg's life, something he never forgot. He also never stopped blaming me for taking his place, insisting that I had something to do with his downfall. I knew he was out there, biding his time and licking his wounds, but I hadn't really given him much thought over the past several thousand years. Truthfully, I hadn't even considered he might have taken up a new career as an assassin, but you know what they say, it's never too late to follow your dreams.

That, in case you are wondering, is why I never called Meg a dick. He was too far removed from the term thanks to one really pissed off sage.

Now with this context, Ahalya was understandably mad. I suppose being a stone in a forest for ten thousand years, give or take, must have been pretty tedious. Animals peeing over you, having a thousand human buttocks resting on your face, wondering if that would be the rest of your life. At the very least, I could appear sympathetic.

Except ... she had nearly caved K's head in with a crowbar! It was hard to muster up any sympathy for this psychopath.

I gave her my best smile. 'Hey Ahalya, I should have recognised you from the stony looks you've been giving me.'

She slowly licked the blade, her eyes never leaving my face.

Maybe my brand of humour was too sophisticated for this audience.

Those who described Ahalya as the most beautiful woman in the world were probably just sex starved at the time. Or the pool of available women was quite small.

Ahalya continued to glare at me for a while. When she spoke, her voice came out almost whispery, like she was choking on the words.

'Did you know Rishi Gautama used to regret having cursed me? He spent many nights by the river bank sitting and talking to me, telling me how much he regretted cursing me.'

Play nice, Akran!

'Sounds like a good husband,' I offered. 'You know, except the cursing-you-to-be-a-rock part.'

'He often spoke about that day he caught us. It turns out that by himself, he may never even have noticed my affair with Indra.'

Okay, I knew where she is going with this.

'It turns out Indra had a malicious enemy, a Yaksha of dubious origins, who decided to inform my husband about the affair. '

Dubious origins sounded a little harsh, but now was not the time to quibble. 'Ahalya ... I ...'

'That damned fool of a Yaksha decided to meddle in my affairs. He made me a pawn in his feud with Indra.

'Rishi Gautama was an honourable man. If I had confessed to him, he might have forgiven me. But once he knew that others knew about it, it stung his pride and he decided to make an example of me.' She glared at me. 'You wouldn't happen to know who that Yaksha was, would you?'

Even I knew that was a rhetorical question at this point.

'So, thanks to you, my one harmless transgression came to his notice, and because he was doubly humiliated, his punishment was HARSHER THAN EVER.' She screamed the last bit, spittle flying from her mouth as she glared at me.

I couldn't possibly reason with her if she was going to be this way.

'Ahalya,' I began 'I know we got off to a rocky start ...'

She sneered. 'Fuck you.'

'You are being too sedimental. We haven't reached rock bottom yet ...'

Her eyes flashed fire. 'Enough with the fucking puns. You ruined my life, you bastard!' she hissed. 'I was innocent. You and your fucking power games with Indra, and I'm the one who got caught in the middle.'

'Back up a moment. I'm happy to accept a share of the blame, but ... Innocent? Really? Did you trip over a stone and fall on his dick?'

'Indra got cursed, and recovered. You got promoted. I became a literal piece of stone. Tell me how that is justice, Yaksha!'

'It isn't. And again, your anger should be directed towards the man who actually turned you into a rock.'

She sneered 'Who do you think was the first person I killed?'

Right!

'There have been many others over time. Other Rishis who knew what happened and never lifted a finger to help. They've all fallen to my blade!' She smiled chillingly. 'I saved you for last, Akran.'

'I'm flattered Ahalya, really, but you shouldn't have gone to all this trouble.'

'Oh, it's no trouble at all, she purred … you deserved a special death. I've been planning this conversation for decades.'

'If he took you against your will, I saw him punished for it. If not …' I shrugged. 'Meg was scum, Ahalya. Still is, I'm guessing. You were not his first and you certainly wouldn't have been his last. Don't tell me you didn't know his reputation back then!'

'I was seduced by a God! There was nobody I could have complained to! I was in an impossible position!'

'Under him, with your legs in the air, you mean? Sure, I can see how difficult that might have been. But you've certainly made a choice now, haven't you? You have chosen to join forces with your lover and kill people for a living. I'm not buying the blameless martyr act!'

'Act? You have no inkling of what it is to be an ambitious Rishi's wife!' She was hissing as she spoke. 'Rishi Gautama married me, but refused to sleep with me; he was always too busy with his penance and meditation, so I succumbed to Indra's advances.'

I wanted to say she had taken her husband for granite, but being the wise and mature Yaksha that I am, I refrained.

I shook my head. 'I'm sorry you got punished for your infidelity, but that really is between you, Gautama and Indra. And maybe a couple's counsellor.'

She gave a disgusted snort, 'Ever the asshole, Akran! You say you are reformed, but you've not changed one whit— making jokes while people suffer from your past mistakes.'

'You want me to admit I was a dick back then? Fine! I was. I was young, reckless and full of myself. I didn't think much of humans and had my head up my own ass for most of my life.' I paused. 'But here's the difference between us. We have both been scarred by divine politics, but we've chosen different paths forward. I'm doing what I can to save lives—but you've chosen murder and mayhem!'

'Yes, you are a paragon of virtue now, aren't you?' She sneered. 'The great Celestial protector of Mumbai. Akran the Magnificent! The Yaksha who can do no wrong!'

'Like I said, I am trying. My eyes were opened when I got exiled from the Celestial court.' I took a deep breath. 'You are right Ahalya, this apology is long overdue. You were someone caught in the crossfire of the feud between Meg and me. I shouldn't have gotten you involved and I am sorry for that.'

'Too little, too late, Yaksha,' she spat.

'You feel the need to kill me? I get it. But the people or person who hired you? They are trying to trigger the end of the Kali Yuga! Millions will die. Is your revenge really worth that much death?'

'That and more,' she answered grimly. 'The Gods you idolise, don't care about us. At least now I choose my own destruction. I don't care about the fucking humans, or the Devas or the Asuras or even the Nagas … this whole world can go down in fire and blood, and I will dance on its ashes.'

She was clearly insane. In her eyes was a psychopathic desire to hurt every living creature. There would be no reasoning with her.

Which actually made me feel a bit better. If she was someone seeking revenge on me, I got it. It was no more than what I deserved. But targeting innocents? She had crossed into the same morally grey territory I did, the only difference being one of scale—my sin was of tattling on one unfaithful wife, while hers was closer to genocide.

I was going to die making puns. There were worse ways to go, I supposed, but probably better times to discover I had a death wish.

'Okay, wait,' I said. 'I have one last thing to say. This might actually convince you that I was in the right. You think I'm being insensitive? Fair enough. But answer me this. Your choice was between being faithful to your husband and sitting on Indra's penis, right? You know what that means?'

She gave me a wary look.

'You were caught between a rock and …' I paused dramatically. '…a hard place!'

Okay, seriously, I'm very proud of that last one. It wasn't my fault my audience was so lacking in humour. Ahalya's face had turned an ugly shade of purple.

You know when they would have found it funnier? If they were stoned!

I really should be writing this all down. This was comedy gold!

Meg interjected with an exaggerated yawn. 'If we are all caught up with this walk down memory lane, perhaps we can get on with it. His skin isn't going to flay itself.' He sauntered closer, grinning at me. 'I can't tell you how much I'm going to enjoy this.'

I was almost out of time. I just had to hope it was enough.

Meg smirked. 'Any last words, Akran?'

I sighed. 'Yeah. Maybe just three of them.' I removed the amulet concealed within my shirt and dropped it on the floor as I stepped out of the summoning circle. 'Go fuck yourselves!'

CHAPTER TWELVE

'*Did none of you notice her slip up? Most of us don't know you were once an Indra. You didn't even know that an Indra is half human. Yet when you told her your plan, she didn't even blink. She immediately figured you were going to cut out your human side.*'
(Conversation with Sars before the warehouse visit.)
—The Private Journals of Akran

Twenty-four Hours Earlier, Mira Road Farmhouse.
Tamara gave me a wry glance. 'Life for everyone else I know happens in the moments in which they live. For me, it lies between those moments. In the realm of possibilities. Where uncertainties abound.' She sighed wearily. 'Sometimes, it feels like I spend my whole life in the in-between place. Nudging moments to make the best outcomes.'

Sars came back looking fit to burst, her face red with excitement.

'Sars, you had something to tell us?'

'K called.'

'It worked?' I asked.

She smiled triumphantly. 'It worked! She panicked and made a call. Tamara was the wildcard that threw her plans out of whack.'

'Yet they left Durvasa here!'

'Durvasa isn't part of their crew, he's just a patsy gullible enough to believe that they all want the same thing, i.e., to close the rift.' Sars shot a quick glance at Tamara. 'I think she figured that if they fought and Durvasa won, Tamara would be taken off the board. If Tamara won, Durvasa couldn't tell us anything we wouldn't piece together anyway.'

'What made you suspect her?' Tamara asked.

Sars began counting off on her fingers. 'First, the RBs. They were definitely after Akran, not her. They surrounded him at the club and barely glanced at her. But how did they know that was where they would find him?'

'Couldn't they have just followed you there?'

I grinned. 'Lyla made one fatal error. She does not know anything about Sars and her powers. Almost nobody does because Sars keeps to herself. But she will extract every scrap of knowledge available and go after a mystery like a dog with a bone.'

Sars blushed at the compliment. 'The night of the attack on the club, I checked every traffic cam between Akran's place, the club and the RB chapter house. We also have concealed security cams around the building pointing at the main entrance, on side streets, and not connected to the main grid. None of them indicated that Akran and K were being followed. Which meant someone close to Takshaka tipped them off. Possibly Takshaka himself.'

Tamara listened with rapt attention.

'The next was the firebombing of the safehouses. They struck three of the places I owned yet missed the one I spent the most time at. It's unlikely they didn't know about it. Not if they knew where the others were.'

'Maybe it was too well defended. Or too public a location.'

'Possibly. But then Takshaka asked us to keep Lyla with us in a safe place. It seemed too convenient. They were trying to box me in. I would naturally go to my penthouse, which is very well protected.'

'Unless you have someone inside ready to bring down its defences if needed.' Sars finished.

'She could have attacked you at the club though, right?' We had described everything that had happened in some detail to Tamara, so she was reasonably caught up. 'Why go through this entire charade if she could get you out in the open? No, wait, don't tell me! It's the first law thingy.'

'That's right.' She wouldn't want to expose herself,' I said. 'But if you are still not convinced, how's this? There are no photos of Lyla anywhere. Takshaka is featured in the press when there are mentions of his club but Lyla only seems to have emerged now.'

'And the choker she is wearing?' Sars added. 'That's pretty powerful magic. Nagas don't flaunt the magical items they have, they prefer hoarding them. It's one of their personality quirks—they are more likely to bury their treasure than risk exposing it to people because they always try to steal it. It's a shade too convenient that she has that on, and we cannot see what she looks like on the higher planes.'

'Not to mention, every woman I know will take off her jewellery when she goes to bed. Lyla was dressed in her nightclothes when Tamara came over but she still had the choker on.'

'That generalisation's a bit offensive,' Sars said, and I threw my hands up. 'That last bit wasn't even something I thought of. K told it to me. Regardless. Separately, this is all circumstantial evidence and pretty thin but when you link the pieces all together, it looks quite suspicious. For instance, when K and I wanted to exit the club through a back entrance, she was trying to goad us to fight. Why would she do that? On one hand she pretends she is terrified, and on the other she is egging us on to deal head-on with the demons in the club. No Naga would encourage us to risk trashing their place of business.'

'Ergo, she doesn't really care what happened to Takshaka's club. Which means she isn't really his daughter at all.'

'That would explain the severely constipated look Takshaka had on his face all through our meeting. He was being forced to enact this charade. I would bet he is an unwilling participant.'

'Also, she was scared when Tamara joined! Her snide comment about us needing more people to protect her … If she was worried for her safety, she wouldn't bitch and moan about extra protection!'

'She hasn't done anything so far,' Tamara pointed out, looking doubtful. 'If all you've said is true, and she's been in your house two nights now, what stopped her from attempting to kill you?

I grinned. 'You have! She wasn't expecting someone like you to be present. That's put her plans out of sync.'

'Also, Akran,' Sars added, 'The display at the club; she didn't know about Narada. That fight was completely out of your league. If she had been studying your abilities for a while, she would have been expecting a mediocre performance at best. What she saw threw her off.'

'We aren't usually this paranoid,' I explained. 'The knowledge of this assassination contract made us pay closer attention to our surroundings. And so, when we decided to attack the farmhouse, K doubled back to eavesdrop on her. He's been in the house the whole time. My guess was that she would tip someone off, and we would return and confront her.'

'It would have been easier if you had just attacked the farmhouse without telling her! You could have nabbed her accomplice and then confronted her!'

Sars and I exchanged a sheepish look. 'That would have been ideal. But, once you told us about the farmhouse while she was around, us not investigating it would have been suspicious. She would have tipped off her accomplice and escaped.'

Tamara looked lost in thought for a minute. It was a lot to process. I was feeling pretty pleased with myself.

'There's one thing that you probably haven't realised,' Tamara said slowly. 'Durvasa said his hex was a simple tracking spell. So why is everything else not working for you?'

I gave her a bewildered look. 'Didn't you tell us that the hex on me was causing problems?'

'I said it was *probably* the hex,' Tamara corrected me. 'All the symptoms are still there. Your aura seems to have black soot clinging to it. It is sapping your will and your power. But what I'm looking at are the symptoms, not the cause. I only assumed it was the hex.'

Sars snapped her fingers. 'I knew I had forgotten something. You mentioned Takshaka was having the same problem.'

I nodded. 'Lyla said so. What were you thinking?'

'Hang on, let me try something.' Sars placed her hand on my shoulder, which had the scars that hadn't healed yet.

I felt a searing pain. Sars was channelling pure mana directly into the wound.

'Ow! Sars, what the fuck?' I yelled as I jerked away. My whole body felt like it was on fire. Mercifully, the feeling subsided quickly, leaving only a stinging sensation. My arm felt numb and rubbery.

'We are idiots, Akran! It was right in front of us the whole time!' Sars said, shaking her head in disgust. 'Try one of your card tricks now!'

I picked a card from my back pocket and flicked it in my hand. It lit up, bright and shiny like teeth in a dental ad.

'What did you just do?' I asked, rubbing my shoulder gingerly. It had hurt like the devil, but she had managed to cauterise the wound. Already, pale pink skin formed over the scars. 'And how exactly did you heal me?'

'We assumed your wound wasn't healing because you had lost your abilities. We were wrong. You lost your abilities because of that wound! She fucking poisoned you!'

I stared at her open-mouthed. 'She did what?'

'It was so convenient. Think about it! Every Celestial is so worried about the magic leaking out, nobody even suspected that you might have lost your abilities because of anything else!'

'Poison,' I repeated numbly.

'Not the fatal kind. Just enough to drive you crazy over a few weeks. A slow, insidious kind, sapping away at your will to live.'

Tamara was looking wide-eyed at me. 'How did she poison him?'

'When did you first lose your powers?'

I thought back to that moment. 'At the club,' I said slowly. 'Right after …'

'She dug her nails into your shoulder!' Sars snarled. I had never seen her so mad. 'That's what was coursing through your veins! And that's what Tamara spotted.' Sars was pacing up and down like a hungry tiger. 'She was covering her tracks when she said Takshaka also experienced something similar. Making us think she was on our side. This clinches it! When I get my hands on her …'

'Sars, calm down. Let's not reveal our hand just yet.' I could feel my mana pool again. Channelling mana had obviously burnt the poison within. Just touching that trickle made me feel whole once more.

'This is it! Everything before this was circumstantial. Now we have proof!'

'I'm betting she is the junior accomplice in the mix. I want the big one, the green-eyed bastard I suspect is also involved.'

'I have an idea,' I said, and turned to Tamara. 'And I'll definitely need your help.'

'For sure. What do you need?'

'An honourable demon. One I can reach an accommodation with.'

'Huh?'

'Durvasa gave me an idea. He looked aghast at the thought I might be cavorting with demons.'

I pointed at her neck. 'The amulet you have. May I try it on?'

She slipped it off and handed it to me. 'I don't think it will work for you. It recognises me because of the taint I added to my soul when I travelled into hell. Literally, not metaphorically speaking.'

'I don't need its abilities. This amulet has demonic energy emanating from it.' I wore it and tucked the amulet underneath my vest. 'I want to look like I have a demon trapped within.'

'Why?'

'The summoning circles here and at Nahusha's place. They know how to make one. They also think I am much stronger than they are, which is why they haven't made their move yet.'

'You want to dangle yourself as bait.' Sars said slowly.

'I need to put myself in a vulnerable position of some kind to let them think they have a chance.'

'There's only one problem with that plan,' said Sars. 'You are pretty weak.' She gave me an apologetic look. 'No offence.'

'I'm not too worried about that,' I said with a confidence I didn't feel. 'As long as Tamara is here, I will be safe.'

I didn't want to risk my neck on the chance that Tamara and her prophecies were accurate. But I was running out of patience and ideas.

'I have it!' exclaimed Sars. 'We tell her Tamara is leaving.'

'Okay. And then?'

Sars turned to Tamara. 'Can you mimic K's invisibility? Or mine?'

'Yours, yes. K's, no. It's different.'

'Which is fine. We tell her you'll be back in a few days. She will spring her trap quickly.'

'But I can't stay invisible for too long. I was telling Akran just now how I need to conserve my power for the right moment.'

'It won't be for very long. Trust me on this,' said Sars.

I fastened the clasp of the amulet behind my back and tucked it under my vest. 'How do I look?'

Sars scanned me on the different planes of existence. 'You definitely look tainted'. She clapped her hands in glee. 'I think we can pull this off!'

CHAPTER THIRTEEN

Okay fine. So, I'm an unreliable narrator. Sue me!

I can't help but leave out little bits and add them in later when I remember them. You try journalling your existence for thousands of years, and let's see how many details get skipped.

—The Private Journals of Akran

In retrospect, this was a dumb choice.

I could have stepped out of the summoning circle anytime I wanted. I should have done so when their backs were turned and when they least expected it.

But this felt more … satisfying. Especially when Meg handed me such a killer response right on a platter. Also, K would never forgive me if I didn't display some panache as I walked out of that little trap.

Ahalya's face was an O of surprise as I moved. Despite her raw, visceral hatred, she wasn't my target; she could glare at my back all she wanted. Battlefield tactics 101: take out the big guns first.

Meg was the first to react. All Indras have lightning-quick reflexes. You don't get to be a war leader for the Gods if you can't think on your feet. He had already raised his hand and I could see lightning crackle on his fingertips.

I punched his nose to a satisfying crunch below my fist, and I felt the bridge of his nose shatter. Blood gushed out as he screamed and grabbed his face, buying me a few seconds. His face was already knitting itself together. But a few seconds was all I needed.

To her credit, Ahalya was no slouch either. A career in assassinations had taught her to cope when the situation got away from her. As I punched Meg, Ahalya moved closer behind me, dagger raised, poised to strike. Which is when a hammer slammed into the side of her head.

Though I was expecting them, their sudden appearance was still a surprise. I couldn't help but be relieved as they emerged from their invisibility.

Sars and Tamara were dressed identically in black crop tops and jeans. Sars rushed over to K to help him up while Tamara squared off against Ahalya.

'What took you so long?' I asked, even though I knew the answer. They were keeping their distance to conserve Tamara's limited power. They had probably missed all of Ahalya's crazy talk.

Sars ignored my question. 'Here, catch'. She threw Mas's experimental metal bracelet at me. I snapped it around my arm and spun just in time as Meg rose from the floor and threw a lightning bolt deadly enough to power half of Mumbai for a week. It should have incinerated me—even

Celestials can't survive a million volts of electricity at point-blank range.

Except it didn't. The bracelet glowed as the bolt hit, twisting and bending it around, leaving me unharmed.

Meg's jaw dropped. I gave him my best smile. Christmas had come early this year.

'No powers, Meg, just you and me,' I said as I closed the distance between us. 'This has been a long time coming.'

To his credit, Meg didn't flinch. He flung another bolt of lightning, this time at Sars.

Sars ignored him. The second bracelet was around her arm. As the lightning crackled around her, she extracted a tiny bottle from her back pocket that looked like a vial of perfume. She placed it under K's nose. He groaned as his eyes slowly focused.

I wasn't going to give Meg any more chances. And let's be honest, that first punch had felt delightful. I closed in and punched him again, finishing the job this time.

He was shrieking in agony, cupping his broken nose. 'Not so good without your powers, huh?' I taunted as I kneed him in the groin. He fell over, retching. His fault, really. He should have anticipated that I would go after the low-hanging fruits.

Tamara was kneeling next to Takshaka's prone body, her hands on his head, muttering to herself. I guessed she was trying to burn out the poison in his veins, kind of like what she had done with me.

Meg lunged at my throat with a stone dagger that appeared similar to Lyla's ruby one, but didn't seem to have any special magical properties. I was able to grab his arm and snake my foot behind his, pulling him to the ground. We rolled on the floor, trading punches and clawing ineffectually at each other.

There was no question in my mind that I was stronger than him. I was also the better fighter, had faster reflexes, and more muscle. I had lived through centuries of being branded a 'fugitive', having to fight for survival. Meg might have been a big deal in his day, but I guessed a few centuries with vaginas, and then eyes, all over his body might've interfered with his exercise routine. His movements were not as quick or coordinated as before.

All of this was compensated by the fact that in terms of sheer power, he had an advantage. His body had an accelerated rate of healing, and punching him, satisfying though it was, was simply not viable as a long-term plan. I needed to cause catastrophic damage—an injury so severe that his healing factor wouldn't fix it before life was snuffed out of him.

'Is there any chance at all that Takshaka's daughter is alive?' I demanded as I scratched at his eye.

'What do you think?' he rasped as he tried unsuccessfully, for the third time, to stab me.

I snapped his left pinky as I rammed his head back onto the floor. The knife slipped out of his hand. I grabbed it before his desperately seeking fingers could find it.

There were quite a few ways to cause catastrophic damage to a Celestial, provided you had the right tools. With a little knife, there was only one way that occurred to me.

I was sitting on his chest, and he couldn't break free.

'Akran, listen to me,' he gasped as I raised the knife. 'I'll make you a deal. My life in exchange for information. Who I'm working for, what the elder Gods are planning, all of it!'

If I had been more like one of those comic book superheroes who plant a big symbol on their chest and float around in bright colours, I might have stayed my hand. I could understand maintaining an image with your adoring fans.

But, no. I was more likely to paint a giant skull on my chest rather than a symbol of hope. Not only was I despised by most of my peers, there was nobody else in this cold damp warehouse I wanted to impress. I also didn't believe that all life was precious or any of that other BS. As far as I was concerned, Meg was scum. He deserved to die.

'Fuck you and your elder Gods,' I replied. The knife hovered at the tip of his eye as I steeled myself to ram it in. A sharp object through the eye socket and into his brain would be too much for his healing factor to recover from.

'His daughter is alive. I can take you to her,' he yelled.

I hesitated. That split-second delay cost me dearly.

With his left hand, Meg ripped the bracelet off my arm, placed his right hand on my chest, and pushed. Lightning arced from his fingers and poured into my chest.

Pain shot through my body as the lightning threw me back. I landed six feet away, twisted up and feeling like I had been burnt alive.

Meg rose to his feet as I lay curled in a foetal position on the floor. I couldn't move. My whole body was on fire. There were fourth degree burns all over my chest. The lightning had ripped through flesh and bone and I sprawled, broken, as my limited healing factor tried to stitch me up.

'Soft-hearted as always,' he mocked. 'Willing to throw your life away on the chance that his daughter was alive?'

From my prone position, I could see Ahalya stirring. I would have called anyone who could help, but my body was refusing to listen to my brain. K had once told me that burns like this don't hurt since your nerve endings are also incinerated. He was clearly deluded. This hurt. A lot more than I could have possibly imagined.

Someone knelt beside me. I saw spots as my vision began to dim. This was it then.

I felt her breath, warm yet pleasant as it tickled my cheek, right next to my ear.

'You'll be okay, Akran,' she whispered. 'This is it. The right moment I was telling you about. The one that matters.' She pressed three fingers down on my face, and suddenly the intense heat was gone. I felt an ice-cold tingling where she had placed her fingers. The spots in front of my eyes began to recede.

'Thought you couldn't heal people,' I slurred as my vocal cords and brain reconnected.

She smiled but didn't answer. Slowly she rose to her feet, her eyes locked on Meg.

He hadn't moved an inch. There was sardonic amusement on his face as Tamara knelt beside me. He might have hoped she would shed a tear for my wounds.

Watching her rise to her feet, her eyes cold and unblinking, was not what he was expecting. He sneered as she walked towards him.

'You are his friend, the witch? I'm going to make him watch as I break you.'

There's a long-standing tradition of banter amongst primates before you engage in battle. Threats, insults, anatomical impossibilities—we trade them as we work up our courage to actually fight. Meg was certainly doing his part. For all his bluster, he wasn't used to facing somebody who didn't cower before him.

Either Tamara was unaware of our basic chest-thumping rituals before combat or she simply couldn't be bothered. To her, he was just another Andrew Tate wannabe with small dick energy. She walked forward, unafraid, swiftly closing the distance between them.

Blue fire gushed out of Meg's arm. I could feel sensation returning to my arms and legs, but I was still unable to do more than twitch and flop uselessly.

The fire had no effect on her. It rushed into her and, impossibly, seemed to get absorbed into her skin. Her body tinged blue for a few seconds before it faded away.

I saw Meg's jaw drop. Tamara closed the distance between them and grabbed his neck, chanting softly as she held him upright. Something about that picture looked wrong. He was a head and shoulders taller than her, and far more imposing and muscular. He should've been able to snap her like a twig. Somehow, with her hand on his neck, he looked helpless. His eyes rolled into the back of his head and his body slumped forward. One of his arms tried to grab her shoulder but there was no strength in it.

Ahalya was now sitting up. The blow to her temple hadn't knocked her out completely. Either she had turned her head in time, or Tamara hadn't struck her hard enough. She sat up, dazed, and looked around. Her eyes narrowed as she saw Tamara and Meg propped up together in an awkward pose. Like lovers embracing, except one of them was unconscious.

Blue fire poured out of Tamara's hand and into Meg's mouth, the same fire with which he had tried to immolate her. Meg's eyes snapped wide open. He tried to push her away, but he couldn't move. I watched him as he flailed helplessly, trying one moment to push her away, the next to pound on her with his fists. Nothing worked. He made a brief inarticulate scream as the inferno ate his insides. It looked like a painful way to die, but I couldn't think of anyone else on the planet who deserved it more than he did. I was willing to watch till the very end.

It didn't take too long to approach the end. When Tamara released him, Meg's body dissolved into smoke and ash. Nothing remained, not even a whisper of his existence. Which meant I had only one more crazy, psychotic killer to deal with.

Tamara slumped to the floor, and her eyes rolled into the back of her head. The strain of the ritual had taken its toll. I crawled up to her, reached out, and felt her pulse. It was still steady. The even, rhythmic heaving of her chest also told me she was alive.

My ears popped. Something had changed. It's impossible to describe in the context of five senses, but somewhere in the ether, a door had shut, and a steadily blowing draught had ceased.

Tamara had closed the rift.

I rose to my feet. It was all over. Indra Meghavana, a thorn in my side, and possibly the man who hated me the most across all realms, was dead. Something shifted within me. I could feel a cold, damp spot in the middle of my chest, expanding to fill my body. It was an odd sensation, like soaking in a hot tub after a long, hard day.

All that remained was to deal with his mad lover, and this would be behind us.

But nobody had told the mad lover that this was over. Ahalya got to her feet.

'You think you've won?' she spat. 'Watch now how your victory turns to ashes.'

I was too far away to stop what happened next.

Sars had propped K up next to one of the boxes in the warehouse and was holding up a couple of fingers for him. She still hadn't registered the threat behind her.

Clutching the ruby knife in one hand, Ahalya crossed the room in two long strides and reached Sars.

Time slowed down. A nameless dread filled me.

Ahalya seized Sars by her hair, and pulled her back by her head. Her hand went around her throat. A drop of blood blossomed where the red blade met Sars's skin.

'Ahalya, don't!' I screamed.

With a savage rictus of a smile, Ahalya slashed viciously at Sars's throat. Blood spurted like a fountain as Sars fell gasping to the floor. There was a look of vicious hatred on Ahalya's face.

My world turned red.

CHAPTER FOURTEEN

'If she lives, one of your closest friends will die while she watches. The fates are rarely clear about many things, but this is an absolute certainty.'
Duke Dulgath of the Fay as he urged us to kill Tamara
—The Private Journals of Akran

Rage engulfed me.

I was drowning in a white-hot fury that turned my mind completely blank except for one thought; kill the @#$%^ who killed my friend.

I had thought she was crazy when she said she would dance on the ashes of the world for revenge. And I got it now. I would split this world in half if it meant ending her existence.

Lightning poured out of my hands, shooting towards her, a tidal wave of raw, unconstrained energy, incinerating everything in its path.

It should have burnt her to a crisp, erased every trace of her existence so I would derive a measure of satisfaction that would fill the gaping void in the pit of my chest.

Except, somehow, it didn't. The lightning crackled and bent around her without so much as singeing her skin. The choker around her neck gleamed a bright red as my power bled and wasted around her.

'You think I didn't plan for this?' she taunted. 'I've been dreaming about my revenge for millennia, Yaksha. Centuries of penance and prayer have seeped into the stones.'

I was no longer starving for mana. Sars was right. Raw primal anger and hatred had burst the dam holding my powers back, and now they were flooding into me. I could feel it thrumming all around, in the air, in the sky and in the ground below my feet. I could feel the pulse of a flock of birds flying above us in the sky, life essence in the flowers, grass and trees all around, in the heartbeats of a million creatures burrowing under the soil. I could tap into it, all of it, and shove it down her throat. We would see if that damned necklace could defend against the atomic shitstorm I was going to bring down on her head.

Someone somewhere near me was shouting, but I couldn't hear what was being said. The ringing in my ears intensified. What I was attempting had never been done before. It would turn the city into a wasteland, but I would have my revenge. A fair trade. Ahalya's bloody corpse and all it would cost me was Sars, K …

And abruptly, it was gone. The rage was still there, but it no longer threatened to choke and overwhelm me. Like a bucket of ice-cold water had been poured into my veins.

I shut my eyes and counted to five. I could feel someone's hand on my arm.

'Akran,' K yelled. From the looks of it, he had been yelling for a while. Tears ran down his face. His clothes were splattered with Sars's blood, his face white from shock and pain.

'Whatever you are doing, you need to stop now!' He winced as if he was in physical agony.

I looked around and noticed the devastation my fury had wrought. The walls and roof of the room had collapsed. Nearly all the wood had turned into splinters and ash.

I had pulled mana from all around me. No exceptions, not even Celestials. It would've be lethal to K if I hadn't stopped.

'Your eyes were obsidian a moment ago,' K said. He choked back a sob. 'Akran … Sars is de—'

'I know,' I interrupted brusquely. Now was not the time to grieve. Now was the time for vengeance. To relish every moment of torment I would inflict on this person in front of me who had killed my friend. Grief was a private affair I could handle on my own.

What I felt for Ahalya now was very different from just a few minutes ago. That was unthinking rage. Wild and volcanic like the pits of Tartarus. This was a glacier of cold, unstoppable hate. Despite her planning, Tamara was able to hit her with a hammer. Her own amulet couldn't protect her against physical attacks. Maybe Ahalya's necklace worked on the same principle.

Something must have shown in my expression, for Ahalya took a wary step back. All the arrogance left her face, I saw a flicker of fear.

The time for mercy had passed.

The ground below us shook until a massive crack formed. I began to tear out huge chunks of the floor, each piece larger than the rest. The air vibrated with power as I felt every fragment in my mind. Concrete boulders rose from the ground and spread apart, encircling her.

Ahalya shrieked, throwing her hands up to protect herself. I spun the pieces around, gathering momentum, and orienting the most jagged edges towards her. One hit her side, hard enough to rupture her kidneys. Another tore into the back of her spine, while a third shattered her head like an eggshell.

Through my power, I felt each blow as it struck her. I felt her heartbeat, high and anxious, before it collapsed and her life ebbed out onto the floor right where she fell. There was nothing she could do to survive this. I revelled in the bloodlust that overtook me at that moment. This was what I was born for.

Killing her should have made me feel better.

It didn't.

There was an aching hollowness in my heart as I lowered my hands. Sars was more than just a friend to me. She and K were among the closest thing I had to a family. I couldn't bear the thought of seeing her lying there on the floor, but I owed it to her. I turned to look, my eyes stinging with tears.

Sars sat up. Alive. A great, bloody gash across her neck. A gash that had transformed from the gushing fountain a few minutes ago into an angry pink scar right across her neck.

Besides her sat the one person of whom I had been suspicious since the very start. The one I should never have taken my eyes off. For his being here confirmed that he had a hand in all this.

Still wearing that same ash-grey suit and with that same condescending smile, Narada waved at me. 'Hello, Akran. What a pleasant surprise meeting you here.'

CHAPTER FIFTEEN

Something has changed within me.
Something is not the same.
I'm tired of playing by the rules of someone else's game.
*　　　　—Elphaba to Gilda, Broadway Musical, Wicked.*

I know exactly what she meant. Fucking Narada!! @#$%^!!!!
^&()^%$$*

*　　　　　　—The Private Journals of Akran*

Maybe I should have been surprised.

But the sight of him only fuelled my rage. My already tenuous grip on my temper threatened to give way entirely. His being here suggested foreknowledge of how things would play out.

He seemed to sense what I was thinking, for he raised his palms in supplication. 'Peace, yaksha, I am not your enemy.'

'No? From where I am standing, it looks like you've been behind all of this from the beginning.'

He shook his head. 'Whatever you may think of me and my methods, we both know and worship the same supreme being. On my life, I give you my word, I had nothing to do with your friend's death.'

I looked at Sars. She nodded once, her eyes beseeching me to not start a fight.

'She won't be able to speak for a few days, and that scar is likely to take longer to heal, but overall, she is none the worse for wear.'

'Akran, he saved her life,' K said softly. He sat by her side, clutching her tightly around her shoulder as if she was a fragile piece of porcelain he was afraid to break. His cheeks were wet with tears.

'Like your friend over there, I too lack the ability to heal,' Narada said. 'But this is a trick I learned that should serve just as well.' He picked up a piece of stone from the debris on the floor, and it crumpled into dust. 'You may want to teach her how it is done.' He sighed. 'I suspect she has more trials coming her way.'

I remembered the first night when we met him in the club. Narada's power was time dilation. He could speed up or slow time down in a specific location. That's how he turned the stone to dust. And healed Sars neck. He had accelerated the speed of her healing abilities.

Slowly, I unclenched my fists and lowered my hands.

'I apologise for my behaviour, Rishi Narada,' I said stiffly. This apologies business was harder than I thought. 'Thank you for saving her life.'

He shrugged it away. 'I see you have finally ascended,' he commented.

I looked down. I was brimming with power, and I could feel it all around me. In my berserker rage, with a red film around my eyes, I hadn't stopped to question how I was suddenly able to access this power. Was watching Sars die the traumatic event I needed to unlock my powers?

Or was this Tamara's doing when she placed her fingers on me?

I had felt like this after my battle with Ashwatthama, but that euphoria had only lasted a week or so. Somehow, I knew this was different. This felt more primal and untamed. It wasn't merely about power.

'You did well this day, Yaksha,' Narada was saying. 'The war rages on, but at least for now, you have struck a grievous blow to our enemies. It may not be enough to turn the tide, but it will give them pause. That counts as a victory in my book.'

A grievous blow? Surely that was an exaggeration.

My confusion must have shown because Narada explained. 'While Ahalya harboured a special hatred for you, she blamed the system as well—sages, Celestials, etc. If left unchecked, she would've assassinated many more people over the next century.' He gave a wry smile. 'I too would have fallen by her blade.'

Narada had mentioned this shadow war as a long game stretching across millennia. How differently we were approaching this—he was thinking in terms of centuries while I couldn't recall what I had last eaten for breakfast.

Behind us, Tamara stirred. I saw her rise from her prone position, clutching her head.

Narada glanced at her.

'I would have greeted your friend, but I think she has absorbed enough abilities for one day.'

I could understand that. Tamara's set of powers was already terrifying. If she learned to manipulate time like Narada could, and then if she ever went to the dark side, so to speak, she might become unstoppable. Besides, Narada had centuries of practice to refine his powers. Tamara seemed to be learning new abilities and implementing them on the fly.

Or maybe he knew she was a 'wild spark' and wanted plausible deniability. He didn't want to 'out' her to the Celestial council. I wouldn't get myself all tied up in knots trying to figure out what was going through Narada's head.

Narada was still speaking. 'It was a wise move, bringing her in. It forced their hand. They didn't know how to deal with her powers.'

Was it clever of me? One of the cards I remembered from that night had an old woman held prisoner in a cell, and a young girl with her back to me, chatting earnestly with her. I couldn't be certain, but I was fairly sure that girl was Tamara. Was this something the cards showed me, or did Narada nudge me towards recalling her?

He had also hinted that I had done him a favour by eliminating Ahalya. How much of what had happened till date was because of him manipulating events in the shadows? Because he was using me as a cat's paw to get his dirty work done?

'A word of advice: while your friend was helpful this time around, it may not be advisable to lean on her too much. To quote a phrase you might be familiar with "when you stare into the abyss, sometimes, it stares right back".'

'Do you know something about her future that I don't?'

'I could show you a reading if you'd like,' Narada began but I was having none of that.

'No readings! No tricks, no answers that beat around the bush. For once, answer us clearly instead of speaking in riddles!'

He grinned. 'You think I'm choosing to let you walk down a twisted path instead of giving you a straight answer?'

I didn't deign to reply. His smile grew broader still.

'Here's the most fundamental truth about life, the universe and everything that's in it. The answer isn't forty-two, or something equally mundane. The truth is that there are no straight answers.'

I scowled at him and he relented. 'Very well, Yaksha, here's an answer that won't twist you up in knots. What do you know about avatars?'

'I know the nine avatars of Vishnu that have walked the earth and that the tenth, Kalki, is yet to come.'

'That's not what I mean. Forget about the avatars of Hinduism. What do you know about avatars in general? What traits do they possess?'

I did not know of any avatars outside of Hinduism. And this felt like he was already deviating from a straight answer.

'Indulge me for a little while longer then, Akran. You knew Krishna from when he was a little boy, didn't you? Tell me, as a child was he the same as when he was an adult? Full of purpose, completely certain of his abilities, eloquent and persuasive when he needed to be? Or did that come later?'

I thought about it for a moment. I was one of Krishna's Celestial guards since the time he was a baby. Growing up, he was a trickster, a lover, a hero and a ruler. He was wise beyond his years, yet also a schemer who would exploit a loophole if he ever saw one. He was a matchless warrior, and a kind and compassionate lover.

But as a child? Krishna was a precocious devil, full of mischief. He stole the clothes of the gopis when they went to bathe in the river. He was forever stealing butter from the household and sharing it with the other cowherds. He was a trickster, sly and cunning, he managed to manipulate each and everyone around him, wrapped them around his little finger. So, no, he was very different as a child than as an adult.

Narada answered his own question. 'An avatar, despite being the living embodiment of the deity he is from, does not retain his abilities or memories when he is born. In the beginning, he or she is purposeless. A carefully orchestrated chain of events need to take place that set the avatar on the path to fulfil his destiny.'

I could understand that. The Vanara Hanuman, often worshipped as a God in his own right, was an avatar of Lord Shiva of the Trinity. Despite his prowess he restricted himself to the kingdom of Kishkindhya until he met Ram. That was a transformative experience for him and he became a principal player in the events that followed, including finding Ram's abducted wife Sita, saving Lakshman from Indrajit's poisoned arrows, and slaughtering several demons in Ravana's army, including a few sons of Ravana.

'To ensure the avatar stays true to his path and isn't killed, or even worse, corrupted and turned before he comes into power, he or she needs guardians, protectors who look after the avatar. Setting things in motion, ensuring everyone is in the right place to help the avatar when he needs it, requires decades, sometimes centuries, of planning.

Krishna was born in the dungeons of the household of his maternal uncle who had sworn to kill him. Getting him out of there and to a safe home had required dozens of layered plots, some of which were setup months in advance. I had spent several years disguised as a boy about his age, befriending him and helping to keep him safe.

'As far as I remember, Krishna, even as a baby, was able to ward off several assassination attempts.' K observed. 'There was that demoness with poisoned breast milk, Putana, who Krishna at five days of age managed to kill by sucking the life out of her.'

'They still have their powers.' Narada replied. 'Not in their entirety, since the body they are born into cannot hold it all. It takes time for their bodies to adapt and be able to take on their due power. But even at a young age, they display abilities far more potent than anyone else around them.' He cast a meaningful glance at Tamara. 'To people around them, it might look like they have an incredible reality-bending field that leaves them unharmed.'

I should have put two and two together the moment he began rambling about avatars but I guess dealing with Meg and Ahalya had really taken it out of me.

'You are telling me she is an avatar?' I looked at Tamara. She was leaning against a wall, her eyes shut. In that moment, she looked as far removed from one as I could possibly imagine. She looked vulnerable.

'I'm telling you that is one possibility which explains how a child comes into this world bearing so much power. It's up to you to draw your own conclusions.'

None of the avatars in the Hindu mythos had been born outside the Indian subcontinent.

'She isn't one of ours, Narada,' I said with absolute certainty. 'Which means ...'

'Which means,' Narada interrupted, 'that entwining her too closely to your own life risks disrupting the purpose she was meant to serve, whatever it may be. You are used to having avatars on your side. What if her role is to prepare the path for others who come after? Being around her only makes you more vulnerable to her abilities. It makes you the strawman to absorb her enemies' arrows. Your life may become a footnote, a stepping stone in the path of a powerful avatar.'

There was a pause as we digested his words.

'All of this is assuming this is a benevolent God's avatar,' K said. 'Not all Gods are benign. There are plenty of malevolent ones out there too.'

That I knew all too well. Xipe Totec, known as 'the Flayed One'; Keres, Goddess of Plagues; the list was endless.

'They don't even need to be malevolent,' Narada said. 'Before you bring a God into your midst, you should ask yourselves if you are ready for what that entails.' His eyes flickered to Sars before resting on me. 'There are plenty of heroic tales about divine beings and their exploits. Not enough words are devoted to those whose only purpose is to die so that the hero has a suitable tragedy in their lives to inspire them.'

'But which God is she an avatar of?' I finally asked.

'We could ask her,' suggested K.

Narada shook his head. 'Since they don't retain their memories, the avatar also doesn't know the reason why the deity chose to be born on Earth. It is only later when they find their purpose that it will all make sense.'

'Maybe we could infer who she is by looking at her abilities?' I suggested.

Narada smiled. 'That brings me to the final characteristic of avatars. Like Aspects, they usually retain the abilities that the deity they belong to is known for. For instance, Valmiki and Vyas were both said to be avatars of Brahma, the God of creation and knowledge. Valmiki composed the Ramyana while Vyas wrote the Mahabharata.'

'I do not know of any Gods across any mythos in our Universe with the ability to mimic and absorb the powers of others,' I said.

Narada stood up. 'Then this would be an excellent time, Yaksha, for you to start reading up.' The three of us stood as well.

Surprisingly, I did not want him to leave. Not now, after he had started giving us answers.

'Why did you save Sars?' I asked.

'You were ready to burn down the world for her. I simply chose to save it instead. It seemed like the better alternative, dont you think?'

I shook my head. 'There's more to it than that and you know it. Last time we met, you said you did not want to use your powers. You spoke about how you would gladly sacrifice us—how victory required someone like you to be unnoticed.'

'Call me sentimental then,' he said, his smile still playing on his lips. 'Is that so hard to believe? That after meeting you all I decided I didn't want you to die?

'I asked for one bloody straight answer, Narada! You doing this risked everything—something you chose to berate me about. I want to know why you chose risking the other players. What changed?'

It seemed like he flinched at the accusation in my words. Something I had said had gotten through. He said nothing for a long moment.

'You are more human than you realise, Yaksha,' he said at last. 'Very well. Your straight answer, as you desired.'

He paused. 'All that we are doing here today is to preserve what makes us, us. Our free will. Our right to existence. Our humanity.

'It's easy when you've lived thousands of years to forget what that means. Even Gods can forget this. Especially Gods.'

'Yes, I could walk away, but at what cost? I would be throwing away everything that we are fighting for, by letting her die when I could prevent it. That's not what being human is.'

'Tell me,' he continued. 'What do we gain if winning costs us our souls? What life is worth living if we become the very monsters we sought to defeat?'

He gave me a sad smile … of what use is victory if our humanity is lost?

'A few days ago, I had brooded over how humans, in their zeal to persecute those different from them, often turned into monsters themselves. Ironic that I had been about to do the same thing.'

Maybe we weren't so different after all

'My use of my powers here may or may not get overlooked. It's a small case of the use of magic as compared to … well …'

He waved his hand. 'The results speak for themselves.'

There wasn't much I could say. To be honest, I was embarrassed. I had lost control and nearly killed K, possibly even Sars. In my anger, I might have turned the city into a wasteland. The city I had sworn to protect. It was a humbling thought that I was a lot more human than I gave myself credit for.

'Nevertheless. Thank you for saving Sars's life. I have misjudged you.'

He clapped me on my shoulder. 'It's like your friend said: maybe you aren't the hero of this story after all. Maybe your life's purpose is merely to protect someone else.' He cast a meaningful look at Sars who was trying to tell K something through her hands. 'Someone who will make a real difference in the shadow war.'

Wait, he was eavesdropping on us? And what did that mean? Was Sars …

Narada gave me a soul-searching look. Whatever he was looking for, he must have found, for he smiled again. I could have been reading too much into the curl of his lips, but this time around, his smile looked genuine.

'You have a long journey ahead of you, Akran. But you've also come a long way.'

Great. More trite observations.

'Keep your companions safe. I will not be around the next time.'

'Wait,' I asked as he turned to leave. He shot me a quizzical look.

'Before you go, the Elder Gods that Ahalya was blabbering about—are those the players you meant? Or were those just the ravings of a crazy woman?'

He smiled again. 'If you choose to not believe in the sun, does it make the sun any less real?'

A low involuntary growl rose from my throat. I was in no mood for this. Narada paid it no heed.

'You are now one of the few people who knows about this conflict. Anyone you choose to tell will be forced to take sides. It's not an easy decision to make, dragging others into this conflict.'

'You are saying this was real! There are Elder Gods, older than the Trinity, making their way back to our Universe. Yes or no?'

He smiled again as he raised his hand, palm facing outwards towards me. It was a symbol of blessing. And a dismissal. 'May you someday find all the answers you seek,' he said.

In other words, he was choosing to ignore my question and walk away. Fucking sages. Every one of them was a pain in the ass.

Then he was gone, and the three of us and Tamara were alone once more.

CHAPTER SIXTEEN

Valmiki's transformation from bandit to revered sage, quietly and without any fanfare, proved that career changes were possible even without announcing it to the world.

Those of you constantly shitposting on LinkedIn just to get yourselves noticed: Be like Valmiki!

—The Private Journals of Akran

Something awaited me at my doorstep a day later. A simple scroll with a blood-stained silver coin stuck to the centre using celestial wax. I recognised the flowery script on the inside which simply read Nahum 1:2–3.

I was unfamiliar with the reference, but that's why I had a room in my house filled with tomes that dealt with stuff like this. I found the verse and passage within a few minutes of searching.

'*The Lord takes vengeance on his foes and vents his wrath against his enemies. He is slow to anger but great in power; he will not leave the guilty unpunished.*'

Flowery words, but the message was clear.

It was a gauntlet being thrown.

The Celestial Host had just declared war.

CHAPTER SEVENTEEN

Okay, I think I finally get it.

The reason why prophecies get such a bad rep is because we have no timeline. Look too far into the future and everything fractures into a skein of possibilities—you only end up seeing one and it may not be the one that comes to pass.

But look at one too close to the present and that's almost certainly bound to happen. There are very limited possibilities.

Meeting Tamara meant someone had to die. Narada had to let it play out the way it was supposed to happen. The harder you fight a current, the more tired you get, until eventually it wins.

And so, he bid his time and then snatched her from the jaws of death, possibly fulfilling the conditions without severing the thread of fate.

At least I think he did. It could also be that he defied the fates and it will result in unexpected consequences.

I'm just going to add it as another problem to be fixed somewhere down the road.

—The Private Journals of Akran

Six Weeks Later, United Coffee House, Delhi

I sat there, waiting for the first of my two meetings of the day, neither of which I was particularly enthused about. It was 5:30 p.m., and I was early, so I couldn't complain.

Tamara was back in Haiti. She had swapped bodies immediately after the ritual and we had to deal with a very confused aspiring actress with singed eyebrows who couldn't remember the last two days of her life.

Sars had recovered though the angry red scar on her neck remained. K had decided he did not want to leave Mumbai, so I was in Delhi alone.

Much as I disliked leaving Mumbai, it was the right decision.

There was no point trying to explain that her visit was a one-off. Tamara's body swapping had gone completely unnoticed, right until my actions had literally sent a beacon to the heavens. The whole incident had embarrassed the Celestial host. They were now convinced she and I had been colluding all along in some conspiracy right under their noses, and laughing at them.

Micah was in exile, having fallen out of favour somehow. Uriah and three dozen of the Celestial host were scouring through the city, looking for me even now. I had been tempted to stay behind and trade blows, but Sars wouldn't let me start another battle. I was going to be far more useful here while I learned how to control my powers.

The city annoyed me. It was hot and noisy, and the people were … angrier. People in Mumbai were indifferent, too absorbed in their own lives and problems. Here, everyone had an opinion and was keen to express it. With their fists, if not by yelling. I couldn't imagine living here without losing my temper.

Still, the food was pretty good. I had ordered the Railway Mutton and the Darjeeling Pork and both were mind-bogglingly good. I was just done with my meal when my first appointment walked in.

He was dressed like me in jeans and a t-shirt. He had no tattoos, piercings, or any jewellery except a simple gold chain around his neck. He sat down in front of me and smiled politely as he ordered a drink for himself.

I watched him in silence. He had well-manicured hands and a genial smile. He spoke courteously to the waiter and chose to skip the meal, going straight for the dessert: a dish called the Atomic Kala Jamun that was the size of a baby's head.

Maybe he thought we were going to bond over our choice of dessert. It certainly looked too big to finish all by himself.

The silence stretched between us like a yoga instructor with something to prove.

It was only after I finished my food and pushed the plate away that he cleared his throat.

'Thank you for agreeing to meet, Akran.'

I shrugged. This meeting had been forced upon us by the Celestial Council. Our feud was dangerously close to breaking the First Law, and the Council's top henchman had personally visited me and told me in no uncertain terms that we needed to find a way to talk things over before blood got spilt in the streets.

'We made a mistake taking up that contract on you. Please understand it was not personal.'

Was he the original? He certainly carried himself in a more regal manner, with his stately poise and affectations of sincerity.

'You tried to kill me. As far as I'm concerned, that makes it very personal to me.'

He nodded. 'I understand, which is why I am hoping we can talk things over and find a way to cease hostilities.'

After the event at the warehouse, a lightning strike destroyed the RB chapter house in Mumbai. Then for good measure, I visited three more Indian cities and torched each of their holdings there. They may have had deep pockets, but I could destroy their hideouts faster than they could rebuild.

Raktabija handed me a blue manila folder. 'This is what we wish to offer in compensation. Full reimbursement for all your safehouses that were destroyed. Adequate compensation for the families and victims of anyone hurt in targeting those buildings. The entire fee that we were paid will be given to a charity of your choice.' He looked me squarely in the eye. 'In return, you will stop attacking our organisation, and we will promise to stay away from your affairs.'

It was a good offer. Better than I had expected, actually.

'This works.' My voice took on an edge as I added, 'for starters.'

If he was surprised, he hid it well. 'What do you propose?'

'If anyone approaches you with a contract on my friends or me in the future, you will let us know. Immediately. No exceptions.'

He nodded. 'I've already put the word out that you and your friends are off-limits. I doubt anyone will approach us, but if they do, you will be informed. This will cost us in terms of credibility and clientele, but your request is reasonable, and we will accommodate it.'

'Second,' I said, ignoring his little speech. 'I may need your services in the near future. I would expect you to be willing to take us on standard client rates.'

He smiled, showing pearly white teeth. 'What would the protector of Mumbai need with a lowly demon such as myself?'

This had been Sars's idea. Ahalya's rant and Narada's cryptic comments had lead us to believe that worse was coming. Elder Gods. More assassins. Having a paramilitary outfit that I could call on might be useful in the future.

Sars nearly dying had left me raw. It was taking a lot of self-control for me to not unleash a thunderstorm right here and now, and damn the consequences.

His smile disappeared. Perhaps he sensed how close I was to responding with violence. 'Your money is as good as anyone else's.'

I pushed my seat back. 'Then we have an agreement.' We shook hands and I held on longer than he must've expected. 'There's one more thing, Raktabija.'

Still holding his hand, I leaned forward and whispered, 'You may have gotten away lightly this time. It's not going to happen again. Try to pull something like this again, and you'll see just how much of a shitstorm we can raise.'

Raktabija's face hardened at my tone. 'You torched four of my businesses. I have compensated you for the attacks on your properties. How exactly do you think I've gotten away lightly?'

'Cry me a fucking river. If it wasn't for the Celestial Court intervening, I would have dedicated the rest of my life to wiping out every trace of you from this planet.'

I saw a brief flash of fear cross his face. 'Are you going to renege on our agreement, then?'

'I will honour our agreement, demon, because I am known for keeping my word. But here's one more promise I make. If you indulge in any illegal activities in my city, then First Law or not, I will exterminate you. Are we clear?'

He blanched. 'We are clear, Akran,' he said haltingly as he disengaged his arm gently from my grip. 'Thank you,' and walked away, looking shaken.

On some fundamental level, my relationship with other Celestials had changed. It was not like I had simply regained my powers like last time. In addition to my own, Meg's powers had somehow transferred to me. I could sense wind currents, feel the most minute changes in temperature, and call rain and hail with a flick of my hands. I had a whole new set of powers, and it would take weeks to figure them all out.

Quite simply, I was at this moment, several orders of magnitude more powerful than I was before ascending.

Which would not make any difference in my next meeting.

The man who walked in was nearly seven feet tall. He was dressed in a long sleeved t-shirt and had a giant battle axe strapped to his back.

Enough to create a scene, even in a city like Delhi. But except for a couple of curious glances, most people simply ignored him and continued with their meals.

Parashuram placed the axe on the table, next to me. 'The axe is visible only to those I wish should see it,' he said by way of explanation.

Figures. Then again, it was Delhi. I wouldn't have been surprised if people could see the axe and were just humouring him.

I had heard stories about that weapon. According to legend, it had shed enough blood to fill five enormous lakes. A soft whisper emanated from deep within. Something about it made the hair on my arms stand on end.

'Pick me up, Pick me up, Pick me up,' it chanted.

'Stop that,' said Parashuram sharply. I froze. My hand was halfway towards the axe, and I had no idea how it had got there. Guiltily, I slipped my hand back below the table.

It turned out he wasn't speaking to me after all. He was speaking to the axe. With a final low murmur, the axe went quiet.

Parashuram drummed his fingers on the side of the table, looking lost in thought.

'Hard day at work?' I ventured politely.

His cool blue eyes turned to me.

When dealing with Celestials who can crush you like a gnat, it's wise to be silent. Despite my ascension, Parashuram could exterminate me without much difficulty. He was the sixth avatar of Vishnu, but unlike the other avatars, he had chosen to stay behind on Earth to defend against evil whenever he was called. He was not one to waste time on pleasantries.

'It's recently gotten better,' he answered.

'It has?' I enquired brightly, with an enthusiasm I didn't feel.

'I've spent the last three centuries hunting down a cult of demon-worshipping fanatics. They always managed to stay one step ahead. For every solid lead that worked out, there were a dozen or more false paths.'

'A cult? Isn't that a little below your pay grade?'

He frowned. 'I don't get paid for this. I do it because it is necessary.'

Gods! It was like talking to Sheldon Cooper. Besides, a cult is just a religion that hasn't gone mainstream yet. It doesn't mean it's not worth paying attention to.

'Right, absolutely, I'm with you there.'

'And they already have thousands of followers, so it's closer to organised religion than you might suspect.'

I regretted asking him how his day was already.

I gave a polite smile and a nod to show how interesting his problems were. He didn't seem to care either way.

'Their high priestess was like a ghost; here one moment, gone the next. It was like chasing shadows. Except these shadows could kill you if you weren't careful.'

I couldn't begin to imagine what could kill Parashuram, so I made the appropriate tutting noises. Knowing him, if I opened my mouth, he would seize that as another conversation topic and natter on for another thirty minutes.

'I had given up hope on ever rooting them out until a few weeks ago.'

Thank the Gods! This story looked like it was nearing an end!

'What happened?' I asked, feigning interest.

'Apparently, she hated one Yaksha so much she was willing to step out of the shadows to have him killed.'

Aah, right. The story had a point after all.

'Ahalya is dead, and I owe you a debt of thanks.'

He gave me a look that I could imagine was him trying to smile, but it just made my blood freeze. His features weren't exactly conducive to smiling.

'I have been at this a long time, Akran. My work isn't done, and I don't imagine it will be for another thousand years or so.'

This conversation felt like it had been going on for a thousand years already.

He paused. 'It occurred to me that if I could train a disciple who could carry on the fight after I'm gone, it might not be a bad thing.'

Holy shit! He wanted me to be his disciple.

Parashuram had taken on three disciples before the Great War. All three had gone on to become legends. They were:

1. The grandsire of the Kuru Dynasty—Bhishma, son of Ganga. He was considered unbeatable but was defeated on the tenth day of the war by trickery. Arjun challenged him to a duel and hid behind Shikhandi. Since Bhishma had sworn never to fight a woman, he refused to fight back and was vanquished.

2. Dronacharya, father of Ashwatthama and teacher of the Pandavas and the Kauravas. He was defeated only because he lost heart, thinking his son was dead, and lay down his weapons.

3. And finally, Kunti's oldest son who fought on the side of Duryodhan, Karna. He was defeated because Parashuram cursed him to forget all that he had learnt at a crucial point in his life. Also because he got out of his chariot to fix its wheel, trusting that Arjun wouldn't shoot him while he did so.

All three of Parashuram's disciples were matchless warriors. Legends who were immortalised in myth and worship.

And now I was being invited to go fourth.

There was a sense of gravitas about this moment. Maybe all of Parashuram's disciples were fated to die in ignoble ways. Accepting this offer might set me on a path that they remembered me fondly for, at least for a while, before finding myself lying face down in a shallow ditch.

Parashuram was still speaking. 'I enjoy the thrill of the fight, Akran, but not the hunt. The more time I spend seeking them, the more they indulge in grisly rituals. Human sacrifice, tantric enslavement, all of it. I wish to put an end to them. Together we could crush this cult before it rises to seriously threaten the world.'

I chose my words carefully. 'I am honoured that you even considered me. May I ask why you thought I would serve as a suitable candidate?'

'Because frankly, Yaksha, you are the most annoying Celestial I have ever met.' He said it without rancour, like he was telling me about a piece of gunk he had pulled off his shoe. 'You are rude, obnoxious, short-tempered and possibly even a little off in the head. You were given charge of the sacred weapons, and you lost them. You were tasked with keeping Krishna safe, and you let him get shot.'

I should never have asked.

'You have a list of enemies that's a mile long, yet you walk around in broad daylight announcing you are the protector of Mumbai.' He shook his head. 'I can't imagine how you've survived so long.'

This was getting embarrassing.

'Ahalya knew I was hunting her. The fact that she chose to come out of hiding to get a crack at you should tell you how much hate you are able to stir up.'

'You are right,' I said politely. 'I'm an embarrassment, I get it! There's no point in beating a dead horse.'

Parashuram's face softened. 'You misunderstand me, Yaksha. What I am trying to say is that somehow you seem to fall upwards. No matter how dire the situation or how completely out of depth you are, pit against overwhelming odds, you come out better and stronger than before. Twice now, you've found yourself battling forces beyond your ken, and each time, on the verge of defeat, your powers come back. Does that seem like a coincidence?'

When you looked at it from that angle, it did seem awfully convenient. I hadn't read too much into my powers coming back the first time since there was a magical gem involved, the Syamantaka, which could supposedly 'clear one's mind'. I also didn't read too much into the re-emergence of my powers because ascension is a pretty rare event. Nobody really knows what it entails, except … It's like one day, you are an unknown actor getting his eyes gouged out in the most painful way on television, and the next you are nicknamed the Internet's daddy and fighting on-screen enemies ranging from drug lords to aliens and fungi zombies.'

'The first time it happened,' I said slowly, 'there was a magic jewel involved. This time …'

Parashuram smiled indulgently. 'You are too old to believe those fairy tales, my boy. You know what has happened … you are just denying it.'

***

I thought there were perfectly rational explanations in both cases. But now? I wasn't so sure anymore.

'Some God watches over you, Akran! There can be no other explanation for someone like you still being alive.'

'Parashuram, please. I know this may be hard, but you really shouldn't spare my feelings. Stop beating around the bush and tell me what you really think of me!'

He frowned. I had a feeling my sarcasm had flown right past his very tall head.

'You defeated Ashwatthama, Ahalya and Indra.' He chuckled. 'From what I heard, you also gave Durvasa a massive fright. It was time someone took him down a peg.' He sobered. 'Nobody is going to believe this bumbling clown routine anymore. You have got to stop hiding and take your place in the light! You will be the distraction while the real hunters use the cover of darkness.' He sniffed. 'With your current skills, it is a worthy role for you. I had hoped you could have done better, but each to his own abilities.'

Okay, I knew what he was doing. He was applying reverse psychology to goad me. Even worse, it was working.

'You are saying I am a pawn,' I said slowly. Being cast in one role after the next by invisible players pulling my strings. All the while, blissfully unaware of what was happening in the wider game while I kept limping on ahead.

Just like Narada described.

To his credit, Parashuram didn't try to deny it.

'Every pawn has a role to play, Akran. With proper planning, you can take over the board.' He leaned closer as if confiding a great secret. 'You aren't just a pawn, though. Look at the two of us sitting here. Has it occurred to you that I could kill you with just a thought?'

Occurred to me? I never stopped thinking about it!

'Yet, is your behaviour deferential? Or grovelling even? No! You hold yourself up. You have looked me straight in the eyes without flinching. You even act like a damned fool and try to touch my axe.'

That last one, I couldn't help, but it was impossible to get a word in edgeways.

'You've got a spine, Akran! I respect that. All my disciples have grit. There's a fire within them that burns bright. They are forged in iron and blood.'

Okay, I was feeling better about myself.

'When I met Narada …'

I knew it. Fucking Narada!

'… he told me that despite everything, you might be the missing ingredient we need to root out these cultists once and for all.'

'This cult you are speaking about. Ahalya described them as worshipping Elder Gods, a group older than the Trinity who first walked this Earth several millennia ago.'

He waved his hand dismissively. 'Elder Gods, demons, it doesn't matter. There is nothing that came before the Trinity. I will deal with these cultists and whoever they worship the way I've always done.' He caressed the blade of his weapon lovingly. 'With my axe!'

His single-minded belief, this black-and-white world of absolutes he lived in, was … admirable …

'What do you need me to do?'

'I am going to train you. Let me tell you now, it will be the most brutal regimen you have ever undertaken. When I pronounce you ready, you can go back to doing whatever it is you do on a regular basis. We will let them know that you killed their priestess. That you are the single greatest impediment standing in their way. Your death will allow them to bring their masters back into this world.'

So basically, bait. He wanted to dangle me like a carrot and hope someone would bite.

Not the most ideal of scenarios.

And yet.

I would be lying if I said the thought didn't excite me. A chance to unleash these new powers, fight the good fight again. More importantly, it would give me some much-needed space from everyone else. I couldn't look at Sars without feeling guilty. She didn't hold it against me, but I blamed myself.

Then there was K. It was my plan for K to walk in with me, despite knowing fully well that Lyla might be plotting something. If she had hit a little harder, I would have lost my best friend forever.

K didn't blame me either. He was doing what fertility Gods did best—hanging out at singles bars and celebrating life two women at a time.

And then there was me. A Yaksha, born and bred for war, in a densely populated city, living a shadow of my former life.

I had the closest friends I could ever hope to have. In every way that mattered, I should've been content.

But I wasn't. There was a restless yearning in me that could not be sated by a life of passivity.

Going after this elder Gods' cult could be exactly what I needed.

'I will not repeat myself, Yaksha. Either you are in, or I walk away now, and this offer is forever rescinded. Will you join me?'

'I am in,' I said. 'Let's finish these bastards once and for all.'

EPILOGUE

Somewhere Else.

The Dread Queen stirred. Her tentacles writhed, slick with ichor, each tipped with a staring eye that wept black tears as she schemed.

There was a feeling deep within her. The thoughts and emotions of an Elder God were too far removed from human language and comprehension. The closest you come to understanding the welling of emotion in her breast would be frustration. Alien and vast and intermingled with rage but deeper.

She had nearly breached the Earth. Her acolytes whispered promises of her return, their rituals thick with blood. Yet she remained trapped in this realm of shadows and darkness, hungry for the taste of living flesh. The mortals they sent—shivering, broken souls—only teased her hunger.

Something had gone awry. Something small and insignificant had managed to thwart her schemes.

She had been planning this for millennia, waiting was not new to her. That which was hidden would soon come to light.

For now, she would study this tiny, pathetic creature, this fleeting gnat that had thwarted her plans. She would unravel its soul.

'Yakshaaaaa,' she hissed in the darkness.

THE END FOR NOW

AUTHOR'S NOTES

In May this year, I was at *Shakespeare in the Park*, a performance put up annually by the Singapore Repository Theatre. It's a fun thing to attend if you bring a picnic basket and enjoy listening to dialogues like 'Wouldst thou wert clean enough to be spat upon' and 'Thou art as fat as butter' being delivered in all earnestness.

In front of me in the queue were two young Gen Z women.

Person #1—So, what's this play about?

Her companion—I think he kills his wife. All his plays are like that!

That, to me, in its own odd way, reminds me of Indian mythological stories. There are a ton of really cool ones out there, but most people are as aware of them as these two young women discussing Macbeth.

One of my goals while writing this series was to bring some of those stories to life—not retell the most popular ones, which is what usually happens, but instead approach them from a different perspective. That's how Akran's adventures came into being—a foul-mouthed, world weary yaksha who happens to have lived in the time of the epics and can provide his own unique perspective on events from then with a more contemporary sardonic viewpoint.

So there you have it. Book 2 of the Celestial Chronicles.

It's been an interesting journey till date. I took a break from working with a tech start-up in Jan 2022 to write the novel that was brewing in my head. I had two stories running in parallel, both involving Akran and K, and I couldn't write one without constantly thinking of the other. So, I wrote them both at the same time. A thousand words a day on *A Necessary Evil* and another thousand words or so for *Shadows Revealed*.

Altogether, this has taken six months to write and another two to edit. It would have finished sooner if it wasn't for my kids having school holidays for a month and me rediscovering *XCOM 2: War of the Chosen* which took up three weeks of my time to replay.

One of my biggest concerns, as far as writing Akran goes, is about how fond of profanity he is. As I write about his adventures, the curses flow naturally from his lips—or, if you want to get metaphysical about it, from my fingers as I type on the keyboard. However, readers don't seem to care and frankly, neither does Akran.

In case you are feeling like Tamara deserves more of a backstory or that her presence is like bringing a gun to a knife fight, then yes I agree with you. Tamara is an important character in the larger mythos. The book I wrote in parallel to this one, titled *A Necessary Evil*, has six short stories about individual characters such as a ghost, a dreamwalker, a voodoo priestess, and a Tibetan monk among others and an MCU Avengers Event where they all meet. The story is set in London and deals with antagonists from Irish mythology.

Due to the way things work in the real world, I was forced to choose which book to publish right after Shadows

Rising (I had a two-book contract) and so I've opted for this one—not everyone is familiar or interested in the Tuatha Dé Danann, but most people in India have more than a passing knowledge of the Ramayana. It was a hard decision but I ensured that there was no pertinent information missing in this. If this does well, I am hopeful that *A Necessary Evil* will get published and you get to enjoy that particular story of how Akran makes a new bunch of enemies and earns Tamara's loyalty.

Sars came *this* close to dying (imagine I'm holding two fingers a millimetre apart). However, her story isn't done and killing her too early would just make her another example of the 'women in refrigerators' literary trope. I've mentioned before how Sars and Kama are both my favourite characters. With Akran away in Delhi for a little while, Book 3 is very much about Kama and Sars. And without giving anything away, the ending of that one has massive ramifications across the Yakshaverse.

I don't usually have a clear plan at the start as to how the story will end. Narada started off as a random whimsical character I chose to add in and he became an integral part of the story. From what I've read, he really is a shit-stirrer.

Around the fifty-thousand-word mark, I started researching Elder Gods (in the X-Com game series, the alien overlords are called Elders.) I found a six-book series by Will Wight about Elder Gods which I really enjoyed. And Zamil Akhtar wrote a fabulous Eldritch God horror/fantasy series that I read right after this that I highly recommend. If you liked this book, you may want to give those a try, though Will Wight's books have pirates and ninjas and Zamil's have a more Arabic fantasy vibe.

Thank you for reading and I look forward to writing the next instalment soon.

Rohan Monteiro

NOTES AND REFERENCES
TO THE MYTHOS

When I finished writing Book 1, I knew right then that I wanted to write another story—this one touching upon the Ramayana. At that time, there was no unifying plot for the series—it was a stand-alone adventure of the Yaksha and his companions. I was about 70 per cent into this story when the idea struck me about the larger overarching series and how this would play out.

But before we get to that, let's look at why I wanted to talk about the Ramayana.

The key difference between the Ramayana and the Mahabharata is that they show two very different facets of human behaviour. All the characters in the Mahabharata are grey—good people commit dark deeds, and the bad guys look less reprehensible than how they are painted. Krishna, the Vishnu avatar, was open to achieving his goals through trickery—be it making Jayadratha think the sun had set or getting Bhim to break the laws of mace fighting. He played a role in the defeat of every one of the Kaurava commanders.

The Ramayana, on the other hand, does exactly the opposite. It strives to show us the standard you should live up to. Ram exemplifies the pinnacle of human perfection

(Purushottama), embodying all the virtues that one would aspire to possess. His impeccable moral character is reflected in the way he fulfils all his moral obligations (Maryada). The Ramayana literally translates to 'Ram's journey'—the path that is followed by Prince Ram when confronted with adversity so that his choices and actions can be held up as a shining example to the world at large of how one should behave in times of strife. It is an easy story to love. And millions of people in India believe whole heartedly in this tale.

There's only one tiny problem. There are people who believe in it so much they obsess over it to the point that they feel the need to force others to venerate Ram as well.[1]

Epics often explore dharma (duty, righteousness) in all its ambiguity. Ram isn't a flawless figure—he's the 'ideal man', but not the 'perfect man'. The story tests how ideals function in a messy world. These events aren't endorsements—they highlight how dharma can conflict with compassion or personal morality.

Akrans's POV on the Ramayan is not unique. Several other writers before me have expressed similar thoughts and critiques of the original story by Valmiki. While there are quite a number to list; *Sita Sings the Blues* is one example that you might find and watch on YouTube.

On the other side of the equation, Ravana isn't characterised as an evil king with no redeeming qualities. He is a brahmin, a faithful devotee of Shiva, a loyal brother, and a capable king and administrator. He was well versed in the Shastras and the Vedas. The Shiva Tandava Stotra, a

---

[1] https://clarionindia.net/jai-shri-ram-has-become-a-murderous-chant-to-kill-muslims/

devotional prayer in praise of Shiva, is traditionally attributed to Ravana. There are multiple temples in India that venerate Ravana because of these very qualities.

The village of Bisrakh Jalalpur in Uttar Pradesh (supposedly the birthplace of Ravana) treats Dusshera (the traditional celebration across India of Ram's victory over Ravana) as a day of mourning. Ultimately, though, his lineage and talents don't matter. His deeds, i.e., abducting Sita, leads to his downfall.

I've not indicated at any point what was Akran's role during the Ramayana. It's something that will get addressed later. Suffice to say he plays an important role.

Two different sets of sons of three Gods—Indra, Surya, and Vayu—are seen in both the Ramayana and the Mahabharata. In the Ramayana, Hanuman is the son of Vayu (Wind), Sugriva is the son of Surya (Sun), and Vali is the son of Indra. In the Mahabharata, Bhim, Karna and Arjun, respectively, are the sons of Vayu, Surya and Indra.

If we believe both the Indian epics are mythological events, we would trust the elongated timelines of centuries between one event and the other. This would explain the improbably long ages of sages like Durvasa, who meets Ram and Lakshman at the end of the Ramayana, then meets Shakuntala, who exists several generations before the Pandavas, then gives Kunti the magic hymn to beget children from the Gods and is seen after the war at Dwarka, cursing Samba and triggering the end of the Yadava race.

On another note, the Kingdom of Ram is said to have lasted eleven thousand years—a golden age of peace and prosperity.

If we regard them as historical events (with human lifespans involved), the appearance of several characters in both epics would indicate that they occurred much more closely than commonly believed. I had written in Book 1 how the commonly held belief was that a day in heaven was equal to a year on earth. Divide eleven thousand years by three hundred and sixty-five and you get a more likely timeline of thirty years of Ram's reign.

Consider the following:

- The Bear King Jambavan assisted Ram in the war against Ravana. He also fought Krishna for the Syamantaka Jewel.
- Hanuman fights in the war against Ravana and later embraces Bhim while the Pandavas are in exile.
- Mayasura is Ravana's father-in-law and built the magnificent palace of Indraprastha for the Pandavas.
- Rishi Bharadwaj gave refuge to Ram and Sita while they were in exile. He is also the father of Dronacharya and the grandfather of Ashwatthama.
- Parashurama appears in the Ramayana challenging Ram to string the Bow of Vishnu (this is right after the Swayamvar of Sita, where he breaks the Bow of Shiva to win her hand). He also appears in the Mahabharata, having trained Drona, Bhishma and Karna in the use of weapons.
- Rishi Agastya gives Drona the gift of the Brahmastra, the most powerful divine Celestial weapon. He also offers Ram a divine bow and arrow and describes the evil nature of Ravana.

- Vibhishana, brother of Ravana and king after his death, met Yudhishthir during his coronation (Rajasuya Yagna).

Think of the oral recollections that make up epic poems as a giant game of 'Chinese whispers' through the centuries—every storyteller along the way adds their own twist to the tale, bringing in popular characters from one epic into the next. Both epics have had significant revision along the way, so much so that the Bala Kanda (Ram's birth) and the Uttara Kanda (Epilogue) are believed by some scholars to have been added much later and not by Valmiki, since the style and composition is very different.[2]

But I digress. Let me address the specific elements within the story.

Ch 2: K's cryptic phrase here is a reference to Robert E. Howards' *Kull* story titled *The Shadow Kingdom*. The characters in that book are snake-men, not lizard-men, but since nagas are present in Indian myths, he just got confused.

Interlude: The entire Interlude with Micah and the other angels was added after a couple of reviews on Amazon mentioned how interesting it was to see the other religions also being depicted instead of keeping this as a bubble. One of the ideas I'm playing around with in my head at the moment is a duology about Micah and some of the threats he needs to deal with. Maybe he's in charge of the souls from

---

[2] https://scroll.in/article/820198/why-the-uttara-kanda-changes-the-way-the-ramayana-should-be-read

the subcontinent, which explains his presence here. It's still a very rough sketch I would love to experiment with. Given that Judeo-Christian angels are typically described with wings of fire, cloaked in the armour of light and righteousness, carrying flaming swords and speaking in terrible voices that can lead to madness—they felt like an interesting enemy to introduce. Maybe there's a place for them in the future of the series.

It is interesting that three of the world's largest monotheistic religions all originated within a thousand square miles of each other (Mount Sinai, the Judaean desert (Israel) and the Cave of Hira). There are also the other coincidences that Akran mentions, such as them being weak with hunger and thirst at the time.

Benny Shanon, an Israeli professor of cognitive philosophy, first proposed a theory in 2008 that the burning bush in the Bible was a hallucination. This is more popularly known as the Biblical entheogen hypothesis.

The use of cannabis, specifically at the Tel Arad shrine, also indicates that hallucinogens were used at the time.[3]

Chapter 4.1: There are three key visions that the cards show Akran.

A blue-skinned warrior fired an arrow that penetrated three shining mounds in the sky that I knew were somehow meant to be cities.

---

[3] https://abcnews.go.com/Health/story?id=4392361&page=1#:~:text=The%20description%20in%20The%20Book,fueled%20hallucination%2C%20according%20to%20Shanon.

https://www.smithsonianmag.com/smart-news/cannabis-found-altar-ancient-israeli-shrine-180975016/

A short story I wrote, which remains unpublished, is about a girl in a post-apocalyptic future who sees visions. One of those visions is exactly the description above, except the blue-skinned warrior turns and smiles at her.

The warrior is Shiva and that scene is from the story of the mythical three cities of Tripura.

Tripura was a collection of three mythical cities created by Mayasura. The cities belonged to the sons of Tarakasura (refer to the opening of chapter ten for who Tarakasura was). The boon they had received from Brahma was that the cities could only be destroyed by a single arrow fired at all three cities together. As the cities were floating and constantly moving, they would only be aligned once every thousand years for a few moments. At the request of the Devas, Shiva shot the arrow that destroyed the three cities.

Why the blue skin?

Shiva, Vishnu, Ram and Krishna have traditionally been depicted as having blue skin.

Amar Chitra Katha, India's most popular comic book publisher and a ready reckoner for all things mythological, always portrayed these four in blue.

There are multiple theories as to why artists and illustrators depicted them this way. A likely explanation in a country obsessed with fairness is that dusky or dark-coloured skin was portrayed as blue. In 2009, the 'Dark is Beautiful' campaign was launched in India to draw attention to skin colour bias. In 2018, a Facebook photo series called 'Dark is Divine' showed all of these Hindu Gods (traditionally depicted in blue) in dark/dusky skin tones, which is visually quite stunning.[4]

---

[4] https://scroll.in/magazine/863825/dark-is-divine-a-photographer-is-using-his-camera-to-challenge-indias-obsession-with-fairness

Additionally, Shiva is depicted with a blue throat because he swallowed the Halahala poison that emerged while churning the ocean. He is thus known as Neelkanth (the one with a blue throat). A statue at the Bangkok International Airport depicts this scene.

'A half-man, half-lion burst forth from a pillar.'

The second vision is that of Narsimha, the fourth avatar of Vishnu. The demon Hiranyakashipu, the father of Prahalad, had received a boon that he could not be killed by man, beast, God or Asura, during night or day, indoors or outdoors. Vishnu emerged from a pillar as a half-man, half-lion, dragged him to the threshold of his house, which was neither inside nor outside, and ate him at twilight.

A young woman stepped into a massive pyre as all around her, monkeys armed with weapons wailed and screamed.

This is the 'purity test' that Sita underwent after her rescue. Sita entered a pyre, saying that if she had remained faithful to Ram throughout all the time they were separated, may she emerge unscathed from the flames. Spoiler Alert: She was unharmed.

Ch 4.2 – Most Greek Heroes had tragic endings. Jason of the golden fleece—died lonely and unhappy when the rotting mast of the Argo fell on his head. Hercules went mad and killed his family. Perseus, who slew Medusa, eventually looked at her head and died. Theseus of Minotaur fame? Thrown off a cliff. Bellerophon, who captured Pegasus? Fell off his flying horse into a thorn bush and lived in misery till he died. Most of the Heroes of the Iliad also suffered ignoble deaths, including Agamemnon (killed by his wife), Ajax the Greater (madness and suicide), Ajax the lesser (drowned by Poseidon), etc.

Chapter 5 – The world's first known record of compound interest appears on a Sumerian clay tablet known as the Enmetena Foundation Cone, dated to around 2400 BCE, from the city-state of Lagash in Mesopotamia. The tablet records that the city-state of Umma borrowed 1 gur (300 litres) of barley from Lagash. The debt, unpaid for years, was calculated with interest—and the final amount after 7 years owed had grown to 4.5 gurs, which matches the formula for compound interest.[5]

The point I'm making? If you are a Celestial living on earth, you should definitely be rich.

Ch 6.0 – The Ashvamedha yagna is a weird one by modern standards because after the horse was sacrificed, the queen or a female member of the royal family was expected to lie with the corpse of the horse. I don't mean lie as in chastely without the naughty bits touching—it was a fertility ritual, so the horse's penis was 'coaxed', though it was dead. More details can be found here.[6]

Ch 6.1 – Parikshit's son Janamejaya decided to conduct a yagna to destroy all snakes. In Book 1 of the Yaksha chronicles, I narrated the story of Uttanka, a sage who was forced to go into the underworld to recover the earrings that were stolen by Takshaka. Uttanka had his own grudge to settle, and he was one of the main sages at the yagna. Fearing for his life, Takshaka ran to Indra for help. Indra told Takshaka to coil

---

[5] https://www.bbc.com/news/business-39870485

[6] https://vedkabhed.com/index.php/2018/05/14/ashvamedha-yajna-the-obscene-ritual/

himself around the royal throne of heaven. However, as the yagna intensified, the throne itself started getting pulled from heaven and towards the sacrificial fires. Seeing this, Indra jumped off the throne. Finally, the yagna was stopped through the intervention of a young rishi named Astika. That day is celebrated in India today as Nag Panchami.

Ch 6.2 – Snakes are revered in Hindu mythology because of their mystic symbolism of virility and Kundalini, aka divine feminine energy (I freely admit I have no idea what this means). Several temples dedicated to snakes are present in India, including the Bhujang Nag Temple in Gujarat and the Nagaraja Temple in Tamil Nadu.

Ch 6.3 – There is one final tale in the Uttanka Indra stories. Story 1 was about how Indra helped Uttanka against Takshaka (who stole the earrings). Story 2 was about how Uttanka helped King Janamejaya kill all the snakes, and Indra helped Takshaka and nearly lost his own life when Uttanka's yagna almost consumed Indra's throne as well.

The third and final story is of Uttanka receiving a boon from Krishna that he would find water whenever he was thirsty if he thought of Krishna. Krishna was pleased with the sage and asked Indra to give him Amrit, the nectar of immortality, the next time Uttanka was thirsty and thought of Krishna. Indra did not want to share the nectar and so appeared in front of Uttanka dressed like a chandala (a handler of corpses). Shocked, Uttanka refused the water—a sage, being of the highest brahmin caste, would not drink water from a chandala, who was effectively among the lowest—the Untouchables. Krishna then appeared and scolded Uttanka for refusing the water. He kept his word to Uttanka by making it so that rain clouds would appear at his bidding whenever he was thirsty. Today, rain clouds in the desert areas of Rajasthan are called Uttanka megha (Uttanka's clouds).

Ch 7 – There are seven Chiranjeevi's (immortals). One of them you'll have already met in Book 1—Ashwatthama. The remaining (in no particular order) are Kripa, Hanuman, Vyas, Parashuram, Vibhishana and Mahabali.

The bit about Gods being unable to bestow immortality, and doing so only through nectar, is a bit of creative licensing on my part. I am unaware of any legends where immortality was granted as a boon (except in the case of the seven Chiranjeevi's, who will remain alive till the end of the Kali Yuga—hence more long-lived than immortal). Further, if the ability to grant immortality were possible, it would negate the need for the churning of the ocean.

Ch 8 – The secret to good Maggi is to boil all the water away. Soupy Maggi tastes terrible. I learnt this far too late in life; around the time I was writing this book. Also, it tastes wonderful when you add butter and onions. I spent three months in KSA in 2008, where there were no food delivery apps or restaurants close by, so we often ate Maggi—sometimes with butter, sometimes with cheese, and at one point, Nutella was seriously considered.

Ch 10.1 – Kate's friend 'Jane' has some other excellent observations to make, namely, 'There is nothing like staying at home, for real comfort' and 'The person, be it gentleman or lady, who has not pleasure in a good novel, must be intolerably stupid'—sadly, there was only one quote that I was able to include.

The pieces of Sati's body fell in fifty-one places, according to scriptures. Each of these places are now worshipped as sacred sites. Most of these locations are in India, but there are seven in Bangladesh, three in Pakistan, three in Nepal, and one in Tibet and Sri Lanka.[7]

Ch 10.2 – I could probably write a whole chapter about Durvasa and his curses, but for the most part, there were two very important ones.

The first is mentioned in Chapter 105 of the Uttara Kanda. Ram was in a meeting with Yama, the God of death, and had instructed Lakshman to guard the door, warning that anyone who interrupted the meeting would die. Durvasa came and demanded entrance. When Lakshman refused, Durvasa threatened to curse all of Ayodhya. Deciding that he should rather die than have the entire city suffering, Lakshman interrupted the meeting (If I were in his place, I would have told Durvasa to go inside). To fulfil Ram's word, Lakshman went to the river Sarayu to drown himself (the poetic ending of this tale, in some versions, is that Indra took him to heaven while he was still alive).

The second major event that Durvasa was directly responsible for was the destruction of the Yadava race (mentioned in the Mausala Parva). The Yadavas decided

---

[7] https://www.indiatoday.in/travel/festivals/story/navratri-durga-puja-51-shakti-peeths-shiva-sati-amarnath-kamakhya-kolkata-kalighat-lifetr-1050105-2017-09-23

to play a prank by dressing one of their own (Samba) as a pregnant woman and asking Durvasa the sex of the child—a really stupid move given Durvasa's temper. Durvasa cursed them that Samba would bear an actual weapon that would destroy the Yadava race. I detailed the consequences of this in part one of the *Celestial Chronicles.*

I should mention a couple of interesting factoids about Durvasa: his father (the sage who adopted him) gave him a boon that every time he curses someone, his life extends. So, though he was tossing curses like lies at a Trump rally, he may have been doing so to prolong his own life as well.

The second was that while Durvasa cursed a lot of women, there were a couple of recorded curses that proved he wasn't being sexist.

He cursed Indra, weakening him and the Devas, which made the Devas decide to partner with the Asuras to churn the ocean and get the nectar of immortality. He was thus an agent of change in his own way.

Durvasa, thus, is also one of the few sages who lived through at least three of the yugas (Satya, Treta and Dvapara)

Ch 11.1 – I didn't make up the wisecrack about snakes having two willies—here is the evidence from Nat Geo.[8]

Ahalya's story first gets mentioned in the Adi Kanda—the first book of the Ramayana.

Ch 11.2 – It goes without saying that many stories are mythological and should not be interpreted literally (which

____

[8] https://www.nationalgeographic.com/animals/article/snakes-alligators-reptiles-genitalia-animals

is also why we don't judge past cultures with present day morality). That said, the stories themselves yield fascinating clues about a particular time's culture, and prevalent practices and ideas.

There are many, many things wrong with the story of Ahalya when viewed with a contemporary lens. There's child marriage (married when she hit puberty), grooming (raised by the sage as a child and then married to him), her husband (chosen by a contest rather than based on her choice) and of course, punishing her for Indra's actions (the scriptures differ about whether she was unfaithful or raped). Most glaring is how disproportionate the punishment is for the crime. Sadly, a lot of these practices are still prevalent in India today. According to a 2023 Lancet Global Health study, 22.3 per cent of women aged 20–24 in India (about 13.4 million) were married before age 18 in 2023, making it home to the world's largest number of child brides.[9]

You, as a reader, can support UNICEF and its efforts to protect children by contributing to https://help.unicef.org/.

A 2022 UN report noted that at least 22 million people globally were in forced marriages, with nearly two-thirds (14.2 million) in Asia-Pacific, India being a major contributor to the statistics.[10]

Similar tales of divine seduction appear in Greek mythology—Zeus sleeps with Alcmene (mother of Hercules) by disguising himself as her husband. The same happened with Leda (mother of Helen), Danaë (mother of Perseus),

---

[9] https://www.forbes.com/sites/anuradhavaranasi/ 2023/12/31/ one-in-five-underage-girls-forced-into-marriage-in-india-lancet/.

[10] https://thelogicalindian.com/gender/india-has-high-incidence-of-forced-marriage-of-minors-un-report-37423.

Europa (mother of Minos), Lamia (mother of Scylla, the sea monster), Leto (mother of Artemis and Apollo) and several more. What's interesting in the case of Greek mythology is that Zeus's promiscuity was a way to explain heroic demigods; the seduction is, therefore, a precursor to the main event—it sets in motion the hero's journey. In the case of Indra and Ahalya, their story is essentially about Vedic era values—don't be unfaithful to your husband, and most importantly, don't cuckold sages, or they will curse you in some horribly creative way.

A final loop to be closed on Ahalya—the common belief is that she was innocent and not how she has been portrayed here. She is one of the Panchkanya—a group of five iconic women based on Hindu mythology. All five women are regarded in the scriptures as archetypes of ideal women and female chastity. The chastity bit is ironic since each of the five is associated with more than one man.

- Ahalya—wife of Gautama and lover of Indra.
- Tara—Wife of Vali, later of Sugriva. (According to some references, she was originally Sugriva's wife)
- Mandodari—Wife of Ravana, later of Vibhishana.
- Draupadi—Wife of all five Pandavas
- Kunti—Wife of Pandu, later had kids with four different Gods.

TLDR: Ahalya is an important character in the legends and the only reason I have interpreted her this way is because there is enough ambiguity about her story to allow her to play the role of a villain.

These stories were penned by men in patriarchal setups, so the women's roles reflect the biases of the time. Childbearing was a societal cornerstone, wars needed scapegoats, and damsels made Heroes look good. Yet, the irony isn't lost: these 'secondary' characters often drive the narrative more than the sword-swinging bros. Ahalya's brief episode in the Ramayana sets up Ram's divine compassion; Helen's elopement (or abduction) triggers the entire Iliad. If these stories were a Vedic sacrifice, the women would be the ghee—quietly fuelling the fire while the priests take credit for the flames.

Ch13.1 – Valmiki and Vyas being avatars of Vishnu is not part of Vedic scriptures. This belief is ascribed to Guru Gobind Singh, the ninth Guru of the Sikhs. He composed the *Brahm Avatar*, an informal composition containing three hundred and forty-three verses included in the *Dasam Granth*, which is recognised as a Sikh scripture. In this, he describes seven supreme poets and skilful writers as avatars of Brahma. I have taken the liberty of using that as a reference here though, in Vedic literature, there is no reference to Valmiki or Vyas being Brahma avatars.

According to legend, Valmiki saw a hunter shoot down a bird, and witnessing the grief of the widowed bird reminded him of the sorrow felt by Ram and Sita as they were separated. He expressed this grief spontaneously in a shloka (a thirty two-line verse that consists of four quarter verses of eight syllables each). The shloka became the de facto verse form for nearly all Sanskrit literature going forward, including the Ramayana (that he wrote), the Mahabharata, the Puranas, Smritis, etc. For this, he was given the name Adivati (the first poet).

Aubrey Menen's *The Ramayana*, which was the first book to be banned in Independent India had a rather amusing way to describe the story of Valmiki.

In his blog *Wait But Why*, Tim Urban *did* an excellent cartoon titled *How Religion Got in the Way* that explores the idea that humans created Gods, not the other way around.

Ascension can best be described as Malcolm Gladwell's tipping point, aka the moment of critical mass, the boiling point, applied in a magical context.

Narada's first words when he meets Akran is a little joke referring to how he is traditionally depicted as chanting one of Vishnu's many names (Narayan).

Akran's signature line, i.e. 'Go fuck yourself', has its origins in the Russia-Ukraine War. As the war began, a Russian warship approached Snake Island, a Ukrainian military outpost, and demanded their surrender. After the second call to surrender, a Ukrainian soldier grabbed the radio and responded: Russian warship, go fuck yourself.

Later, this became a rallying cry for the Ukrainian resistance—the army and the public.

You tend to end up liking some scenes more than others—it can't be helped. In my case, my favourite scene happens to be the one where Akran is making all the bad puns (I had great fun writing it). The second favourite is the one where Narada showed them visions of the future—that is probably the scene I rewrote and edited the most. The *Malazan Book of the Fallen* series has a character, Fiddler of the Bridgeburners, who uses a deck of cards called Deck of Dragons in a similar fashion, though those showed more cryptic interpretations. My goal in that scene was to establish clearly the path that was unfolding ahead of Akran, leading us to that scene right at the end.

A final point I want to make is based on a question asked of me by a reader: Why would you subvert a perfectly wonderful and timeless story by taking them from the myths and putting them in modern Mumbai?

The answer is why wouldn't we?

Ashok Banker made an interesting point when I reached out to him after *Shadows Rising* released last year. His advice then was, 'Either write for money or write what makes you happy—don't try to do both.' Writing for money in the genre of mythological fantasy is about not going against the grain. It's about avoiding any sort of cognitive dissonance in the minds of the readers. They expect, when they pick up a book about Indian mythology, to find covers with shirtless, muscular men shooting bows and arrows in a Bronze Age setting.

Fantasy, the way it is understood anywhere else in the world, is non-existent in India. All we have, categorised under fantasy, are endless retellings of existing myths, from different points of view—whether it is Karna, his wife, Kaikeyi, Krishna, Ravan, Indrajit, Mandodari, etc. You could classify them as mythological fantasy, but they don't create completely new stories—they reinvent existing tales.

The technical term for the sub-genre I'm writing in, which falls under urban fantasy, is mythpunk. Mythpunk blends traditional mythology and folklore with postmodern literary techniques. Unlike classical retellings, mythpunk stories often subvert or deconstruct these myths, incorporating modern themes, diverse perspectives and non-linear storytelling.

The overarching goal is to build a shared urban fantasy universe, tapping into unique stories from our heritage and folklore, yet at the same time pushing the envelope in terms of nudging fantasy along. That's part of the reason why Akran moved to Delhi—I'm breaking him (and myself) out of the comfort zone we are in to focus on stories that tap into the unique cultural elements of that city.

Why not create completely new stories in fantasy with zero connection to mythology? To that, the only answer have is … Stay tuned!

I've just wrapped up two—a horror story based on Indian folklore, set in Uttar Pradesh, and a noir detective story with fantasy elements blended in, set in Bangalore. Expect one of them by end of this year, and the other whenever the publishing Gods look upon me more favourably.

Here ends Book 2 (or 3, depending on how things go).

ACKNOWLEDGEMENTS

As always, this book was only possible with the help of some very important people. My wife Sharon—struggling authors need hardworking spouses in the background to keep a roof over our heads. I am especially grateful for all her efforts in supporting and encouraging me to pursue my dreams while she puts food on the table. She also fended off everyone who expressed shock at my pursuing such a dismal career by patiently explaining that we should all be encouraged to follow our passions.

My kids are now eight and ten. I am really hoping that they will read my books and be super impressed. Don't get me wrong, I'm excited about everyone out there reading what I've written, but especially them. More than the rest of you all.

To Sanghamitra Biswas from Westland, who took a chance on this book and made it a reality. The editing process was managed by Sonia Madan and publishing legend V. K. Karthika, which was very exciting. Like Haley's Comet, her name has been streaking past me for over ten years since my first book but I finally managed to see her in 2025.

Also, all the other people at Westland—Amrita Talwar (Marketing), Saurabh Garge (Design), Satish Sundaram (Sales)—thank you all.

My gratitude to the amazing authors who took time out of their busy lives and agreed to read this manuscript and provide a quote if they liked it.

Special thanks to the beta readers. They've dropped like flies until only one last stalwart has remained. Vivek Thoopal has diligently read most of what I've written so far.

This past year, I reconnected with an old friend from school and her husband, Ketan Pandit, has also become one of my beta readers. A big thanks to him as well.

And finally, a big, heartfelt thank you to all the readers, even you pirates and freeloaders. I've been on your side of the fence with too many books I want and too little money to spend. If this book actually gets pirated, it's likely a sign that it is successful and that would be a good thing. Unless you are very talented or very lucky, writing is one of those callings that is endlessly frustrating because you believe deep down that the story you wish to tell is wonderful; but somehow, the teeming millions all around you cannot see it. It takes dedication and commitment to read a book from cover to cover, and if you have reached all the way to the very end with me rambling on, then I am definitely grateful for your support. I would request that if you like the book, kindly rate it on Amazon and Goodreads. Every little bit helps, but no pressure. I had several readers reach out on Instagram @author_rohanm and it was a pleasure interacting with them and answering their queries. Please don't spam the two young women on TikTok with the same name, because I have absolutely no idea who they are.

Thank you once again. This journey is only beginning.